LOVE TRIUMPHS

A bouquet of traditional love stories

Susan D. Brooks   Tami D. Cowden
Su Kopil   Betsy Norman
Carolee Joy

Fusion Press

Published by Dream Street Prose,
In cooperation with Fusion Press,
A publishing service of Authorlink
(http://www.authorlink.com)
3720 Millswood Dr.
Irving, Texas 75062, USA

First published by Dream Street Prose
In cooperation with Fusion Press,
A publishing service of Authorlink
First Printing, February, 2000

Printed in the United States of America

ISBN 1 928704 72 7

Dedication

For our husbands,
Ben, Steve, Jake, Tony and Mark,
our every day heroes.

Author's Notes

This is a work of fiction. All the names, characters, organizations, and events portrayed in this book are either the product of the author's imagination or are used fictitiously for verisimilitude. Any other resemblance to any organization, event, or actual person, living or dead, is unintended and entirely coincidental.

Table of Contents

A ROSE A DAY

Carolee Joy

Lori Williams longed to skip February 14th. Maybe Cupid wouldn't mind postponing Valentine's Day until her heart finished healing. While she was wishing, she might even ask to cancel the first two weeks of February. Never mind that it was the best sales day of the year for her flower shop.

There was no way to get through another Valentine's season without thinking about Mack. Not only the day, the weeks before promised to be just as painful with the hearts, the advertising, the restaurant, jewelry and lingerie specials in the upscale retail neighborhood where her shop was located.

Why couldn't he have waited to make her a widow? About fifty years, at least. Given her a lifetime of love, instead of just five years.

Everyone said she'd stop grieving. Eventually. How much longer would she have to wait? Three years had passed, and she still missed him as much as if it had only been yesterday since he'd been taken from her.

How would she get through the hearts and flowers and all the memories they evoked?

Then on the day she flipped the calendar to February, a stranger came into the shop and bought a red rose. Eyes as green as the leaves on the long stemmed rose he selected, he gave her a quirky little smile, as if he knew some secret that should be obvious to her, but wasn't.

She slid the cash register drawer shut and gazed after him. Red for love triumphant. What a lucky guy. He must be new in the neighborhood, too, or just passing through. She would have remembered seeing him before, otherwise. Most of the customers at Dream Street Roses-N-Such were regulars.

The next day, he returned and bought another rose. Deep pink, this time. Gratitude, or appreciation?

"Nice shop," he commented, again paying in cash and lingering on his way out the door.

"Thank you," she called, unable to think of anything more to say.

The third day he chose a pale apricot bud. Admiration. She wondered who the lucky recipient was. The same woman he appreciated passionately? The pattern continued for the rest of the week as the man ran through the color spectrum of roses. After he'd chosen one in every color and every emotion would he disappear? Or return for another red rose?

Lori almost hated the fact that the shop would be closed

on Sunday. Usually she looked forward to her only day off, but her increasing curiosity over the stranger made her long for Monday.

Scolding herself for being ridiculous, she tried to immerse herself in tending her greenhouse on Sunday afternoon. After all, a man who bought flowers every day definitely had obligations. He'd probably messed up big time and was buying roses to assuage a guilty conscience. Even Mack had given flowers only to soothe, and he'd had a hundred blossoms at his fingertips every day. He'd been strictly a chocolates man for special occasions.

Monday arrived, but the handsome stranger did not show up at nine as he had every day the previous week. Determined to put her foolish curiosity aside, she spent the rest of the morning in the design room preparing the afternoon deliveries and let Mack's nephew, Jimmy, handle the front counter.

Just before noon, he drifted into the back where Lori was coaxing an Enchantment lily into the center of a large arrangement ordered for a hospital patient.

"I swear that guy has cruised past the window fifteen times! If he wants something, why doesn't he just come in?"

Lori's hand froze over the pink petals. Her heart skipped, then beat a little faster. "What guy?"

"The One A Day Man. Maybe he's starting to balk at the increasing cost of roses."

"Maybe." Lori kept her tone light and avoided Jimmy's gaze. "They all do. It's just a perfect case of supply and demand, and yet everyone acts like the florist is trying to make a killing on Valentine's Day." She put the finishing touches on the arrangement. "Why don't you load the van? This last one is for a new mother. You'll need the little pink teddy bear to go with it. I'll go out front and handle the noon crowd."

She'd barely had time to rearrange the vases of flowers on display when the door chimed. Filled with anticipation, she looked up into the kindly gaze of Mrs Goodbee, one of her most faithful customers and the owner of the bagel shop next door.

"Good morning, dear. I need to pick out something for my sister. She's been sick the past few days."

Lori helped her select a sunny bouquet of carnations and daisies in a teapot with packets of herbal teas hidden among the greenery. "This should be just what your sister needs to perk up." She smiled at the older woman.

Mrs Goodbee chatted a few moments about the rain expected for later in the week and the proposed Sidewalk Days planned for the merchants in mid-March. She lightly touched the back of Lori's hand before she left. "The holidays are always the hardest, but someday it won't seem so difficult."

Lori blinked against the tears suddenly filling her eyes. Maybe, but Mack had proposed to her on Valentine's Day. What could possibly happen to keep her from thinking about that?

Several more customers kept her busy for the next half hour. Then the door chimed again.

The rose guy. He wandered the perimeter of the shop, as if deep in contemplation of the silk plants arranged near the wall.

A flutter of elation quickened her pulse, but she smothered the sensation. How foolish! The man was, after all, just a customer. But she couldn't stop the tiniest sense of guilt from creeping in to mar the pleasure his smile gave her.

"Any yellow roses?" He stood before the cooler, apparently checking the selection of prepared vases.

He must be joyful today. "Not in there, but I have some pink tipped yellow ones in the back. How many do you need?"

"Uh," the faintest hint of color rose in his face. "Just one."

"Okay, I'll put some greenery with it and wrap it up."

She turned and headed for the back room, surprised to realize he was right on her heels. "Did you want to see it first?"

"Oh. No." He stopped, the color in his face deepening a little more. "I'm sure it will be fine."

In the design room, she quickly added a spray of baby's breath and feathery green fern, then wrapped the flower up in a cellophane sheet and secured it with a bow the same vibrant color as the petal tips.

Jimmy hovered nearby for a moment, then peeked out between the curtain partitioning the room off from the front of the store. "He's a competitor. He's sampling all the varieties of roses you carry so that he can outdo you."

"There aren't any other flower shops within our business area."

"Well, I bet he's planning on changing that. Don't give away any trade secrets," he whispered as she passed him.

"Maybe I should put a 'bug' in the rose." She couldn't resist teasing. Jimmy had hopes of being accepted into law enforcement work just like Uncle Mack once he finished his college degree. He already had the suspicious nature of a detective. Amazing how much he reminded her of how enthusiastic Mack had been when they were younger.

"Laugh all you want, but he wants something." He raised a dark brow with the self-assurance of a twenty-year-old who thinks all the answers can be found in a textbook.

She patted his arm. "I'll keep that in mind." Jimmy was a nice young man, and he'd appointed himself her advisor when Mack died. She found it comforting, if somewhat irritating at times.

Mr Green Eyes stood at the counter, looking over the selection of business cards and brochures. "Are you the owner?"

"Yes." She held the rose out for his approval and warmed at the way his gaze lingered on her before he seemed to remember the flower he'd come in for.

He looked disappointed, and for a moment she thought

the flower didn't appeal to him. Or maybe Jimmy was right and he was simply sizing up the competition. "You're Mrs Williams."

"That's right. And you are…." she held out her hand and took the credit card he extended for the first time. "Brandon Wells." At last a name to go with the charming smile and eyes that seemed to peer deeply into her soul. "Do you work in the neighborhood, Mr Wells?"

"No, I mean yes. I live in the neighborhood. Just moved in above the shop, actually, and plan to be settled into work by next week."

Before she could ask him about his business, Jimmy caught her gaze from across the room and arched a brow as if to say, see? He's a corporate spy!

Several more customers entered the shop, diverting Jimmy's attention. Lori's lips twitched with a suppressed smile as she processed the order and gave the man the credit slip to sign.

Brandon leaned over the counter slightly and lowered his voice, giving her the feeling they were in an intimate setting instead of a busy floral shop. "Why don't you just set that smile free? Someone else may need it more than you do."

She had to laugh. "You, I suppose?"

"Maybe." He let the pen clatter to the counter, picked up his rose and left without saying anything more.

Pretending to rearrange a few of the plants near the window, Lori watched him walk down the street.

"Want me to tail him?" Jimmy's voice near her ear made her jump. She turned to face him.

"I'm sure that won't be necessary. Now, how about making deliveries before someone sends out an APB on those flowers?"

The next day, Brandon bought one humble white rose, but the shop was crowded with other customers, precluding any chance for conversation. Not, she assured herself, that it mattered one way or another. Mr Wells was turning into a dependable customer, for whatever peculiar reason he needed a daily rose.

Two days later, he managed to catch her alone as he selected and paid for a pale lavender rose.

"So does Mr Williams work with you?"

Lori bit her lip before replying. "My husband died three years ago. And no, he wasn't much of a flower person. He was a policeman."

Brandon's gaze softened. "I'm sorry. Line of duty?"

She took a steadying breath, although the pain she usually felt didn't seem quite so bad under Brandon's sympathetic smile. "Yes. He caught a robbery in progress while he was on his way here. Just down the street actually. So even though he was off duty, he got caught in the cross fire."

"That's rough."

"It's so unfair." And it was her fault. She bit her lip to keep her feelings in control.

His fingertips barely grazed the back of her hand where it rested on the glass case. "I'm sorry."

The moment stretched out. Lori blinked back tears.

Brandon's voice dropped to a comforting whisper. "You feel as if you were somehow to blame, don't you?"

She jerked her gaze up to meet his. He was the first person to recognize the guilt she felt over Mack's death. After all, if he hadn't been on his way to her shop, he wouldn't have even been in the neighborhood. If she hadn't insisted on being one of the first merchants to set up business in the newly reclaimed downtown area before it became the safe place it was now; if she hadn't been working so late against his wishes, Mack would still be alive.

"Yes," she whispered.

"Don't," he said, then left when the door chimed and several customers streamed in.

She thought about him off and on for the rest of the day. How had he so quickly recognized feelings she had never shared with anyone else? Why had his understanding words eased her sorrow?

She wondered what his story was. If he came in tomorrow, she would ask.

The next day when he came in during a brief morning lull, she seized the opportunity while she was waiting for authorization on his credit card for the orange rose he'd selected. Ah, ha, now he was feeling enthusiasm and... desire. Her heart beat a little faster. She chased the thought away before it could take root in her relentlessly fertile imagination.

"I've been thinking about what you said the other day. About the guilt. How did you know that about me? Have you ever been married?" He wore a gold band with a single diamond embedded in it but on his right hand. The left was bare, not even marred by the telltale white stripe of a married man on the prowl.

His eyes filled with sadness making her regret her hasty question. "A long time ago," he said finally.

"Sorry, I didn't mean to pry." She slid the credit card slip and a pen across the counter toward him.

He signed his name, then looked up. "It's okay. She died ten years ago. That's why I know all about the guilt. It goes away eventually, if you let it."

"I'll keep that in mind." She took the pen, startled when his fingers brushed against hers. An accident? Not judging by the look in his eyes. To hide her nervous reaction, she blurted out the first thing that popped into her mind. "What are you doing with all these roses, anyway?"

He smiled, transforming the gloom that had settled between them into a radiance that squeezed her heart with pleasure. "I'll show you, if you'd like."

"When?"

"Saturday night."

"That's Valentine's Day."

He glanced at the calendar hanging up behind the

counter. "So it is." Another area merchant came in and stood impatiently behind Brandon. "We could have dinner."

When she hesitated, he rushed on, as if afraid she'd say no before she heard his suggestion. "Every restaurant in town will be crowded and overbooked, but my place will be ready by then. I make a great lasagna."

Old Mr Phenster from the pharmacy on the corner leaned forward. "Just say yes, Lori! I only have a few minutes here."

"Okay. Saturday will be fine."

Brandon smiled and left.

Lori spent the rest of the afternoon in a daze. A date! She actually had a date. And on the dreaded holiday of romance, no less. At least it would give her something else to think about between now and then.

Like, what did one wear to a casual dinner cooked by a man who bought a dozen roses one at a time? In different colors? She wished he would have told her what he did for a living. He certainly kept odd hours. Just like Mack had.

The day before Valentine's, Lori emerged from the back room to find Jimmy engrossed in conversation with Brandon.

"No kidding? How many did you shoot?" Jimmy leaned across the counter, avidly listening to some story of Brandon's.

Lori's blood ran cold. Only one thing engrossed Jimmy that much. Law enforcement. Her mind raced, while panic ran rampant through her. There weren't any new businesses in the area, she'd checked and hadn't found any. She'd assumed Brandon simply hadn't put his sign out yet, but now she realized how wrong she'd been.

Brandon Wells must be one of the policemen who took turns staffing the "cop shop", a neighborhood watch office established after Mack's death.

Hoping he hadn't seen her, but too upset to do anything if he had, Lori ducked back into the design room. She couldn't get involved with another policeman, she wouldn't!

Grabbing her purse and two arrangements needing to be delivered, she called out to Jimmy that she would make the afternoon deliveries. Then she left.

Just her miserable luck. The only man who had caught her eye since Mack would have to be a policeman. One thing for certain, she had to get out of their "date" tomorrow night.

At the police office, she left a note for him explaining something had come up, and she wouldn't be able to join him for dinner, after all.

So she was a coward. How many times did a person have to suffer a broken heart, anyway?

Saturday she let the extra staff she'd hired handle the customers while she stayed in the back preparing arrangements, restocking the design room and loading the van with flowers. If Brandon came in that morning for his daily rose, she intended to be too busy to talk to him. Hopefully, he'd get her message and realize she wasn't ready to socialize, especially on this, the most romantic day of the year.

"Why did you change your mind?" Brandon's voice made her whirl toward the doorway.

"I didn't really change it. I didn't feel right about it from the start." She supposed it was better to just be as honest as possible. He seemed like a nice man; it wasn't his fault he was in the wrong occupation for her.

He stepped inside, making the small room seem airless and too heavy with the perfume of dozens of flowers. "Lucky for me Sgt Connor knew where to find me."

"Why wouldn't he? Is today your day off or something?"

He held the crumpled note in his fist. "You left this at the cop shop."

"Of course I did, isn't that where you work?"

Understanding dawned in his eyes. Tension eased from him as his gaze met and held hers. "You think I'm a cop. That's why you cancelled our dinner."

"Can you blame me?" After all the compassion he'd

shown, surely he could understand why she couldn't risk being emotionally involved with a policeman again.

"Why did you think that?"

She twisted a piece of floral wire between her fingers. "I heard you talking to Jimmy. About a shooting you were involved in."

Shaking his head, he chuckled and held out his hand. "Let Jimmy watch the shop and come with me. Just for a minute. I promise it won't be dangerous."

She hesitated. Should she trust him? Could she? *Trust your instincts,* she could almost hear Mack whisper

She'd been drawn to Brandon from the first day he entered her shop. Despite her doubts, she had to have faith in him. And herself. She slowly extended her fingers. His wrapped around hers, then he led her out the back way.

Six doors down, he unlocked a heavy door and stepped back to allow her to enter. Trails of electrical cords lay on the floor like dozens of black snakes. A platform draped with gauze material occupied one corner. Pull down backdrops and large professional lighting fixtures crowded another. Other props and set designs leaned against the far wall.

For a moment, she couldn't fathom what everything was for, then it hit her. "You're a photographer!"

He laughed softly. "Very perceptive. And the shootings Jimmy was asking me about were the ones I'm using all of your lovely roses for."

Relinquishing her hand, he showed her the photographs displayed on a table in the front of the shop. "I do some portrait work, but more catalog shoots. I'm doing one for the National Rose Society. They sent me silk ones, but I didn't like the way the artificial petals photographed. So the first day at your shop was strictly to buy a rose for that day's work. After that...." He shrugged.

"Then what?" She couldn't believe the elation threading through her and wanted him to say what she needed to hear.

"Then it was just to see you."

"What were you going to do when I ran out of colors?"

He laughed. "Start over with red. I finished the shots up last week, anyway, but couldn't come up with a better reason to pop into your shop every day."

"You could have just asked me out."

He smiled, tender and full of awareness. "You would have said no. Am I right?"

She stared down at the floor. Was he? If she had known from the first that Brandon was so subtly trying to court her, what would she have done? Hidden in the design room? "Probably," she whispered.

"What will you say if I ask you again about tonight?"

She raised her gaze to meet his. She already knew what she wanted, but couldn't resist teasing him just a bit. "Can you really make lasagna?"

"I already did. Along with a strawberry cheesecake that will make you beg for mercy. It's all awaiting your pleasure later tonight." His warm, inviting smile chased away the last of her doubts and filled her with hope for the future.

"Then I accept." She took a step toward him, thrilled and expectant when he closed the distance and took her hands in his. "And Brandon, I'll bring the roses."

"Make them red," he said. "For love triumphs."

ENGRAVED MEMORIES

Betsy Norman

They're destroying the last romantic remnants of my marriage, Lucy thought.

The city workers fired up their chainsaws. Chin in her hands, she sat on the steps of her front porch and watched. One by one, the gnarled limbs of the ancient oak standing sentinel across the street crashed to the ground to make room for an expanded playground.

"What are you sulking about?" Her husband's voice interrupted Lucy's melancholia. Virgil stepped partway out from behind the screen door and onto the porch to take a look. "It's about time they cut down that old eyesore, anyway." The frame banged shut as he disappeared back inside.

Lucy stifled the sob stuck in her throat. Virgil didn't

seem to remember, but she did. Tomorrow would be fifty years to the day he carved their initials in that "old eyesore."

She'd been sixteen when Virgil came courting and asked permission to take her on an evening walk. He had worn his Sunday shirt and suspenders and toted a handful of late summer field flowers. Lucy remembered it as if it were yesterday.

"I have something to show you, Lucy." His teenage voice cracked in nervousness, and his palm blindfolded her vision. "Close your eyes."

She could only giggle, her shy step falling in tow with his guidance. He brought her to the park, illuminated by only the fat harvest moon presiding over the sky. Scents of lilacs and the last smoky coals of a bonfire wafted in the air.

"Here!" His excited whisper tickled one ear. The moist hand unmasked her vision and held tight to one shoulder. "See? 'VC loves LW' I carved it with my Swiss army knife. It means Virgil Croy loves Lucy Wendell." His eyes were bright and intent on hers. Expectation, fear, and elation all mixed into one.

"Do you love me too, Lucy? Will you be my girl always?" Virgil didn't wait for her reply. His arm swooped outward toward the adjacent field. "I'll build you a big house! Right there—so you can always look at this tree and know how much I love you."

He'd made good on his promise, but now the tree would be gone. How could he forget what it represented? Lucy sighed and stood up. She didn't want to watch them cut down the trunk and reduce her engraved memories to sawdust.

It surprised her that Virgil had even surfaced long enough from his workshop to take notice of the tree's removal. Since his retirement two months ago, he'd become a mole-man, buried down in the basement with his wood shavings and sandpaper.

After forty-seven years of marriage, these were supposed

to be their golden years. They'd weathered lean times together before getting their feet firmly on the ground. Three kids one after the other, with a fledgling carpentry business; they struggled to make ends meet. Cash-poor, but rich in love, time for each other sometimes got put off for later, but not forever.

Croy and Son's now belonged to Frank, their eldest, with his twins alongside him. Lucy had reached a comfortable spot in life with her husband, and now that he was retired, she wanted to rediscover the man she'd fallen in love with. It hurt her to think all he wanted to do was rediscover the intricacies of his lathe.

When she stepped inside, the house was unusually quiet, devoid of the banging and sawing from the basement. Most likely he's off to the hardware store for another file bit, Lucy snorted. Did he ever stop to consider she might like to go with him? They could have had lunch at the new café by the lake.

No, he was too busy with his project.

She spent the rest of the day in a funk, aimlessly tidying up, and lonely, wishing for Virgil to talk to. When he didn't come up for dinner, she called down to him about his food getting cold.

"In a minute," he replied.

Later came and went, and after three more "In a minute's," she decided to go to bed without him for the first time.

Lucy paused at their bedroom door. Her sad expression mourned back in the full-length mirror opposite. Did she really look that old?

Fifty years. She thought Virgil would remember such an important date, but how could he when she no longer resembled his high school sweetheart enough to remind him?

Stepping inside, she sat down on the bed. The sagging springs creaked.

"Oh, this old bed!" She bounced on it a couple of times,

sending the warped joints into an out of tune symphony of complaints. There was a time she and Virgil delighted in making the old bed sing. Now…Well, now it had lost its voice.

An empty pillow greeted her the next morning. No warm smile or good morning kisses, and no warm Virgil to snuggle up with for some pillow talk. Lucy buried her head under the covers and began to cry.

"I've got something to show you, Lucy." Virgil's hand tugged at her shoulder.

"What?" She sniffled and gave him a confused look.

"Close your eyes." Anticipation shone in his expression —a schoolboy excitement she hardly recognized it had been dormant for so long.

Virgil helped her out of bed. She felt foolish being led around blindly in a violet sprigged flannel nightgown, but giddiness overtook embarrassment.

"Virgil Croy, what are you up to?"

"Shhhhhh."

She followed his lead. The sharp tang of cut wood and staining chemicals filled her nostrils. Stopping short, she realized he'd led her to the top of the stairs to his workshop.

"You want to show me something down there?" Flabbergasted and disappointed, she refused to budge. "I'm not interested in anything that's kept you holed up in that dirty basement all night, and that's that!"

Lucy shook off Virgil's hand and stormed back to the bedroom, ignoring his pleas to reconsider. She got dressed and flounced out of the house before her frustrated tears betrayed her.

Once she reached town, she did by herself all the things she'd wanted to do with Virgil. A walk by the lake, luncheon at the fancy café. She even bought a small bouquet of flowers from a street vendor. It wasn't the same. She missed Virgil.

So we've gotten a little too old for spur of the moment

romance, Lucy told herself. Maybe he just got preoccupied spending time doing what he loves. Maybe she should have asked him if they could go out for awhile and do something together. A few kind words instead of a childish temper tantrum.

The night by the tree she'd promised to love him always, no matter what. Comfortable, familiar Virgil was just as loveable as romantic, spontaneous Virgil. Lucy felt ashamed of the way she'd acted.

When she got home, the house was dark and ominously quiet again. The basement light was off, so she knew it was Virgil who'd gone to bed without her tonight. She twirled the limp bundle of posies in her hand, trying to compose an apology.

"Lucy?" Lamplight flooded the hall from their bedroom. Virgil stood in the doorframe, wringing his hands. "I was worried about you."

"I'm sorry. Oh, Virgil, I'm so sorry. I was being selfish and crotchety. Can you ever forgive me?" Tears stung Lucy's eyes.

"C'mere, sweetheart." Virgil held out his hands and welcomed her into his embrace. "Shhhh. Close your eyes."

"What?" Startled, Lucy tried to read his expression, but Virgil placed a callused hand over her eyes.

"Turn around." She did, and they both stepped into the bedroom. "Now, open them."

Inside, a brand new spindled oak bed gleamed, the headboard handcrafted with interwoven hearts. In the center hung a plaque made from the very same lopsided heart with the initials "VC loves LW" engraved inside—taken from their oak tree.

"It's not our wedding anniversary, but it is the day you promised to be my girl, Lucy." Virgil's soft voice tickled her ear, his hands hugging her shoulders. "Fifty years ago today."

"You remembered! Oh, Virgil! Is that what you wanted

to show me in the basement? How on earth did you get it up here?" Lucy cried out in joy, hugging him fiercely, laughing at her own foolishness.

"The twins came by to bring it up. I'm sorry I've been so busy in the workshop lately. I wanted to get the new bed done in time, and I was too excited to wait for the boys' help. I wanted it to be a surprise. When I found out they were going to be cutting down our tree, I asked the workers to spare our keepsake. I couldn't bear the thought of losing it."

"Thank you, Virgil." Her tears overflowed with happiness. "And here I thought you'd lost every romantic notion you ever had!"

"Not every." He grinned and sat down on the new mattress, patting the seat beside him. "Hmmm. No squeak. I think maybe this new bed could use some breaking in, don't you?"

"Oh, Virgil! We're too old!"

"Funny, I don't feel old, and you look just like the pretty little Lucy Wendell whose initials I carved." He gestured to the plaque. "And gave her first kiss to under this tree."

Lucy giggled, feeling sixteen again, lighthearted and in love, and ready to create some new memories.

KISS ME, YOU FOOL

Tami D. Cowden

Angela lavishly spread scarlet lipstick across her mouth. Then she eyed the crowd to find the best beneficiary of her talents.

Lusty wenches had to be choosy, after all.

She favored the conservative sort. Men who blushed always pleased the crowd.

Spotting a particularly buttoned-down type patiently waiting at the refreshment stand, she pranced up behind him, careful to keep out of his line of vision.

Despite the suit and tie he'd worn to the Renaissance Festival, close up he didn't look quite so much like an accountant. The suit jacket he held over his shoulder was of high quality material, but his tan hadn't come from days spent pushing pencils. And his fine white shirt barely seemed to cover the well-muscled shoulders underneath. A hair tie set with a Celtic design held back his ponytail of thick dark hair.

Not what she expected from Mr Conservative.

But here he was on a Saturday afternoon, wearing a suit to a medieval festival.

That made him fair game.

Confident she had the attention of the nearby crowd, Angela mimed passion for the oblivious fellow, casting adoring looks at the back of his head, and laying her hand across her heart. Snickers and applause began among the onlookers. She blew a kiss to the man's back, while he, unaware, studied the refreshment stand's menu.

The crowd roared with laughter. Her target glanced around, looking for the cause of the amusement, but she ducked down, pretending to adjust her leather slipper. He looked forward once more.

More giggles erupted as she rolled her eyes at the audience. Springing erect, she danced behind him, smacked her lips and batted her eyelashes. Finally, when she was sure the crowd was at the height of their glee, she tapped him on the shoulder.

When he turned to look behind him, she grasped both sides of his face in her lacy gloved hands and pulled his head down to hers. Standing on tiptoe, she gave him a resounding kiss. His skin was warm against her fingertips. Even through the creamy lipstick, she felt a spark as her lips touched him.

Startled gray eyes stared back into hers, causing a flutter in her heart.

A real flutter, this time.

Her own eyes widened in response before she remembered her role. She winked and stepped back, flourishing her hands to present her victim's face to the crowd. The bright red imprint of her lips graced his cheek. The crowd whistled and applauded, as she twirled about, eyes closed and hands clasped as though in ecstasy. She curtsied.

Through it all, her conservative fellow had said nothing, only stared at her with those wide gray eyes. But as she gave her last bow and prepared to scurry off to another part of the fair, his hand stayed her. Holding her fast beside him, he raised her hand.

"But I claim the right to return your kiss, my lady."

His voice was low, but it resounded in her ears. Her lips formed a small "o" as she stared back at him.

His eyes never left hers as he slipped the wispy lace glove away and pressed a gentle kiss on the back of her hand. Shivers raced up and down her spine as she again felt a shock as his lips touched her.

"A small kiss, my lady, to treasure until we meet again." She felt bereft when he suddenly released her.

Bowing, he backed away. He never glanced at the roaring crowd.

For a moment Angela stared at him, holding her freshly kissed hand to her heart. But as her swain melted into the crowd, she remembered her duties and ran off.

For the rest of the day, as she played her part throughout the fair, she constantly scanned the crowd for a glimpse of her handsome swain. But alas, he was nowhere to be found. She went home alone that night, to dream of a bold knight in a well tailored suit.

The following day, Angela worked the crowd again, strolling the grounds of the fair and planting evidence of her kisses wherever she went. Her mind replayed the previous day's performance, even as she gained her usual share of laughs and cheers.

She began her pantomime of infatuation with a bald man in Bermuda shorts, but soon realized the crowd seemed to be laughing at the wrong times. Glancing around, she discovered the cause. Another player had set upon her as his victim.

He sported the standard harlequin costume the fair's jesters wore. But none of the players she knew had ever filled out the costume so well. The black and white triangles seemed to accentuate muscled calves, arms, and shoulders. Paint of the same color disguised his features, and a bright belled jester's cap covered his hair.

She had no idea who he was, and frankly, she didn't care! His pretense of infatuation was horning into her act.

"Go away," she hissed under her breath, even as she dramatically turned up her nose at him for the chortling crowd's benefit.

"Nay! I shall never leave my lady's side." The thrilling accents with which he intoned these words caused her to veer her head back to look at him. "At least, not without another of my lady's kisses!"

She frowned. That voice was familiar. Looking closely, her heart skipped a beat as she recognized those gray eyes.

"You!" She looked him up and down. "You've changed your clothes."

"Yesterday I auditioned. Today I perform!" He bowed low, touching his lips to the hem of her skirt. Looking at her sideways, he added for her ears alone, "But this is no performance."

Forgetting all about the man in Bermuda shorts, she grinned.

"Well, what are you waiting for?" Raising her voice for the benefit of cheering spectators, she urged, "Kiss me, you fool."

The crowd roared approval.

Angela closed her eyes and welcomed the now familiar spark evoked by their touching lips.

Sometimes, angels rush in after fools.

TAG SALE FIND

Su Kopil

"Exquisite," said a low, rumbling voice.

Caitlin stopped writing price tags and turned to the man who stood beside her in the nearly empty living room. Dark wavy hair looked as though it had been raked through with his fingers more than once. The tails of his cotton shirt were tucked neatly inside faded blue jeans.

"Excuse me, sir," she said.

He turned his attention away from the armoire he'd been admiring to look at her.

She drew in a breath as a pair of intense blue eyes rimmed with dark lashes peered at her. A flash of emotion, gone too quickly to be identified, crossed his tanned face.

"Yes?"

"I'm sorry but the armoire isn't for sale."

"Oh." His hand, which had been caressing the cherry wood, dropped to his side. "I thought the sign on the road said contents of house for sale."

"It did." She moved closer to the armoire as though protecting it from his touch. "Everything except this piece."

She saw the disappointment in his eyes and fought to keep the defensiveness from her tone. Selling off the items in her parents' home had been harder than she'd expected. She hadn't lived here in over ten years, yet watching strangers critically eye and touch her mother's cherished possessions brought an overwhelming sadness. Her sister, Elizabeth, was much better at handling these things. It was Elizabeth who made the funeral arrangements and Elizabeth who suggested the tag sale.

"Are you sure you don't want to sell it?" The blue eyed stranger flashed an impish grin but she refused to let his homegrown good looks affect her.

"I'm sorry. This is a family heirloom. There's a nice bureau in the other room, part of a three piece set, perhaps–"

"Sold it!"

Caitlin jumped at the sound of her sister's voice floating across the room along with the echo of her heels clicking on the polished wood floor.

"A young couple just bought it. Isn't that great?" She smiled at Caitlin before turning her attention to their potential customer. "I'm afraid the early bird catches the worm around here but there's still a lot to choose from, like this beautiful piece." She gestured to the armoire.

"You don't mean this ancient, over-sized closet?" Caitlin repeated the description her sister had used earlier in the day.

Elizabeth glared at Caitlin. "Don't mind my sister. Selling our mother's house and furniture has been too much for her."

Heat flooded Caitlin's cheeks, and she had to turn away from the man's compassionate gaze.

"I'll take ten percent off the asking price," Elizabeth continued.

"You will not!"

"Your sister," the man nodded toward Caitlin, "informed me that this piece isn't for sale. Excuse me, but I'm a bit confused. Is it for sale or not?"

"No!"

"Yes!"

"Grandma's armoire is coming home with me. It's not for sale."

"Perhaps I'll just look around some more." Looking decidedly uncomfortable, the man headed for the kitchen.

"Really, Caitlin, I don't know what has gotten into you." Elizabeth stalked off.

Retrieving the pen she'd been using earlier and a clean sheet of paper, Caitlin folded it in half and wrote "not for sale" on one side. Then she propped it on the knobs of the armoire.

She could have saved everyone a headache if she'd made a sign earlier, only she didn't realize just how much she'd wanted to keep Grandmother's armoire until she'd nearly lost it. Either way she supposed she owed the man an apology or, at the very least, an explanation.

She found him in the kitchen admiring a china tea set.

"Pretty, isn't it?" she said.

He replaced the cup to its saucer so quickly she almost thought hot tea had sloshed over the rim.

"Don't tell me, the tea set isn't for sale." The corners of his mouth lifted.

She dropped her gaze, once again feeling the heat rise in her cheeks. "The tea set is for sale," she said. "I only wanted to apologize for my behavior before."

"You mean you've changed your mind about the armoire?" His eyes lit up.

"No, no," she quickly replied. "I thought after the way I acted the least I could do was offer you an explanation."

"That's not necessary." He grinned. "Although I appreciate the thought."

"I want to." She smiled back sensing his interest. Somehow, she knew he would understand. "You see, my grandfather fell in love with my grandmother the moment they met. He always told us kids she cast a spell on him."

"Like a witch?" he chuckled.

"More like a magical fairy." Caitlin grinned. "Grandma was a tiny woman. Anyway, he began building the armoire that very day. He'd already decided to marry grandma but felt as though he didn't have much to offer her. He wanted her to have something special, something exquisite to start their new life together, so–"

"He built her the armoire. Your grandfather sounds like a romantic fellow."

"You don't know the half of it." On impulse, she grabbed his hand. "Come see."

She brought him to the armoire, removed the sign, and lovingly opened its double doors. "Look." She pointed to two sets of initials and a date carved into the wood."

"Their wedding date?"

His look sent a shiver along her spine. "No. That's the day they met. Grandpa carved it before he had even asked Grandma to marry him."

His fingers, tracing the carved letters, touched her hand.

A jolt of awareness, deep and unnerving, flashed through her. Holding her breath to still her rapidly beating heart, she counted to ten before he finally broke the connection.

"Confident old coot, huh?" His voice deepened.

Caitlin detected no trace of ridicule in his eyes, only amusement and something else, something she had sensed earlier.

"Thank you for listening." She started to back away from him, from the well of feelings he evoked in her.

"My pleasure. I would've liked to have met your grandfather, seems we'd have had a lot in common." With that he disappeared into a crowd of people who had entered the room, leaving Caitlin to puzzle over his last comment.

Standing at the darkened kitchen window in her apartment, Caitlin turned toward her sister. "Elizabeth, how could you go behind my back? You know what that armoire means to me."

"Look, at this place." Elizabeth waved her arm to indicate the tiny studio apartment. "I did you a favor! There is no way you could have fit that monstrosity in here."

"Grandpa made that monstrosity!"

"Grandpa should have stuck to plumbing." Elizabeth gathered up her purse and stood to leave. "I'm sorry. I don't mean to sound so cold. Keeping my emotions in check is what's getting me through this. I only stopped by to drop off your half of the money since you left early. I'll call you tomorrow."

Looking around her small apartment, Caitlin knew her sister was right. No way would the armoire have fit into her small living space and paying for storage was out of the question. Still she couldn't bear the thought of the piece her grandpa had lovingly built, the piece her grandmother and then her mother had lovingly cherished, sitting in some stranger's house.

When the doorbell buzzed, she considered not answering. The second buzz brought her to her feet. "Who is it?" she called through the door.

"Lou. I was at the sale today. Remember?"

She recognized his voice immediately. "How did you know where I live?"

"I asked your sister before I left, in case–"

Caitlin opened the door. "I'm sorry but my sister sold–"

"The armoire," he finished in a softer tone. "I know. I bought it."

"You–" she gasped.

"She was about to sell it to another man, an antique dealer. I couldn't let that happen."

She looked at him, puzzled.

"I have special plans for that armoire." He smiled. "It wasn't meant to sit in an antique store. It was meant to be loved."

"Oh?" She felt her heart beat faster.

"Do you remember the date your grandfather carved?"

"Of course, October sixth, nineteen–" She stopped as his meaning became clear. Today was October sixth. The days and weeks had collided and melted into one another since her mother's death, and she hadn't given a thought to the date. Until now.

Suddenly, she recognized the emotion that had played across his face since their first meeting. It was the same feeling that had caught her off guard at his look of compassion when he learned of her difficulty in selling her mother's things. The same sensation that had intensified when he listened with such interest to the story behind the armoire and later when their hands touched.

He reached for her hand now and she felt a tingle, then a warmth flow through her.

"Is it coincidence that today is October sixth or is it some kind of magic?"

She laughed softly. "I vote for magic."

LEGENDARY KISS

Susan D. Brooks

"Einstein? No one wants to kiss Einstein." Cheryl stared up at the bronze statue of the brilliant scientist. "He's too bumpy."

"That's it then. I'm out of ideas." Robert looked at his watch. "And we're out of lunch hour." He glanced across Constitution Avenue, squinting into the July sunshine. "I don't see why we can't use one of the soldiers at the Vietnam Memorial. Those are very cool."

"Because they're too—I don't know. New. Besides, there's always someone there. This has to be more private." Cheryl turned and looked toward the Lincoln Memorial. "Lincoln's out of the question. Too big, too public."

"And the park rangers would never allow it." Robert's tone hinted at his frustration.

"Don't give up." Cheryl nudged him with her elbow. "In a city like Washington, where there's almost as many statues as residents, we're certain to find something."

He smiled down at her, his sparkling blue eyes sending her body temperature up a few notches. "Let's head back to work."

They started back up Constitution Avenue toward the Smithsonian Museum's National Air and Space building. Cheryl's long legs easily matched Robert's stride and, as she had each morning for the last month, she marveled at how well they meshed; not just their gait, but their personalities, too. Usually, interns hired for the summer at the museum bored her; most were either still immersed in the college mindset of party, party, party, or so fascinated with the endless collections of flight history memorabilia that they never did anything but work.

From the beginning, though, Robert seemed different. The handsome graduate student introduced himself right away then stopped by each morning on his way to the planetarium where he ran the projector. He'd wink and beg for another story from her inexhaustible supply of tales about the capitol area. At the end of the first week she found herself watching for him at break time and at lunch, but he always ate with someone else, one of the other interns and, several times, her dynamic boss, Lisa.

"What about the Roosevelt Memorial?" Robert's voice brought her back to the present. "On that wall where all the imprints are?"

"All the molded lips and eyes and ears?" Cheryl shook her head. "Not very romantic."

"I suppose not." He frowned and stuffed his hands in the pockets of his khaki pants.

"I could help you better if I knew more about this project of yours." She glanced at him. "All I know is that you want to find a statue that's kissable for some research you're doing. Is this work for your masters degree?"

"Ah, not exactly." The tips of his ears reddened.

"Oh." Cheryl didn't feel that she should probe, so she let the subject drop, but a moment later, he cleared his throat and confessed.

"I'm trying to get someone's attention, but she's so wrapped up in her job she doesn't know I'm alive."

Immediately, Cheryl thought of Lisa. Trim, attractive, and very ambitious, Lisa wanted more out of life than working for the Smithsonian; she dreamed of having her own business. She devoted endless hours to researching franchise opportunities and talking to those already in business for themselves.

Cheryl, on the other hand, couldn't imagine working anywhere but the Smithsonian Institute. She loved the staff who burned with dedication, the tourists who gaped at the displays, the artifacts themselves from America's past.

But the job of assistant gift shop manager barely paid enough to make ends meet, much less allow her to save money to return to college. No, she needed the manager's job, the one now open. The one Lisa would pick the replacement for later this week.

Maybe if I help Robert, Lisa will be grateful and give me the promotion.

She looked again at his handsome profile and decided the job was definitely the lesser of the two prizes.

"I have an idea." She touched his arm.

He turned, eyebrows raised in question.

"The Peace of God."

"The what?"

"A statue in Rock Creek Cemetery." She held up her hands as skepticism appeared on his face. "Hear me out. It's of a woman seated on a bench with her eyes closed. The monument is very beautiful, very old, and the section it's in is secluded. And hey, what has more stories than a cemetery?"

"Okay," he agreed cautiously, "then what?"

"We need to make up a legend."

"Make one up?" Robert sounded appalled.

"Sure. That's how most legends get started anyway."

He appeared to consider this as they waited for a crossing signal at 14th Street and Jefferson Drive. Then he snapped his fingers. "I've got it. You have to place something on the ground in front of her. A rose!"

"A rose?" Cheryl wrinkled her nose as the white light blinked permission to walk. She stepped into the street. "No, too obvious. How about a nosegay? You can buy them in Georgetown. They're romantic and from the same era as the statue."

"I like it. Then what?"

Legend, legend, legend. *Come on, girl, you can think of something.* Cheryl's mind sorted through facts and tales she'd heard. "You lay the flowers down and say something like Peace of God, send my true love." She hesitated.

"And make sure he or she comes on the wings of a dove," Robert finished, his voice rising with excitement. "Then, the next person to call your name is your true love. You have to kiss to make it stick."

"Hey, that's pretty good." Cheryl grinned up at him.

They climbed the steps to the Air and Space Museum.

"Let's go tonight. We can go out to eat in Georgetown afterwards." Robert held open the heavy glass door for her. "Why don't you bring Lisa? And one of those nose things."

Resigned to play the role of Cupid, Cheryl stopped by Lisa's office on the way back to the gift shop. "Hey, I heard the coolest story."

Lisa didn't look around from her computer. "If it's about those people in the White House, I'm not interested."

"No, no, nothing like that." Cheryl eased into the small workspace and perched on a two-drawer file cabinet. "Listen. I heard that if you go to this statue in Rock Creek Cemetery at midnight and lay a nosegay on the ground at her feet, the person who calls your name is your one true love."

Lisa gave her an incredulous look. "That's ridiculous."

Cheryl's heart sank. Pragmatic Lisa wouldn't go for such a thing. Poor Robert.

"It's not a nosegay," her boss continued, "you take three things, a flowering almond for hope, a red rose for love, and ivy for marriage. And you don't have to go at midnight. You can go any time after sunset."

Stupefied, Cheryl stared at her for a full minute. "You know about this legend?"

"Sure." Lisa shrugged. "It's an old one."

"I thought I knew them all." Cheryl shook her head. "Oh well. Have you ever tested it?"

"No."

"Want to? Tonight? Robert wants to go, and we can have dinner afterwards in Georgetown."

"Sounds like fun." Lisa reached for the phone. "Oh, take that box of post cards with you. They go in your store."

That evening, Cheryl followed Lisa through the cemetery gates and paused, a knot of anticipation hard in her stomach. The ivy, flowering almond, and rose shook slightly in her hand. Robert, sending a message through Lisa, said he'd meet them here.

"I don't see him." Lisa shifted impatiently. "Let's just go to the statue. This place isn't so big he couldn't find us."

Cheryl nodded and led the way down the cobblestone walk. Silvery light from the moon illuminated the headstones and well-trimmed shrubs gracing both sides of the path. The night air, soft with summer, caressed her arms, her face. She breathed in deep, catching the scent of the rose.

A romantic night and no romance in sight. *Maybe I'll try this legend out myself after Lisa's taken her turn.* She almost giggled at the thought. Trying out a legend? What a crazy idea.

They stopped in front of a marble lady seated on a bench, head lowered, a cape falling from her shoulders to the ground. Cheryl handed the flowers and vine to Lisa, but her friend shook her head.

"You do it first."

Cheryl hesitated, then realized nothing would be hurt if she went first, so she laid the three items on the ground and stood back.

"Peace of God, send my true love and make sure he comes with the wings of a dove," she chanted softly. Lisa grinned at her.

"Your turn." Cheryl gestured to the flowers.

Lisa shook her head. "You can't use the same ones twice."

"Cheryl." The male voice came from a bush to her left. She turned in time to see a shadow walk toward her. Pale light revealed Robert's smiling face.

"The legend says you have to kiss me." He took her hands in his.

"Me?" Cheryl gaped at him. She glanced over at Lisa. "But—but—"

Lisa burst into laughter. "I've known Robert for years, and there's nothing between us. His older sister and I went to high school together."

"So you were in on this?" Cheryl looked from her boss to Robert and back again.

"From the beginning. I figured he might get you distracted from that barn of a museum long enough to enjoy something else in life besides research." She shook her head. "I never saw anyone worse than me about working."

Cheryl looked up at Robert. "But why all this? Why not just ask me out?"

"Because I wanted to create something you'd remember. Something you'd archive with all the other information in your fact-filled head." His gaze wandered to her mouth. "Besides, I wanted you to always remember our first kiss. A legendary kiss."

His lips met hers, warm and filled with promise.

WON'T YOU BE MINE?

Betsy Norman

Monoliths of snow halted Tara's morning jog through the park. Huge rectangles thrust upward from various sentinel positions around the band gazebo. Small teams of people gathered around each one, axing or chipping their way into the columns. One snowsuit-bound couple worked on tying off the banner that explained the odd snow structures: Winter Carnival Amateur Team Snow Sculpting Contest. The Valentine's theme was: Won't you be mine?

What a waste of time. She sighed over the lonely reminder of the Hallmark holiday that taunted her solitary status. Why put your heart and soul into something, only to have it melt away to nothing? It was an ironic metaphor for her own love life.

It seemed clichéd to categorize all men as commitment impaired, but three fizzled relationships in a row had firmly cemented Tara's opinion. She thought the last boyfriend was The One, until talk turned to starting a family. She wanted one; he didn't. End of story.

By getting too close to the elusive flame of love, she'd smothered it, dashing all her hopes in the process. Better to forget about it and accept being alone. Whenever her maternal instincts popped up, she could pacify them by visiting with her nieces and nephews.

Tara made a decision as she contemplated the formidable white rectangles guarding the park. She'd be more like them, frozen and unyielding, but she'd be smart enough to stay out of the sun. Who needed chocolates and roses, anyway? Soup with noodles seemed much more practical in the dead of winter.

"Oomph!" A corner of the nearest snow giant collapsed and a disembodied male voice grunted from beneath. "A little help here? Please? Anybody there?" A thermal, red-gloved hand flagged for aid.

Another big chunk slid precariously, and Tara realized the man's dilemma. He'd cut too much off at once, and it had tumbled on top of him.

"I'm coming!" She bolted around the opposite side and created a counter-balance for the remainder, safely guiding it away from the prone man. She lugged the largest portion of snow covering his chest away and peered down at his face in concern. "Are you okay?"

"Whew!" The man remained on his back, panting. "Thanks. You're a lifesaver."

He tossed aside his hat, exposing brown hair plastered to his brow, and unzipped the ski jacket. Tara could almost see steam rising off of his chest.

"Are you crazy? Even Hercules couldn't handle all that ice and snow toppling over him." She tried to catch her own breath and plopped down beside him. "Shouldn't someone be helping you—I mean, this is a team competition, isn't it?" She pointed toward the banner.

"Yeah, but my 'teammates' backed out on me to be with their 'sweethearts.'" He rose up on his elbows with an undaunted grin. It went well with the dimples. "One decided painting the new apartment he and his girlfriend are going to rent would make a great Valentine's surprise, and the other's got an expectant wife feeling decidedly unsexy, and he's determined to convince her otherwise."

"Humph." Men like that didn't exist in Tara's opinion. Romantic and domestic. It just didn't happen. What was this guy's story? She noticed he didn't have any ball and chain excuse about keeping him home. Why would he hang around buddies who did?

"This doesn't look like a guys-only type thing," she said, glancing around at the other teams, mostly consisting of affectionate couples. "Shouldn't your 'sweetie' be helping?"

He dusted himself off and rose, offering a soggy gloved hand to assist her up. She took it, surprised at his gesture.

"Well, sure, if I had one." He winked. "I was going to play fifth wheel just for the fun of it, but ended up solo. I'd probably do the same thing if I were in their position. It'd be much nicer holed up warm and cozy at home with a...."

He didn't finish the sentence. Tara stared at him, subconsciously eager for him to continue. He shrugged with a lopsided grin, as if to dismantle the thought before confessing it. "Some guys are just lucky, I guess."

The morning sun came out from behind a cloudbank and played zigzag shadow games through the pine trees surrounding the park. Tara felt its warmth creep over her, a reminder of her vow not ten minutes earlier.

"Smart, more like it. Couldn't you make up some excuse to help you avoid losing your snowball fight with this impenetrable fortress?" Tara budged her weight against the half-begun statue.

"Beats staying home alone. Hey! Careful. You'll ruin

the, the—" He grazed a hand over the area she'd flattened. The quirky grin surfaced again. "The whatever this is going to turn out to be."

Tara considered the misshapen snow sculpture. "It sure doesn't look like much now, does it?" She gave him a dubious glance.

"No, it doesn't, but nothing ever does at first." He reached for his axe again. "I need to chip away the excess and look for its 'heart' before it can look like anything. Isn't that what the professional artists do? Let a sculpture form itself?"

"If you say so." She laughed.

"Stand back," he warned playfully. "And allow this artiste to work."

Tara stepped aside under the pretense of stretching out muscles gone cold from her aborted jogging. She needed to go easy and perform another warm-up before attempting to start over, but her heart wasn't really into it any more.

While he chopped away, she checked out the other projects underway. Most teams had already hacked their way to the core of their blocks and were busy shaping them into elegant sculptures.

His gloomy tower of snow looked lurching and lumpy. He'd never finish it alone, despite his enthusiasm and optimistic attitude. He needed help. Her help.

That thought buzzed through Tara's mind triggering warning bells.

She should continue her jog. She should forget about his wistful labeling of his monogamous friends. She should not be curious to see what his tenaciousness developed, what wondrous secret lay hidden inside the frozen center waiting to be discovered. She should forget it was Valentine's Day and how his smile made her toes tingle. She should remember her promise to remain cold and aloof.

Too bad her insides were already on defrost.

"Need some help?" she asked before her conscience

gagged her.

Her timid offer stopped him mid-swing. He looked genuinely pleased, dropping his axe and thrusting out his hand with a broad smile. The dimples pitting each cheek deepened.

"Boy, do I ever." He gave her hand a vigorous shake. "What's your name, partner?"

The contact was not only physically jolting but also radiated heat up her arm. She was thankful for the sharp wind chapping her cheeks. It hid the blush she felt thawing them. "Tara Sutton."

"Jamie Bigelow. Great to meet you, Tara. Have you ever sculpted snow before?" he asked.

Tara shook her head.

Jamie leaned in conspiratorially. "Me neither!"

His candor was the icebreaker she needed to justify helping him. Or so she told herself. Under Jamie's vague direction, Tara scraped at the ice with an old baking pan he'd pounded ragged nail-holes through. They worked in tandem and often side by side, whittling away at the compacted snow.

He explained even though he'd never created a snow sculpture before, one of his no-show buddies was a veteran at the winter festivals and had given him a few pointers on how to do it and what tools to use.

"He and his wife have kids—two boys. They're hoping for a little girl this time," Jamie chatted amiably. "They've been doing this since the oldest was a toddler."

"Don't the little ones get cold?" she asked.

"Nawww." He waved a hand. "They love it. Chuck builds them a hollowed out igloo fort to block the wind, and they're in heaven. Regular little Eskimos. Couldn't drag them inside last time I babysat."

"You like kids?"

"I love kids. Don't have any of my own yet, so I borrow theirs for practice. They love their 'Uncle' Jamie."

By the time the block had been chipped to a more reasonable size, the sun was high and bright. It shone directly down on Tara, despite her pledge to stay clear of its melting rays.

"Hungry?" Jamie asked.

"Starving!" Tara, still in her Lycra leggings and turtleneck sweatshirt, had completely forgotten about breakfast or that she needed to phone the landlord to fix the broken thermostat in her apartment again. It was always freezing there, and she didn't look forward to returning, especially after basking in the warmth of Jamie's smile.

"C'mon up to the commissary, and we'll grab some cocoa and sandwiches." Jamie took her hand. The taut strength of his melted the last ice reserves of her vow.

"Isn't that for team members only?"

"Aren't we a team?"

He said it with such affable sincerity. Of course, he was only referring to the snow sculpting competition, wasn't he? Just because he hadn't let go of her hand didn't give her a basis to suspect a further possibility. Or did it?

Jamie guided her toward a secluded table to eat their lunch away from the din of the other teams. They settled opposite each other and tore into the pre-wrapped hot beef sandwiches and red-frosted cupcakes.

Tara smiled. "Mmm. I think anything would taste good right now. I didn't exactly plan on taking a detour before eating this morning."

His hand inched toward her elbow, fingers brushing hesitantly against the damp fleece. "You must be soaked through. If you catch a cold on my account, I'd feel obliged to bring you chicken soup every day until you got better." His impish grin surfaced again, this time with a charming sparkle of blue eyes.

On the contrary. Because of Jamie, any chill she harbored dissolved into a shiver that wasn't caused by the weather.

"I'm okay. I haven't played in the snow for ages."

"It is kinda fun, isn't it? I always liked building snowmen when I was a kid."

"Yeah, but then they always melt."

"That's an unavoidable consequence, and you can always build more. Even snowmen can't resist the tempting heat of the sun."

Or snow women, Tara thought.

An awkward silence fell between them, full of adolescent cow-eyed glances and self-conscious sandwich munching. Tara felt like a teenager at a winter party, flushed from sweaty woolen handholding and flying along the ice on figure skates.

"C'mon," Jamie said. "Let's get you thawed out before we tackle that sculpture again."

The irony of his words almost made Tara laugh out loud, but it still didn't hurt to test for any remaining frostbite.

He led her to the fireplace in the corner of the commissary, and she sat on the huge hearthstone. The heat from the fire permeated her limbs. Stoking up a few logs, he scattered the coals into sparks and sat close to her. She felt warm and dry within minutes. Almost too warm, sitting so near Jamie. Tara stretched out a few sore kinks, then sneezed unexpectedly.

"Looks like I might owe you that chicken soup, after all," Jamic said.

"Oh, it's nothing. Probably just the swift temperature change to indoors has my nose running. Or maybe the smoke from the fireplace. I'll be okay once we're back in the fresh air." And not in such close proximity to Jamie that she felt feverish.

He took her hand again and led her toward the door. Intending, she assumed, to help her descend the icy steps, but when he failed to let go until they'd reached their snow block, Tara felt herself liquefy.

So much for being an Ice Queen.

Jamie broke out smaller chisels from his duffel bag so they could begin a detailed shaping of the sculpture, but he still hadn't decided on what it was going to be.

Tara tried to sluff off the achy feeling and drippy nose that kept getting worse, but after another hour or so, she had all the symptoms of a bad cold. She desperately didn't want the afternoon to end, but a sneezing fit knocked her right on her kcister.

Jamie huddled up next to her and put an arm around her shoulders. "Tara. You'd better go home and get some rest. I'm sorry I dragged you into this when you're not even dressed properly to be outside all day. Now you're good and sick, and it's all my fault."

Even though her sinuses were suffering, inside her chest radiated warmth born from the tenderness and comfort of his concern. She didn't really want her heart to become a frozen tundra. She wanted the warm coziness Jamie had kindled inside her, wanted to see if the coals could ignite. She wanted a Valentine that would last.

But what if it turned out to be merely spontaneous combustion, burning itself out as inevitably as all her previous relationships?

"It's not your fault," she sniffed. "But you are right, I better go. But now you'll never know what the sculpture wants to be, will you? Because of me, you won't be able to finish."

"Because of you, I will finish." He gave her a shy grin and thumbed a focal point in the air toward the snow lump. "See there, the crude bulbous shapes?" he asked.

"Yes," she nodded. "But what are they supposed to be?"

He hopped up and scraped away some of the loose snow, smoothing and rounding the sculpture beneath his hands carefully. "Two hearts uniting. Can you see it now? Its practically finished itself!"

"You're right." She pointed to the contest banner theme. "Won't you be mine? It's perfect." Tara smiled at him, and he beamed back.

So, he'd found the "heart" beneath the frigid, unyielding ice, after all. Two, in fact. Bleary eyes and a runny nose couldn't overcome her secret delight at Jamie's success. Was it an omen?

"Let me help you home," he said. "You need to be bundled up in a big blanket, pronto."

"No, you go ahead and smooth the rest of it off. My apartment's just a few blocks up. I can make it fine."

"A few blocks up where, exactly? I mean—" There was an edge to his question, as if he felt the same expectations, the same fear. The rush of meeting someone you want to meet again and again, but never will unless you speak up right now. "I mean, well. How am I supposed to know where to bring the soup when I'm done?"

Tara bit her lip. Should she freeze up again and let the icicles around her resolve re-form rather than risk her heart to Jamie?

"With extra noodles?" he coaxed. "I won't let it get cold, I promise. We could rent a video and hole-up together on the couch, or something. And tomorrow there's a classic movie marathon on cable we could watch."

"But tomorrow is Valentine's Day." Tara bit her lower lip.

"So it is." Jamie's voice dropped quietly. "Won't you be mine?"

She turned her face toward the sun, letting the rays melt straight into her soul. Yes, she was sure even cold soup couldn't dull the warmth she felt right now.

"221 Snowdrift Lane, number 3, second floor. With extra noodles, remember?"

"You bet. I'll be there in less than an hour."

Perhaps she wouldn't remind the landlord about the thermostat, after all. The temperature in her apartment was just perfect for "holing-up."

LUCKY

Carolee Joy

"You're so adorable, with those big brown eyes and that curly hair around your sweet face. Why wouldn't I want you to spend the night?" Touching her nose to his, Brooke let the puppy lick her face.

Behind her, the vinyl floor squeaked when Ross, her co-worker, shifted his weight. He cleared his throat. "You're sure this is necessary?"

She nodded and continued to baby talk the puppy. "Aw, sweetness, you'll be a good baby while your daddy is away, won't you? Say yes." Lucky scrambled into her lap and eagerly licked her chin.

Ross knelt and tousled the dog's fur. "I mean it's enough that you agreed to take him while I'm gone for the wedding. The nights before then seem like a terrible imposition."

The wedding. He said it as if going home to get married was something he did every weekend. No big deal. Brooke suppressed her disappointment. She'd expected better of Ross, but she guessed she didn't know him as well as she thought she did. She hadn't even known he was engaged until just a few weeks ago when several co-workers were having coffee, and she'd caught a glimpse of a picture of him and a very pretty blonde he'd shown everyone before Brooke showed up. She'd been so stunned she'd missed the rest of the discussion and only caught his lament about not knowing what he was going to do with his six-month-old puppy while he was gone.

His arm bumped hers, sending a shock wave through her while he petted the dog. Embarrassed at the heat stealing up her neck, Brooke eased the cocker spaniel from her lap and rose. "I thought he'd adapt better if you could come for the next couple of evenings, just so he doesn't feel abandoned. That way when you are gone this weekend, it won't be such a rough transition."

Lucky wagged his tail and bunted his nose against her legs.

Ross stood. "You want me to stop by every night?"

He said it as if it were a prison sentence. Brooke crossed her arms over her chest. For a moment, she almost thought she detected the slightest flicker of interest in his brown eyes. How foolish of her. She chose her words carefully to hide hurt feelings. "If it isn't too much trouble."

"No, no. Of course, not. I just meant." He reached out toward her, then let his arm drop. "You're right, of course. Ease him into the separation. I'll come by after work. Unless," his eyes searched hers.

Hoping she'd tell him not to bother? Well, she wouldn't. When she didn't respond, he gave the dog a last fond pat and made his way to the door.

"Guess I'll see you at work tomorrow."

"Bright and early." Giving him a cheerier smile than she

felt, she closed the door behind him and sighed. Lucky pawed briefly at the door and whined, but then he followed her to the overstuffed chair and scrambled up into her lap.

Brooke absently stroked his silky ears while she channel surfed without seeing anything on the screen. What a sweet puppy, just the kind of dog she'd always wanted.

Just as Ross was the kind of guy she'd always hoped for. But if he hadn't noticed her enough to ask her out after months of working together at the bank, thinking she'd ever be more than a dog sitter to him was like wishing on a star. Absolutely useless. Especially since he already belonged to someone else. At least she could feel good about helping out a friend.

The next night, she had just fed Lucky and was opening a can of soup for her own supper when the doorbell rang.

Ross stood at the door, more appealing in shorts and a golf shirt than a soon-to-be married man had a right to look.

"How's my baby?" His brilliant smile made her heart ache and for the briefest moment she allowed herself to imagine what it would be like if he thought of her that way, but of course he meant the dog. Lucky came running.

As Ross knelt and let the dog greet him with sloppy kisses, Brooke stood mesmerized, soup dripping onto her leg from the spoon she held in her hand.

Lucky's tongue on her calf snapped her back to attention. Brooke started, and Ross chuckled.

"I didn't realize he liked vegetable soup. But then, I've never tried to serve it to him that way."

He stood, so near she felt warmth emanate from his skin.

"I was hoping to catch you before you had dinner."

"It's just soup," she said. "And I haven't heated it yet."

"Then let me take you away from all of this." His arm swept the narrow entryway, and he grinned. "Let me buy supper."

He wanted to take her out? Only because of the dog. The dog! They couldn't leave when she'd already been gone all day. "It wouldn't be fair to Lucky."

"We can bring him a doggie bag." Ross was silent, then snapped his fingers. "I know! That drive-in where they bring the food to your car. They have the best burgers and chocolate shakes in town. Lucky can go with us as long as you promise not to let him have all the fries. How does that sound?"

A peanut butter sandwich sounded good if she could eat it with Ross. He might be getting married in a few days, but that didn't mean she couldn't enjoy his friendship. She smiled, caught up in his enthusiasm. "I'll turn off the stove."

A short time later, she laughed at Ross' jokes and Lucky's antics and bit into the best burger she'd ever had. Or maybe it was because sitting in Ross' convertible with the summer breeze ruffling her hair and a starry sky overhead would have made cardboard taste like prime rib.

The next night, Ross showed up with pizza from her favorite place. How had he known what she liked?

His grin was somewhat sheepish. "I remember you mentioning this place during coffee break a few weeks back."

Warmed all the way to her toes, Brooke let him in while Lucky barked and ran happy circles around Ross' ankles.

Ross had to be the nicest guy she'd met in ages. Maybe ever. He didn't complain that she was an incurable channel surfer. He didn't laugh when she picked all the toppings and cheese off the pizza and left the naked crust on her plate. He stayed until the news came on, then shifted Lucky's sleeping form from his lap to hers.

His fingers brushed her bare thigh, causing a moment of awkward silence. He leaned over her, one arm braced against the couch. For a scary but thrilling moment, she thought he was going to kiss her, but she ducked away and gathered up the dog. She'd heard people tested the water with someone else on the eve of their wedding. This wasn't the eve, but really close. She reminded herself he had already made a commitment.

She cried herself to sleep.

Lucky woke her early Saturday morning with plaintive little cries, whimpering, and prancing from the bed to the door.

Brooke ran a hand through her short hair and jammed her feet into her puppy-dog slippers. She grabbed Lucky's leash, then threw open the door.

Ross stood on the threshold. His brown eyes twinkled as he took in her yellow sleep shirt, mussed hair and furry slippers.

"Ross! I thought you were leaving this morning." She clutched the leash against her chest and wished desperately to be back in bed. With the covers pulled over her head.

He bent and stroked Lucky. "I want you to go with me."

"Me? With you? To your wedding?" She couldn't have been more amazed if he'd asked her to fly to the moon.

He straightened, his expression full of surprise. "My wedding? Whatever made you think I was getting married?"

"Leaving the dog, the picture—" She stammered to a halt.

His brow crinkled for a moment, then his laugh filled her world with sunshine. "My brother is the one getting married. My twin brother."

"Your brother. Of course," was all she could manage through the elation filling her heart.

"So what's your answer, will you go with me? I can't leave you when I'm finally getting a chance to know you. You can sleep in my kid sister's room. My family will love having you."

"What about Lucky?" She leaned a little closer to Ross, drawn by the promises his eyes made.

"He'll come, too. Oh, Dad will fuss, but he'll get over it. Say you'll go. You don't expect me to do without my two best friends on such a beautiful day, do you?"

"Certainly not." She inhaled the fresh scent of him and closed her eyes.

His lips grazed her temple, the corner of her mouth. "You know, getting Lucky was the best thing I've ever done. I thought I'd never get you to notice me."

Amazing. She'd been about to say that she got lucky when she offered to dog sit, but she was too busy enjoying Ross' kiss.

SECOND SUNDAY IN MAY

Tami D. Cowden

Joanie had only the vaguest impression of the events of the previous days.

The long cross-country trip to Jack's Boston home, the arrangements to be made, the crowd of strangers bringing sympathy and casseroles, the funerals, the meeting with the lawyer. And now she was alone. In a strange house that was to be her home.

No, not alone. The children were here.

Three children. Her children, now, courtesy of the drunk driver who had killed her brother, Jack, and his wife, Michele.

Twin nieces, Penny and Patsy. Solemn-eyed, straight-haired, freckled duplicates, at four old enough to understand their parents weren't coming back. One nephew, Tucker, a blond cherub who had just learned to walk and found few things in the world more interesting than his own thumb.

So here she was, the aunt who never even babysat, the only family her brother's children had left in the world.

Except for Max, of course.

Michele's brother had obviously been shocked to discover that the children had been left to her guardianship. She hadn't given him the satisfaction of knowing she'd been shocked, too. Joanie winced as she recalled the scene that had taken place only the day before at the lawyer's office.

The big leather chair enveloped her as she felt her jaw drop lower and lower as the attorney's dry words slowly revealed a fate not of her doing. She was the children's guardian. She had control of a sizable amount of money to rear them. She—who had never even signed a lease because the thought of staying a year in one place was too confining—now owned a large house in a respectable middle-class suburb. A suburb!

"Are you seriously asking me to believe that my sister entrusted her children to that wild gypsy?" Max spoke quietly, yet somehow his words echoed around the room. "She doesn't stay in one place for more than six months at a time."

Had she stayed anywhere even that long? No, she hadn't. Not since she first struck out on her own, heading for Paris with her paints and rolled up canvas in a backpack.

"Say something!" Max's fury turned on her. "Why did they do this? Have you even met the kids before now?"

"Once. I met the twins once." She had no answer to his first question. Why did Jack and Michele do this? She turned her attention to the attorney. "Was it Jack's idea?"

The attorney flushed slightly. "I assure you, both Mr and Mrs Elliot were quite emphatic in their choice of guardian." He cleared his throat. "Frankly, Mr Widner, they both thought you were too concerned with your business pursuits to take on the responsibility of parenthood."

Max's color rose alarmingly. "I would have made the time for Michele's kids." He bit the words out forcefully, enunciating them one by one, before turning away from them to face the window.

Through the grief-stricken haze that clouded her own senses, Joanie realized that Max was not so much upset that she had been chosen, as hurt that he had not.

How ironic.

Because she was wondering what she had ever done to Jack to make her brother want to disrupt her life this way.

She thought with longing of her small studio in Venice, California. Of the ease with which she had always picked up and moved on for all of her adult life. Of her paintings of oceans, mountains, and deserts, of factories and of farmland.

Her paintings were known for their freshness—the novel insight that only a stranger sees.

What would she paint if there were no new vistas? How would she find inspiration if she had to see the same thing day after day for the next seventeen years until these kids were grown?

How could Jack do this to her? Joanie looked at Max out of the corner of her eye. What was wrong with him? Tall, lean, tanned. He looked respectable in his well-cut business suit. Successful in his highly polished shoes and his fashionably longish brown hair. Secure in his place in the world.

He's attractive. She'd thought so at her brother's wedding, and six years later, he was even more so.

Sure, a businessman can be boring, maybe, but wasn't that a good trait in a potential guardian? He looked like the sort of guy anyone would want to raise their children. Why hadn't Jack and Michele chosen Max?

The little she knew about her sister-in-law's twin had not been negative, really. To hear them tell it, he just wasn't much fun. Michele had laughed once that Max had been born forty years old. Was that such a bad thing in a parent?

Would it be better to have one who had never grown up? Isn't that what Jack had always said about his kid sister? Oh sure, he said it with his indulgent laugh and hugs, but he meant it.

So Michele and Jack had had to choose between two extremes and had taken the lesser evil? Feeling secure, as everyone does, that such plans would never have to be realized?

For a long moment, Joanie allowed herself the fantasy of telling Max he was welcome to the responsibility of a ready-made family, thanks very much.

But she remembered her childhood. Jack always shielding her from unpleasant realities. Jack defending his nonconformist sister from the tyrannies of the clone-like high school cliques. On report card days, Jack standing between their stern father and the free-spirited Joanie, saying "You wait, you wait, Dad. Someday she'll come into her own."

And never once had Jack asked for anything in return. Until now.

Payback time. She couldn't let Jack down.

So Joanie stood, leaned over the lawyer's desk, and signed her commitment to her brother's faith in her. She felt Max's furious gaze burning into her the whole time, but she left without a word to him.

That was yesterday.

Today she was trying to dress three kids who could teach eels to be slippery. Keeping one eye on Tucker, toddling about in a diaper that was ominously loose around his waist, she tried to persuade Penny into some clothes.

"I can't wear the blue top, Aunt Joanie. Penny tore her blue top." Patsy squirmed free of the arms attempting to pull a shirt over her head and rolled her eyes in apparent disgust at the fashion ignorance of aunts. Penny silently frowned in sympathy.

"Do the two of you always have to dress alike?"

"'Course we do. We're twins." They spoke in unison.

"Well, how 'bout today we try something diff—" Joanie broke off as she realized that these kids were going to be doing a lot of things differently from now on. Maybe dressing differently didn't have to be so high on the list of priorities. Sighing, she simply asked, "What shirts do you want to wear today?"

As one, four shoulders lifted. Two pairs of hands were raised palm up. Four eyes gazed at her somberly.

"Let's start with Tucker," Joanie muttered. "He doesn't have to match, does he?"

Two small smiles appeared briefly, before two heads shook an answer. Tucker sucked his thumb.

Two hours later, the three kids were finally dressed, and one of them rediapered. Twice. The juice Tucker liked so much was definitely short-term rental property.

"We're hungry!" Penny and Patsy spoke together. Patsy added, "Tucker is hungry, too."

Joanie glanced at the clock. "10:00! I guess I'd better get breakfast going." She lifted Tucker up and led the girls into the kitchen. The mess still left from dinner the night before caused a wince. She'd been too exhausted to clean up.

"Uh, how's cereal sound?" She set the small boy down and looked into the cupboards uncertainly. There were lots of casseroles in the freezer, but otherwise there didn't seem to be much food in the kitchen. She made a mental note to go to the grocery store.

"Cakes!" Tucker yelped and teetered toward his high chair. "Cakes." He grabbed one of the legs and tried to pull his chair to the table.

She kept nosing through the cabinets. "Aha! Cornflakes!" She pulled the box out triumphantly and shook it.

"No! Cakes!" Tucker gave up his effort to bring his chair to the table and sat heavily on his bottom. Jutting out his lower lip ominously, he glared briefly at his aunt before shouting again. "Cakes."

Who would have thought such a little child could have such powerful lungs? "Sorry, kid. I may be new to this parenting stuff, but I am not giving you cake for breakfast." She bent and held the box out for the boy to see. "See the pretty tiger. He wants you to eat the cereal. Yummy."

He slapped a hand at the box, knocking it from her hand. Cornflakes cascaded to the shiny tile floor.

"Tucker!"

Tiny heels drummed on the floor. "Cakes. Want cakes." His face was turning a bright red, making him look like a tomato with a blond wig.

"But—"

"He wants pancakes. Mom always makes us pancakes when we want them." Patsy sniffed audibly before whispering, "Made us pancakes, I mean." Penny put a small arm around her sister's shoulder and contributed a whimper.

A keening wail sounded from below as Tucker lifted his heels too high and fell back, hitting his head on the floor. Penny and Patsy crowded toward their brother and noisily contributed their own cries.

"What the hell is going on here!" Max's deep voice echoed off the kitchen appliances.

Joanie spun around at the sudden shout, slipping in the spilled cereal. She plopped awkwardly to the floor, ending up next to the children. So startled were they by this turn of events, they quieted mid-shriek. Like her, they turned to stare at their uncle.

"Cakes?" whined Tucker.

Looking up at him from her undignified position, she thought Max seemed even taller than usual. Even more capable. And much, much angrier.

"Look at this place. It's a mess. What have you been doing!" Yep, he was definitely angrier than ever.

She struggled to stand up, but her foot slid through the crushed cornflakes. Max shook his head with exasperation.

But apparently his fury didn't make him forget his manners entirely, because he held out a hand to help her up.

Once she was safely on her feet again, however, courtesy was forgotten.

"Sheesh, Joanie, do you have any clue how to take care of these kids?" He waved a hand around the kitchen. "It looks like a bomb went off in here. You're really making a hash of this, just as I expected."

Taking a deep breath, she counted to ten. Looking at the mess and rubbing the sore spot on her tailbone, she kept going up to twenty. The nerve of this guy!

Finally, when she felt she had her own temper under tight control, she answered, "I'm taking care of these children. It is my first day, though, you know. Unless you have some constructive advice, I suggest you keep your opinions to yourself."

There. That sounded pretty good. Calm, cool, and collected. Not at all like Mr I-Can-Do-Anything-Better-Than-You.

"Oh, I have constructive advice, all right. How about you go back to your artist colony and let me raise my sister's kids properly? How's that for constructive advice?"

"Sorry, but your sister obviously didn't think you were good enough to raise my brother's kids!" It was a low blow, she knew, but she was darned if she'd let him come in here and tell her what to do.

He sucked in air, and for a split second she actually thought he might strike her, before she dismissed the thought as absurd. Still, he stared at her, his fists clenched, for a long moment, while she boldly held her ground and his gaze. Finally, a lengthy breath escaped his lips, and he turned away.

Trying again for a calm voice, she continued, "I am as puzzled as you that Michele and Jack gave me this responsibility, but I won't let them down."

He turned and looked her full in the face. She shivered at

the calculating expression in his eyes.

"I'll give you six months. A year at the outside." He nodded as though to himself. "And then you'll be gone."

Her eyes narrowed. "I'm not going to leave, Max."

"We'll see. Meanwhile, I'll keep things from falling apart." He looked around the room and rubbed his hands together. "Well, allrighty then. I guess we ought to get this place cleaned up and these little guys fed. Girls, do you know where the broom is kept?"

Penny scooted to a closet, her sister close behind. Seething, Joanie wanted to interfere with his interference, but the truth was, she could use a little organization. From what she could see, Max was definitely orderly.

So maybe the best thing would be to ignore his needling, and take his help, however ungraciously offered. At least he was pretty to look at.

Smiling grimly to herself, she squared her shoulders. "Fine. I'll get breakfast started."

A small hand grabbed her knee, at the same time tugging Max's slacks. "Cakes?"

The hope in the little boy's voice drew reluctant laughs from his aunt and uncle. Max leaned down and swept the tyke into his arms.

Shooting a look at Joanie over the tousled head, he challenged, "Do you know how to make pancakes?"

Her head shook, but her chin lifted. "No. But I'll learn."

True to her word, the art of pancake making was but the first of many tasks Max watched Joanie master in the coming months.

Still, he was unconvinced. Running a household of four might not be something learned overnight, but he was sure a more stable person, like himself, for example, wouldn't have so many disasters. And his sister wouldn't have had any problem at all.

Like the time he came by just as Tucker was running out the front door naked. Or when all three of the kids got the chicken pox—and she did, too! He and Michele had had the sense to get chicken pox when they were kids.

He'd thought that would be the last straw—surely she'd head for the hills then. But no. She laughed at all their spots. She even painted a picture of them all in their polka dots.

That it was a terrific portrait, full of life, just annoyed him more.

The kids ate macaroni and cheese and hot dogs. Even worse than the easy fix stuff, she had them eating Thai noodles or tortilla rollups, or other new fangled stuff. When his sister was alive, the menu always included roast beef or chicken. Stuff that was good for kids.

He supposed he should be glad the laundry got washed and floors got scrubbed, but he looked forward to the day her old travel lust would call the interloper away.

He only hoped it would be before his lust carried him away.

At first he ignored the attraction he felt for her. Pretended it didn't exist. She was undisciplined, irresponsible, unreliable. Everything he disliked. Just because this wild thing was packaged in the most fantastic body he'd ever seen was no reason he should think about asking her out or anything.

Who cared if he loved the way sunlight hit her hair, turning it from mere brown to a riot of red, gold, and chestnut? Beautiful brunettes were a dime a dozen, and besides, he was sure he preferred blondes.

As for those eyes, so dark they held the mysteries of night, well, that was just stupid. They were brown. Ordinary brown. And the very fact that she was able to make plain old brown eyes seem so exotic, just further proved how unsuitable she was.

Not suitable to be guardian of his sister's children. Not suitable for his interest.

Or so he told himself. He counted the days until she moved on.

But the months passed. He dropped in with increasing frequency to see how the kids were doing, and he discovered that his body had very different ideas of what was suitable. The brief surprise visits, originally intended just to catch the gypsy in some scrape, turned into planned events. Family outings.

"His sister's children" became Penny, Patsy, and Tucker. Not just little kids, but individuals. Small certainly, but already developing distinct personalities, tastes, and opinions. He liked them for their own sakes now.

But he knew, in the farthest reaches of his mind, that he came to see her every bit as much as he came to spend time with the kids.

They had their regularly scheduled Wednesday nights at the pizza place. And when the little ones were tucked in, he savored the hour spent talking with her in front of the fire.

Saturday afternoons at the park yielded a few moments on a bench, watching how high the twins could swing, and how wide Joanie could smile.

And she did smile. At him.

But he knew she'd be gone. It was just a matter of time before she decided that Boston didn't offer the right "vista" as she called it. No new scenes to paint.

In fact, she'd already altered the subject of her paintings. More and more, it was children who appeared. Sometimes happy, sometimes sad, but always she captured the innocence of childhood.

Personally, he thought these paintings were far better than her other work. But he doubted she'd agree.

He said nothing. He pretended he felt nothing.

Every Sunday, with Tucker in the nursery, and the twins in Sunday School, Max found himself sharing a pew with Joanie. And then they all went to brunch. Max told himself that he was merely making sure Tucker, Patsy, and Penny has as normal a home life as possible.

And so it was, on the second Sunday in May, some nine months after the tragedy, he sat near her for the service. Today was a family service, with the children present. Tucker rested on her knee. Patsy sat between them, while Penny leaned against his other side.

"Motherhood is truly a blessed state." The young minister beamed at his congregation. "That is why we celebrate this day in honor of mothers everywhere."

Max sat up straight. Mother's Day? He'd forgotten it was Mother's Day.

This could be a dreadful reminder to the children of Michele's death. Of Jack's death.

He glanced at the children. The girls were sitting politely, listening to Reverend Miller. Tucker was paying attention to the toy car in his hand. No fallout yet. He chanced a look at Joanie, to find her staring back at him, worry written clearly in her eyes as well.

Damn. They should have skipped church this week.

The sermon continued. The many roles a mother undertakes were recounted. The sacrifices she makes listed. The service she performs honored. At the conclusion of the service, the children of the congregation were invited to come forward to obtain flowers to present to their mothers.

"Oh, no." He muttered the words. Here it comes, now the kids would realize they didn't have a mother anymore. He saw Joanie tighten her hold on Tucker's waist, hugging him closer, and he draped his own arms around the twins' shoulders.

But, in unison as ever, the twins stood. "C'mon, Tucker. Let's get the flowers." Tucker slid down from Joanie's lap and took his sisters' hands. They joined the parade of children in the aisles.

"It's okay. Healthy." Fluttering her hands before herself, she whispered, "We'll take them to the cemetery. A nice ritual. It's okay."

Nodding, he swallowed hard. "Yeah. Yeah. Good idea." A knot formed in his throat as he watched the trio. Joanie fumbled in her purse, and glancing her way, he watched her remove a tissue and wipe at her tears. He reached for her hand and squeezed.

The warmth he felt at her touch no longer surprised him. But this time, he acknowledged it, accepted it. She returned the pressure of his grasp, and for the first time, he allowed himself to wonder what she felt for him.

Three small bodies crowded back into the pew right then. Max started to announce the plan to take the flowers to their parent's graves, but he stopped.

Three small hands, two delicate and one chubby, were holding out bright yellow mums to Joanie.

"Happy Mother's Day." The twins' duet was quickly repeated, with enthusiasm if not clarity, by Tucker.

He heard her gasp. Or maybe he heard his own sharp intake of breath. With shock, he realized that he wasn't the only one who had fallen in love with her. The only one who valued her. The only one who needed her. He was just the only one who couldn't admit it.

Until now.

Joanie felt the tears starting in her eyes again at the sight of the three flowers, one stem broken from the tight grasp of Tucker's fist, held out so generously before her. Taking the mums, she pulled the children into her arms, amazed anew at how she could fit all three into her hug. Swiftly administering kisses, she struggled to find another tissue in her bag.

A handkerchief was pressed into her hand.

Max! She stared guiltily at the purse in her lap. If he misunderstood, if he thought his sister was forgotten, he'd be so hurt. So angry.

She didn't want to lose him! The fierce thought startled

her, but she knew it was true. He had become a part of her life. She would make him understand the ability of children to hold onto the security offered them, even in the face of loss.

She'd make him understand how important he was. To the children. To her.

With trepidation, she lifted her eyes to meet Max's, but instead of the glare she expected, she found a warm gaze caressing her.

"I don't have any flowers for you," he said simply.

She shook her head and started to speak, but with a gentle touch of his fingers, he stilled her lips.

His fingers glided to her cheek to wipe away a stray tear. Holding her gaze, he leaned forward and gently kissed her. She breathed in his spicy scent, and knew he understood.

THE SWEETHEART WELL

Su Kopil

Elizabeth glanced nervously up and down the deserted
street. She must look ridiculous in her taffeta gown and
matching pumps, standing in front of the old wishing well,
but thankfully no one could see her. The Holling and Barrett
families would finally be joined forever in less than an hour,
but not in the way she had once envisioned.

She remembered when Forrest Drive used to be the heart
of Logan Falls. Then the supercenters moved in on the
outskirts of town. One by one the Mom and Pop shops
closed down, including her father's hardware store. She'd
been sixteen, in love with Grayson Holling, and devastated
when her mother informed her they were moving west.

She stared at the crumbling stone of what was once

Logan Falls' claim to fame—the Sweetheart Well. Lovers both young and old, her parents included, had flocked to the well with their hopes and dreams and wishes.

Elizabeth touched the splintered wood. Peeling paint gave it a blotchy appearance. Someone had long ago removed the old bucket and rope and boarded up the opening. Tall weeds, growing thick along the base of the well, tickled her stockinged legs.

She remembered the first time she'd visited the Sweetheart Well. She was seven, and Grayson was a very adult eight.

"Make a wish, Lizzie," he said.

"I don't know how," she answered.

He handed her a shiny new penny. "Close your eyes, turn around three times, and throw it. If your penny falls into the well then your wish will come true."

She did as he told her but she'd become disoriented, and her toss went wild, the coin landing in the grass.

Grayson laughed so hard his face turned red, and she thought he would pee in his pants.

She hated when he laughed at her. Right then, she vowed to return to the well by herself, with a roll of pennies, and practice in secret. Next time Grayson told her to make a wish, she'd be ready.

And she was.

It was her freshman year of high school. Grayson had finally noticed she was growing up. When he asked her to the Valentine's Day dance, she was ecstatic. Until Marylou Palmer told her Grayson had asked her first, and she'd turned him down flat. Elizabeth ran out of the dance, but Grayson followed her, and brought her to the Sweetheart Well.

"Make a wish, Lizzie," he said.

"I don't want to," she pouted. Even though she'd waited for this moment all her life, she was too upset with Grayson to care.

"Marylou lied to you." Grayson stared at his feet,

fidgeting with something in his pocket.

She had never seen Grayson Holling nervous before, and despite herself she listened.

"Marylou was just trying to get even with me for not asking her out. You're the only one I asked to the Valentine's dance." His earnest gaze met hers as he handed her a shiny new penny. "Make a wish, Lizzie."

Solemnly, she took the penny, damp from his sweat. She closed her eyes, spun around three times like she'd practiced for years, and lightly tossed the penny. She held her breath until she heard the faint, far-away splash. When she opened her eyes, Grayson stood before her.

Her heart beat wildly in her chest.

Grayson lowered his head to hers and kissed her for the first time.

From that day on they were inseparable. One day they would be married. She knew it was true. All those times she'd secretly practiced, and on that Valentine's Day especially, she'd wished Grayson would kiss her, and he did. The next time, she planned on wishing for Grayson Holling to marry her.

But that was before she stopped believing in fairytales and wishes, before her mother told her they were moving. The last time she saw Grayson was at the Sweetheart Well. It was Valentine's Day, two years after he first asked her out.

"Make a wish, Lizzie," he said and offered her a shiny new penny.

"No, Grayson, wishes are for children. They don't come true." She'd been crying all day, and her eyes were puffy. Her family was leaving in the morning. She knew she would never see Grayson Holling again.

"Please, Lizzie," he pleaded.

She saw the brightness in his eyes, but she couldn't do as he asked. Not this time. She stood on tiptoe and softly kissed him. "Goodbye, Grayson. I'll always love you." She choked back a sob and stumbled away. When she reached the corner she turned back, but he was already gone.

They'd exchanged letters for a time but, as happens at that age, life got in the way.

Now, on Valentine's Day twenty-five years later, her son was marrying Grayson's daughter.

Elizabeth caressed the rough stone. So many wishes, so many dreams. Had she really ever been that young, that naïve? With a sigh, she turned away from the well and headed back to her car.

"Mom, I was starting to get worried." At the church, Elizabeth's son, Michael, paced the small room, glancing at his watch.

Her original flight got cancelled, and she missed the rehearsal dinner the night before. She'd called Michael in a panic. He'd calmly told her everything was under control and to book a morning flight.

Elizabeth felt tears well up in her eyes. She'd often wondered who had taken care of whom after the divorce. Even at ten, her son had been responsible and strong. When he chose a college in the east, it was he who comforted her. And then, he met Cara, his soon-to-be-bride.

"You look so handsome, Michael." She adjusted his black bow tie.

"Now, Mom, you promised." He grinned.

"I know, I know, no tears until the reception." She sniffed.

"I wish Dad had made it."

"I understand." She smiled, attempting to hide her trembling lip. After all they'd been through, it still amazed her that Walter would miss his only son's wedding for a business trip. "I'll see you in a few minutes." She hugged Michael, then left him with his best man.

The murmur of the crowd inside the church rose and fell as everyone took their place, and the organist played the first notes of the "Wedding March." The wide double doors at the back of the church opened. A small gasp rose from the guests as the bride began her long walk down the aisle on the arm of her father.

Elizabeth's heart pounded in her ears drowning out the music. This was the first time she'd seen Grayson Holling in twenty-five years. To her eyes, he looked exactly like that boy she'd left standing at the Sweetheart Well.

He held his daughter's arm, his gaze never wavering from the front of the church, until they were even with Elizabeth's pew. As though he knew exactly where she sat, Grayson's gaze found hers. The air suddenly grew thin, and she found it hard to breathe, but she couldn't turn away.

His eyes were bright, and the smallest of smiles played upon his lips. Then he turned, lifted his daughter's veil, kissed her on both cheeks, and gave her hand to Michael before taking his seat.

Despite her intense desire to concentrate, Elizabeth barely heard the ceremony. She was too aware of Grayson Holling sitting only yards away from her. Although her son's engagement came as a shock, she had months to prepare for the wedding. Even the memories that accompanied her on the long flight didn't prepare her for the strong reaction she had to seeing Grayson again. Michael had told her the Hollings divorced amicably some years ago, but she didn't expect the absurd stab of jealousy at the sight of Grayson and his ex-wife, Marylou, sitting together. She felt like she was fourteen all over again, attending her first Valentine's Day dance.

Halfway through the reception the newlyweds hurriedly left to catch their honeymoon flight and begin their new life together. With the constant interruptions, she and Grayson barely had a chance to say more than a few polite words at dinner, but she'd been aware of him watching her most of the evening.

Elizabeth collapsed into a chair at one of the tables for

what felt like the first time since the couple exchanged vows. Her feet ached from wearing pumps. It had been a long day filled with emotional highs and lows. The band played a slow song, and couples filled the dance floor.

"I believe they're playing our song." Grayson appeared before her and offered his hand.

The pain in her feet receded, and she smiled up at him. "We never had a song."

"Every song was our song." He watched her intently.

She laughed and accepted his hand.

He led her to the dance floor and took her into his arms. If she closed her eyes, she could almost believe it was twenty-five years earlier so intense were the emotions that filled her heart. She really wasn't surprised to realize she'd never stopped loving him. But it was too late. She was no longer that young innocent girl full of hopes and dreams for the future.

All she had was this night—this moment, in the arms of the man she'd once believed in forever with.

"I've missed you, Lizzie," he whispered in her ear.

"I've missed you, too." She closed her eyes, giving herself permission to dream one last time, on this one last Valentine's Day—a day meant for magic and romance.

Song after song, Grayson twirled her about the floor, barely giving her a break between songs. Not that she wanted one. She almost felt as though he was afraid to let her go. At least, that's what she wanted… no, that's what she chose to believe. It was her dream, and she would live it to the fullest. When the band finally packed up and the guests started leaving, she felt like Cinderella. Too soon, her dream would end and reality, stark and lonely, would intrude.

She sensed Grayson's reluctance to end the evening as well, and when he suggested they go somewhere for a drink, she eagerly accepted. They compared memories, talked about their families, and the years in between.

Finally, he asked, "When do you go home?"

"Tomorrow."

"So soon?" He looked distracted.

She was disappointed when he paid their bill. It was almost as if, with her leaving tomorrow, he had already put her out of his mind. And here she had almost dared to hope, dared to believe, the dream might not end.

In the car, for the first time since they danced, he was silent.

She felt awkward and a little foolish. What must he think of her, mooning after him like she'd done as a girl. She didn't pay attention to where they were until he pulled the car over and helped her out. In the beam of the headlights, she recognized the Sweetheart Well. Her heart skipped a beat.

He stood near the well unable to look at her, fidgeting with something in his pocket. If she didn't know better....

"Grayson Holling, I'd swear you were nervous about something." The thought made her feel better, and she laughed.

He looked at her then and grinned. Pulling his hand from his pocket, he held out a shiny new penny. "Make a wish, Lizzie."

"You're joking, right?"

"Please?"

Her breath caught in her throat, and her thoughts swept back twenty-five years. How many times had she regretted not making that last wish before she moved away? How many times had her mind played tricks on her, saying *if only*....

Slowly, she reached for the penny.

Their fingers touched, trembled, then parted.

She closed her eyes and took a deep breath. It had been years since she'd done this. Could she still? Dare she believe? Turning around three times, she lightly tossed the penny, and made a wish. She waited, straining her ears.

A soft thunk sounded as the coin struck the boards of the

well. Then to her amazement, from very far away, she heard a tiny splash. Her penny had slipped through the cracks.

Opening her eyes, she found Grayson standing before her.

Her heart pounded, and the spark of hope burst into brilliant flame.

His head lowered, and his lips captured hers in a kiss that could make wishes come true.

FLOWERS EVERY MONDAY

Carolee Joy

"I moved nine hundred miles to be with you, and now you tell me we should date other people? Say it again, Bill. I want to be sure I heard you right." Pain and anger rising inside her, Kendra bit her lip and smoothed an imaginary wrinkle from the white tee shirt resting on the top of Bill's laundry basket. The rat! If he didn't want to be exclusive, why hadn't he said it before she washed all the clothes he'd brought over to her apartment?

"I only said it wouldn't hurt to date other people for awhile." Awkward silence grew between them. Bill sighed and placed his hands on her shoulders. "Kendra, I swear there isn't someone else, but we're all tangled up in assumptions."

"Well, excuse me for thinking you loved me when you

wanted me to leave Oshkosh for Dallas."

"I do—care about you." He spoke the words as if they stuck in his throat like taffy.

Overwhelmed with hurt, Kendra tensed. "Maybe that's not enough. I uproot my life, and now you're not sure."

"You're twisting things again. I think we could keep our options open, that's all. We could date other people during the week and still see each other weekends. It doesn't help that you live nearly an hour away." His tone became slightly accusing. "Forget what I said." He pulled her closer, but she turned her head, and his lips brushed her temple.

Kendra shrugged out of his embrace, determined not to be swayed this time by his appealing smile. "You're not cuddling your way out of this one. Just tell me, where am I going to meet anybody in suburbia? At the Laundromat? Grocery store? Or should I just wash your socks and bake chocolate chip cookies while you cruise the singles bars, window shopping and taking your time?"

"I never asked you to do all that."

"So what? You never told me not to, either."

Bill frowned. "I didn't want to hurt your feelings, but if you're going to be mad anyway, I'll tell you—stop baking. I'd rather chew on the lava rocks around those shrubs downstairs than eat another of your cookies."

Tears stung her eyes as she searched for a retort. Bill sighed, grabbed his keys and stomped toward the door. "We're getting nowhere fast. We'll talk after you've cooled off."

His footsteps pounded down the outer stairway. Kendra unclenched her hands and caught sight of his forgotten clothes. Grabbing up the basket, she hurried after him.

"Bill! Wait!" He stopped on the sidewalk and looked up. Kendra balanced the basket on the balcony railing. "You forgot your laundry." A shove sent shorts, tee shirts, and socks raining down to the landscape. Kendra dusted off her hands and slammed back into the apartment.

A moment later, the phone rang. Kendra took a deep breath and answered.

"Ken!" James Ethan Davenport's voice exclaimed. "Guess what I've got."

"Whatever it is, Jed, I hope it's not contagious. Unless it's a craving for chocolate."

"Chocolate. You okay?" Immediately, Jed sounded concerned.

"Sure, why?"

"You sound funny. Oh, that's right. Saturday night and Mr Potato Head. Want me to call back tomorrow?"

Kendra burst out laughing, Jed's irreverence chasing the tears away. "He just left. For a long, long walk."

The mobile phone line crackled. "Okay, then grab a sweater and meet me in the parking lot."

Moments later, Jed pulled up in a 1968 Camaro SS. Pausing to admire the classic convertible, Kendra gave it a pat before getting in. "She's a beauty, Jed. Where did you find her?"

"Odessa. Knew that one of these days all that traveling for the company would work to my advantage."

Bill, plucking white Jockey shorts from prickly bushes, looked up. Jed waved. Bill scowled and bent to retrieve a pair of socks from among the cinnamon colored lava rocks.

"What's he doing anyway?" Jed glanced back as he drove.

Kendra stared out the window until they turned onto the freeway. "Scrounging for dessert, I imagine."

"Meaning?"

Lights of oncoming cars blurred from her tears. "He said he'd rather chew rocks than eat my chocolate chip cookies."

Jed laughed. "He just doesn't appreciate dunkers. At least they don't crumble into a dozen pieces when you dip them in coffee. I like 'em."

Kendra smiled and relaxed into the red vinyl upholstery. She'd liked Jed, an equipment salesman for Milford

Engineering, from the day they met in Bill's office. Jed treated her like a buddy and was her resource for learning the political ins and outs of the company. Self-assured to a fault, Bill tolerated their friendship with patronizing amusement, apparently dismissing any possibility of Jed seeing her as more than one of the guys.

Easy going and comfortable to be around, Jed shared her passion for old cars and awakened new enthusiasms for barbecue and Rangers baseball. Studying his profile as he floored the Camaro, Kendra stifled an impulse to smooth back a lock of dark brown hair that had tumbled onto his forehead from the warm spring wind. Strange, the better friends she and Jed became, the less time he spent with Bill. She missed the occasional lunches the three of them had shared at first.

"He's jealous," Jed said softly.

Kendra's mind whirled. "Of—who?" she asked, not daring to hope he meant himself.

"You, of course. You got the project assignment he wanted. Hell, he'd had his mind set on that while you were still at Northwestern University." Jed shook his head. "Never understood how the two of you could work amicably in the same department."

Kendra had considered the wisdom of it too, but eager to see her settled in, Bill insisted they worked well together in college and discounted the possibility of competition. Lately, however, her doubts about their compatibility had increased. Sometimes she wondered if she'd made a huge mistake in moving to Texas, but she thoroughly enjoyed her job.

And her friendship with Jed.

He patted her hand. "Don't worry, Ken. He'll be back with an apology. But in case you get lonely till he is, want to go to the Rangers game tomorrow? I've got great tickets."

Kendra smiled. "I'd like that."

Monday morning Kendra kept to her office and pointedly avoided Bill. Though her anger lingered, she wondered if maybe he was right. Maybe she should have taken an apartment closer to him, but somehow she'd ended up near Jed.

Jed. Her thoughts wandered until she realized she was spinning fantasies, sparked, no doubt by Jed's rare presence in the office. Kendra caught a glimpse of him, striding past her office in stone washed Levi's and a polo shirt the same deep blue as his eyes.

Of course, he didn't have Bill's blond handsomeness, but his rugged looks and easy charm were appealing. Jed teased Bill mercilessly about stealing his girl, but Kendra knew he was just joking. Months ago, she'd dismissed the idea he had more serious intentions, and she valued his friendship too much to idly contemplate her own feelings.

She returned from lunch to find a small vase of flowers on her desk. Kendra smiled. Every Monday afternoon she received a bouquet, usually daisies or carnations, but today yellow roses created a sunny glow in her cubicle. Her favorite, and despite their quarrel, Bill hadn't forgotten. She stowed her purse and looked up to see him standing in the entryway.

He looked appropriately contrite. "Promise not to throw anything at me?"

Kendra pretended to search the top of the desk for a likely missile. "You're safe. Nothing here that will go the distance."

He came in. "I'm sorry, Kendra. I didn't mean to hurt your feelings. But I think we need to finish our talk."

She crossed her arms. "That sounds ominous."

He sighed. "How about if I come over for dinner tonight?"

"No way. You want a heavy duty discussion, then the least you can do is take me out for convenience food."

"Convenience food?"

"That's what Jed calls food that somebody else fixes."

Bill looked disgusted. "Jed. Why do you encourage him?

Seems like he's always hanging around, asking you to pick up his mail, baby-sit his stupid mutt, or help rebuild a carburetor."

Kendra sat still, suddenly feeling like the desk between them loomed as large as the state of Texas. "Well, he was your friend first. I've just been nice, that's all."

Bill shook his head and started for the door. "I hope you know better than to take him seriously."

Kendra smiled and touched a yellow rose petal. "The flowers are especially pretty today."

"What?" Bill turned, glanced at the roses and scowled. "You know, it's a waste to get cut flowers so often."

Her heart fluttered at the sudden click of her thoughts. Why hadn't she realized it sooner? "Always the practical engineer, aren't you? See you later. Seven thirty."

That evening at dinner, Kendra stacked cardboard coasters into miniature towers. Bill had kept up a steady stream of inconsequential shop talk ever since he picked her up. "Enough already. Didn't you have something important to talk about?"

He hesitated, then leaned closer. "Kendra, I really am sorry about Saturday night. Your cooking's not half bad, honestly. It's just that sometimes I've felt, well, smothered."

Smothered! Kendra bristled and opened her mouth to speak, but he held up his hand.

"Please. Let me finish. This isn't easy to say when you've come so far for me already, so I'll just tell you and hope for the best. I've accepted a job in Houston."

"Houston?" Immediately, Kendra's mind churned with her own recent doubts. "Why didn't you tell me before now?"

He shrugged. "Didn't want you getting all upset. The job might not have panned out. I've been disappointed with Milford, and Houston is the center for what I want to do. Of course," Bill continued, apparently misreading her silence and taking her hand. "You're welcome to join me there."

You're welcome to join me. Not, I love you, Kendra, please come with me, I don't want to be without you. What difference did it make? Did she even want to spend any more time with Bill? Anywhere?

Her thoughts shifted to Houston's reputation for nonstop bumper to bumper traffic. The freeway system dubbed the "spaghetti bowl." Humidity so thick, you could wring the atmosphere. Starting over again when she was finally feeling settled right where she was.

He squeezed her hand. "You shouldn't have any trouble finding another job. We can even share expenses. Have a better chance to know each other."

Kendra raised an eyebrow. "Live together? Saturday night you told me we should see other people."

He waved his hand. "I was restless. Besides, I had two nights to think this over. Seeing you drive off with that redneck, Jed, made me realize how lonely you must be."

Kendra shook her head. "Was. But now that I've made a few friends, you want me to give up my job, move to Houston, and be your roommate. Is cooking and laundry duty included in that?"

He looked dismayed. "It's not like that."

"Really? Face it, Bill. You and I have never shared the same interests. We don't even like the same cars."

"You make it sound like the end, Kendra."

"I think it ended long before Saturday." She slipped her hand from his. "But no hard feelings. I wish you the best of luck in Houston."

An hour later, Kendra stood on her balcony watching the flicker of passing headlights. Her breath caught as a shiny red Camaro zipped into the parking lot.

Jed leaped out and looked up. "Ken! Want to go for a drive?"

Her fatigue vanished like mist before the sun. "I'd love it. Let me lock up."

A few minutes later, she walked up to the passenger's

side, surprised to see Jed sitting there. He gave her a lazy grin and tossed the keys to her. "Only thing sexier than a red convertible is a pretty woman driving one."

A blush heated her face from the uncharacteristic compliment as she settled into the driver's seat and turned the key in the ignition. "Any idea where you can find her?"

Jed rested his hand on the back of the seat, not quite touching her neck. His fingers strayed to finger a curly lock of her hair. "Maybe. What did you and Bill decide?"

She turned sideways to face him. "You knew?"

He nodded. "He told me this afternoon. Said he figured you'd either go with him to Houston or go back home to Oshkosh."

Kendra was silent, contemplating his words, surprised at the anxiety he was obviously trying to hide.

Jed drummed his fingers against the dash. "Well?"

She smiled impishly. "I told Bill he needs to find someone else to do his laundry. I'm staying right here."

Jed seized her by the shoulders and kissed her. Although startled at first, she leaned into him, returning the warmth of his mouth as a torrent of heat rushed through her.

His voice was uneven against her ear. "Any idea how long I've been wanting to do that, Kendra?"

She drew back, touched his face and smiled. Shifting the convertible into gear, she revved the engine. "Not really. But I'd like to hear all about it." She adjusted the rearview mirror, turned to smile at Jed, then faced forward, ready to experience her new future. "And Jed, thanks for all the flowers. It took me till now to realize you're the one."

CANDLE OF HOPE

Betsy Norman

Callie fervently hoped the new veterinarian was a miracle worker. The bedraggled kitten her daughter had kept hidden beneath the porch was in dire shape. She jerked the car into park in the driveway of the small-town animal hospital and gently coaxed her daughter to relinquish the limp bundle cradled in her lap.

"Will she be all right, Mommy?" Tears sprang anew across Diedra's rosy cheeks, inching their youthful sorrow into Callie's heart. Her five-year-old daughter had tried to love the bony little gray calico back to health, sneaking it milk and tuna fish, but the kitten was too weak to respond to her daughter's hopeful attempts.

The little girl had so much love to give. Why couldn't her father see that? He only came around when it suited him, and it hadn't suited him for over a year. No wonder Diedra kept the abandoned kitten a secret. She must have looked into the little thing's pitifully large golden eyes and found a soul mate.

Diedra bounded out of the car ahead of Callie and burst into the clustered lobby alcove.

"Diedra, slow down!" Callie entered at a more sedate pace, careful not to jar the kitten. The tall blonde man penciling in something on his desk calendar perked upright at their arrival.

"Diedra, is it?" The edges of his mustache drew into a conspiratorial grin. "As in Diedra Jenkins, Callie Jenkins daughter?" The smile sprawled further still when he looked to Callie. She was too startled to do anything but nod affirmation to his unexpected question.

"That's right! How did you know?" Diedra asked.

"Oh, a little 'Birdie' told me."

He winked at Callie, who blushed at his wordplay. He meant Birdie Butler, of course, the town gossip and matchmaker authority.

Diedra broke into pleas for assistance. "Oh! Can you help us? Paisley's awful sick. She won't die, will she? You won't let her die?"

"Paisley is the kitten Diedra found, Dr Adams." Callie gestured to the towel-wrapped burden in her arms.

"Please, call me Stuart. Let's have a look at Paisley, shall we?" His large, tanned hands reached toward Callie and the kitten, gingerly peeling back the swaddling to take a look. His voice dropped lower. "I guess fate intervened to give me an excuse to finally meet you."

The boyish grin and blue-eyed twinkle enveloped her at close range. Callie flushed again. Birdie was known to exaggerate at times, but she hit right on the mark about Stuart Adams disarming way of smiling.

Stuart towered over her, intent on his inspection, and quite possibly unaware of how intimately close he stood. She didn't expect a man who worked with animals all day to smell like spicy aftershave.

"Can you make Paisley better?" Diedra blurted. "I found her near the creek road. She tries to drink the milk I brought for her, but mostly she just lays and cries. Maybe her daddy left, too."

Stuart looked to Callie, his golden brow arrowed upward in query. Callie glanced away. She didn't owe this man an explanation for her daughter's painful confession. She didn't want to see judgment distort those smiling blue eyes.

"Why do you think Paisley's daddy would do that, Diedra?" Stuart asked.

The little girl scuffed her sandal on the floor, eyes downcast. "I don't know. Maybe he didn't want a family." Her daughter stroked the scruffy fur of the kitten with hesitation before her hands went abruptly to her back pockets.

Callie's expression faltered to see her daughter censure her affection so rigidly. She closed her eyes and bit her lower lip to regain composure. A gentling hand at Callie's shoulder caused her to open them again. Empathy and compassion emanated from Stuart's eyes, not the scorn she expected. Relief flooded her. She knew he understood what both mother and daughter were feeling.

Stuart took the mewling Paisley and crouched next to Diedra. He gave her a reassuring smile, gently patting the bony length of the bedraggled kitten. "You just leave her to me, sweetheart. Looks like Paisley may have found herself a new family."

He rose again and retrieved a cherry sucker from the bowl on his desk and gave it to Diedra. "You keep busy with this for a bit, while your mom helps me with Paisley back in the exam room, okay?" Diedra stuffed the lollipop into her mouth with an anxious nod.

Once the door was closed behind them, he laid Paisley on the railed exam table and withdrew a hypodermic from a drawer. After swabbing a small patch on the kitten's flank with alcohol, he gave her an injection, then scratched behind her ears to temper the sting.

"This is a precautionary antibiotic, to ward off infection." Paisley let out a barely audible raspy purr. Callie watched with her heart in her throat as this large man handled the tiny animal with meticulous tenderness.

Stuart began to shake his head, dragging a rough hand through his hair. "I see this all too often, unwanted litters abandoned to fend for themselves. It's a heartless and cruel thing to do to something so small and vulnerable. This kitten is badly undernourished and dehydrated, Miss Jenkins."

"Please, Callie will do. I'm sure old Birdie has filled us both in on each other enough to be on a first name basis by now."

They exchanged embarrassed grins. Callie knew the elderly woman was exceptionally thorough when pitching one potential candidate to the other.

"Callie." Stuart continued with gravity. "It would be best if you let me keep Paisley overnight for observation. She's in pretty bad shape."

"Oh." Callie was crestfallen. She didn't want the small candle of hope her daughter had lit in adopting the scraggly kitten snuffed out. "If you think it's for the best, all right."

"You might want to prepare Diedra."

"Yes," Callie agreed. "I'm not sure I want to get her hopes worked up, only to have them dashed again."

Stuart nodded, his thoughtful expression unreadable. He began to run warm water into a basin. "I'm going to clean Paisley up, get her warm and dry and see if I can get some nourishment into her. I'll need to get a blood and stool sample to rule out the more dangerous feline diseases. Tomorrow morning I'll give you a call and report on her progress."

"Thank you, Dr Adams."

"Stuart," he reminded.

Callie gathered up her courage and reached for the doorknob before Stuart's hand at her elbow stopped her.

"I'm going to try my best, Callie. It's not fair for your little girl to believe everything she tries to love will leave her." He stepped closer, intensity in his voice. "It's not fair to you, either."

The fierce empathy she saw flare in his eyes reminded Callie of the chronicle of Stuart's arrival Birdie filled her ears with weeks ago. He'd been engaged, and his fiancée left him because she didn't want to be caged into the small town where he planned on setting up his practice.

"He's just a country boy at heart, Callie-girl," she'd warbled. "Content to plant deep roots and nurture a few saplings. That city gal weren't for him no more than that motorcycle hooligan was for you."

Callie was certain Birdie had pronounced the same wisdom to Stuart.

"No, it's not fair." Callie whispered, "But it's how it is, all the same."

The next morning, Diedra's gangly legs paced back and forth through the kitchen. The repetitive motion only twisted Callie's nerves into a knot. She kept begging Callie to call Dr Adams, but Callie couldn't bring herself to do it. She dreaded the bad news that surely kept Stuart from phoning. Instead, she tried to keep her daughter occupied with puzzles and board games, finally resorting to baking cookies and cutting up vegetables for stew. The lazy late summer sun was just kissing the horizon when a triple-rap shook the screen door.

Callie peeked through the kitchen sink front window and caught a glimpse of chambray pulled taut about a broad pair of shoulders. Inching forward to a better look, she saw wheat-blond hair and identified Stuart standing on the front stoop. His head hung, and his posture looked preoccupied. Callie silently commended the man for being noble enough to deliver the bad news in person, knowing how crushed

Diedra would be.

A scatter of footsteps echoed down the hall, and Diedra banged open the screen door and let out a squeal. Callie hurried out of the kitchen into the foyer, prepared to perform damage control. Instead she found the two, heads bent together, cuddling and cooing over a bright-eyed Paisley. The kitten's engine purred loud and clear. Callie put her hand to her mouth, unable to stifle the gasp of relief.

"Stuart, how did you ever manage such a transformation?"

"You've got Paisley to thank. She's got a strong will. She knew just because she was deserted, it didn't mean she wasn't worth loving. She knew Diedra was waiting for her. We humans could take a lesson from animal instinct."

"Isn't Dr Adams wonderful, Mommy? Can he stay for dinner?" Diedra hugged both kitten and man with a child's uninhibited joy. Callie silently agreed. *Yes, he is pretty wonderful.*

Stuart surrendered the squiggly bundle of fur over to her equally squirmy new owner and smiled, embarrassment coloring his expression. Diedra ran off jabbering excited plans on where to put Paisley's food and litter box, and could the kitten please sleep in her room?

Callie was speechless with admiration and beamed a grateful smile at the man who had saved her daughter's faltering hopes.

"How can we ever thank you?" She whispered in awe.

He looked humbled, shrugging a shoulder and pocketing his hands. "It wasn't my doing, really. It was your daughter. That little cat knew there was a bursting heart just craving to love it. That's the best medicine there is."

Callie hugged her arms around herself. "I only hope Paisley can work some magic on Diedra in return. She wants her father's love so badly. I don't think he's ever coming back, and I don't have the heart to tell her."

"Do you want him back?"

"Heaven's no. I was young and naive. He just had trouble with letting dust settle on his heels and didn't want to be tied down." Callie glanced toward her daughter's muted singsong voice chirping upstairs. "He gave me Diedra, though. I'll never regret that. She's become my life, and I plan on raising her here, but this is a small town. Even though Birdie and her matchmaker efforts swear otherwise, the prospects have been mighty slim, so Diedra's all I've got."

"Who says it has to be that way? You would sacrifice your own happiness as well as hers and reject all hopes of a relationship? Maybe it's not just her father she wants, but a father. A family, Callie."

Callie didn't have an answer to that. There was no denying she was lonely. Her daughter was very perceptive, and often mirrored Callie's wistful sighs of solitude. It wasn't that she didn't want a man in her life, there were just none available she could trust with her daughter's innocent heart, much less her own. *Until now*, an elderly woman's voice inside her head prodded.

"Well, old Birdie's got new fat to chew." Stuart parodied the old-timer's drawl, puffing himself up and thumbing imaginary suspenders. "She's all abuzz about the new single veterinarian in town." He strutted down the hall toward the kitchen, eyeing her mischievously over his shoulder. "He's got steady work, ain't goin' nowhere so far as I know. Trustworthy. Family-oriented man—good with cats and kids...." She heard him take a bracing inhale. "And he just loves homemade stew and chocolate chip cookies."

Callie giggled at his capering, despite herself.

"Rumor has it, she's already got him earmarked for that pretty little single gal, Callie Jenkins and her precocious daughter. Oh, she's a bit gun-shy, Birdie says. Requires a gentle hand, but one look at her is all you need to take up the gauntlet. Fine lookin' woman." He grinned over the stew ladle and took a taste. "Good cook, too."

"She says all that, huh?" Callie smoothed her apron and tried to don a proprietary expression, swatting him away from the kettle. "Did Birdie also say this Callie Jenkins doesn't take kindly to guests who don't wash their hands before dinner?"

"No, ma'am, she forgot to tell me that."

"Well. It would be a good thing to remember if you've any hope of being invited back. I also suggest you make yourself useful and set the table."

"I surely will." He made good on his promise and began scrubbing vigorously in the sink before reaching for the dishes in the drying rack. He grabbed an old candlestick off the buffet. "Mind if I light a candle?"

Callie smiled at him. "You already did."

WINTER AWAKENING

Tami D. Cowden

"Wow! Mommy, look at the snow!" Jeffy stuck his tongue out, trying to catch the flakes. The three-year-old stood up in the grocery cart, obviously trying to get a better angle.

"Careful, Tiger. Don't fall out." Despite her son's excitement, Ellie Pierce's heart sank as she pushed the cart through the parking lot. Snow meant the traffic would be worse than usual. By the time she and Jeffy got home, it would be after seven. What with making dinner and doing the laundry, it would be another late night.

She strapped Jeffy into his booster seat and packed the week's shopping in the trunk. A market flyer substituted for the ice scraper, which had disappeared again. She turned the key, only to hear a faint grinding whine. Casting a brave smile at Jeffy, she tried again, but the engine refused to start. A quick check of the dashboard revealed the lights had been left on.

This was all she needed. She rested her forehead against the steering wheel and closed her eyes. Straightening, she brushed a tear from her eye and unfastened the buckle on Jeffy's seat. They'd wait inside the store for the auto club.

A sudden rap on her window snapped her head around. Through the rapidly crusting glass she could just make out a dark figure holding up a pair of jumper cables. She rolled her window down an inch.

The glow of the street light above her car revealed just enough of her would-be rescuer's face to make her catch her breath. Beneath a crown of white snow, dark curls framed features even enough to rival a Greek statute. Eyes the color of a summer sky showed sympathy at her plight.

"I heard you trying to start your car. Sounds like you need a jump?"

"Oh, uh, thank you. I'm going to call the auto club." She started to roll her window up again, but her son's voice stopped her.

"I'm hungry, Mommy. Let's go home."

"On a night like this, it will be hours before a tow truck arrives." Dark brows lifted as he nodded toward Jeffy. "Sounds like you need to get your boy home." He smiled. "It's okay. You don't even need to get out of the car. Just pop the hood, and I'll do the rest."

For a moment, Ellie sat in indecision. She hated to accept help from a stranger. But it could be midnight before the auto club sent someone to jump-start the car.

"Mommy!" There was just enough of a hint of tears behind Jeffy's cry to rouse her to action. She pulled the lever to open the hood.

Within a few short minutes, her car engine was humming. Her knight in a sheepskin coat efficiently detached the cables, closed both hoods, and walked back to her window.

"Thank you very much. It was very kind of you to help."

"Hey, is that you, Ms Nickols? No problem. Glad to help."

She wrinkled her nose in puzzlement at his use of her maiden name. Squinting in the dim light, she studied his features. Recognition hit. Six years ago, when she'd student taught at Burton High, he'd been a senior. "Tommy? Tommy Blackburn?" She rolled the window the rest of the way down.

"I go by Tom these days." He bent down to peer in at Jeffy. "And I guess you're not Ms Nickols anymore."

"No, I married Jim Pierce. You remember him, don't you? He was the track coach when you were in school."

"Yeah, Coach Pierce. He taught social studies, too." He grinned, nodding. But then his eyes clouded. "Oh. I'm sorry. I heard about the accident."

After more than three years, she was able to ignore the familiar clutch at her heart. "Thank you." She was so accustomed to the sympathy, her reply came mechanically.

"Mom-my! Let's. Go. Home." The demand was laden with all the indignation a toddler can muster.

Ellie laughed, grateful for the interruption of further pity. "Tommy, thanks so much for your help." She held out her hand through the window. He clasped her hand and held on to it.

"My pleasure. But it's Tom."

Despite the cold, wet weather, his grasp was warm and dry. Faint calluses tickled her palm. Against her will, her gaze met his. Warmth, barely remembered, coiled within her. With a gasp, she snatched her hand away. Facing forward, she directed her eyes straight over the steering wheel.

"I'd better be getting home now. Thanks." She chanced a peek at him and was struck by the faint shadow lining his jaw. The stubble would tickle against her neck. Heat rose in her cheeks at the direction of her thoughts.

She rolled up the window and put the car in forward. Driving off, she couldn't resist a glance in the rear view mirror. Tommy still stood on the pavement with a hand raised in farewell.

As she carefully maneuvered her car on the icy streets toward home, Ellie silently berated herself. Things had come to a pretty pass if she could actually feel attraction to a student.

Former student, a tiny corner of her mind amended. But that makes no difference, she argued back sternly. Once a student, always a student. Besides, just because Tommy Blackburn had grown into a fine figure of a man was no reason for her to view him as one.

Still, later that night, with Jeffy fed, bathed and tucked into his race car bed, she couldn't help but think a bit more about stubble brushing against her neck. She missed her husband, but she was still a young woman.

The next morning, Ellie awoke suddenly when thirty-five pounds of exuberance landed on her side.

"Sledding, Mommy. Let's go sledding!" A glance out the window near her bed explained Jeffy's excitement. The snow had obviously continued throughout the night. By the looks of it, school would be cancelled.

She flipped on the radio and soon heard the news confirmed. She grinned.

"Okay, Tiger, we'll get the sled out as soon as we've had breakfast." Winter had never been her favorite season, but opportunities to spend a relaxed day of play with her son were too rare to waste on house cleaning. Teaching allowed her more time with Jeffy than most jobs, but raising a son alone still took more hours than a day offered. An unexpected day off was a chance to have some fun time.

And maybe relaxing a bit would help keep her thoughts off one very young former student. Or so she hoped.

Filled with hot cereal, Jeffy actually permitted her to zip

him into his snowsuit. She pulled on an old pair of ski pants, and soon they were headed for the park, dragging a snow saucer behind them.

Despite the early hour, the steep sledding hill was already dotted with brightly dressed children on toboggans, sleds and saucers. Some of the kids simply rolled down the hill, laughing as snow fell down their collars. Ellie kept Jeffy to the smaller slopes, where young mothers half pulled and half pushed well-bundled toddlers over the snow. But Jeffy kept pointing to the long hill.

"Mrs Pierce! Okay, admit it. You went into teaching for the snow days, right?"

So much for keeping her mind off Tommy Blackburn!

She turned toward the sound of his voice. At the sight of him, she nearly fell over from the wave of sheer physical need that swept from the tip of her wind-kissed nose to the toes snuggled in her snow boots. What had been the stuff of dreams in the snowy twilight rivaled any romance novel cover in sunny daylight. The wide breadth of the shoulders stretching the sheepskin jacket suggested many hours lifting weights, while his tight ski pants showed the muscular line of his legs. Ear muffs creased through the thick shock of dark curls. A wide grin split his face. In his aviator glasses, she saw herself, mouth agape, staring at him.

She closed her jaw. "Tommy." Mentally shaking herself, she forced a smile. "Thanks again for your help last night." See, she told herself sternly, he's out playing in the snow with the rest of the kids.

"No problem. But it's Tom." He waited for a second, and then added. "And may I call you Ellie, now?"

"Oh, ah," Two sides of her warred, the prim widowed high school teacher arguing against the young woman who was years from her thirtieth birthday.

The young Adonis before her didn't wait for the outcome. "Great. Ellie." He reached out and straightened Jeffy's knit cap. "Hey, there young fella! You look like you need to take a spin down Parker Hill."

"Oh, no." Ellie tried to tell herself the breathlessness in her voice was at the thought of Jeffy on the steep hill and not because of the stunning example of masculinity at her side. "He's too little for that."

A mutinous pout formed on Jeffy's face. But before any childish temper was displayed, Tom intervened.

"Well, maybe not quite big enough for a solo run, but with a friend?"

She glanced at the hill. The major danger was running into another sledder. With an adult on board, she knew they could either stop or steer clear. She nodded her permission reluctantly.

"Okay, then, kiddo. My name's Tom. What's yours?"

She started to answer, but the boy beat her to it.

"Jeffy Pierce."

Tom held out his hand, and Jeffy solemnly shook hands. "So what do you say, Jeffy, would you like to go down the hill with me?"

Brown eyes, so very like her late husband's, widened with excitement. The small boy started to run toward the hill as fast as his snow boots would carry him, leaving Tom and the sled behind. Tom tucked his sunglasses in a pocket, revealing blue eyes crinkled with laughter.

Picking up the sled, he grinned again, "I'll take that as a yes." His voice lowered, and he added, "Be right back."

Ellie found a tree to lean against and watched the small form in his red snowsuit jump up and down at the top of the hill. The larger, darker figure sat crossed legged on the saucer, and tucked her son onto his lap. From her spot, she could see Tom was talking to Jeffy, who nodded seriously.

The sight made her heart ache. She could provide for her son's physical needs, and give him all the abundant love a mother has, but she could not be a father to him.

She sighed. Neither she nor her husband had any male relatives living. Her retired neighbor, Mr Darrows, sometimes let Jeffy "help" with his gardening, but there was no constant man in Jeffy's life. Jeffy was responding to Tom with as much enthusiasm as her own suddenly awakened hormones were urging on her.

Maybe her sister was right. It was time she started dating again. But someone a little older than Tommy Blackburn! Her Jim had been five years old than her. Just the right age, in her opinion. She mentally reviewed the male teachers at her high school, eliminating the married, the never-gonna-marry, and the nearly retired. That didn't leave many options, but maybe she'd take a chance on one of them. With that tentative plan, she resolved to forget about Tommy Blackburn.

Jeffy raced to her side after his slide down the hill. He bubbled out the joy of his trip while begging for permission for another turn. He ran off eagerly at her nod. She had a feeling nothing short of exhaustion would drag him away from the park. Resigned to a lengthy wait, she knelt to begin a snow man.

After a few more runs downhill on the sled, and uphill on short legs, little Jeffy was ready for a rest. He and Tom joined Ellie in building the giant snowman.

"That's the way, Jeffy." Tom helped her boost the boy high enough to place the round head onto the torso of the snowman. She could see that Tom held most of the large snowball, but from Jeffy's grunts, she knew her son believed he was lifting the heavy snow all on his own.

She was touched by Tom's patience. So many men had trouble relating to very small children. He was going to make a wonderful father someday.

A few branches for arms, pebbles for eyes, and bits of bark for mouth, and the snowman was complete. It stood like a sentry, gray eyes staring toward Winton Hill.

"There now. He'll enjoy watching all the kids slide down the hill, don't you think, Jeffy?" The little boy nodded but knuckled his eyes with wet mittened hands and leaned against Ellie.

She laughed and scooped him up in her arms. "I think it's time for us to head back. He's not the only one who needs some time in bed." She'd spoken unthinkingly, but saw a flicker in Tom's eyes. Good heavens. He hadn't though that an invitation, had he?

But all he said was, "Maybe next snow day, you'll take a slide down the hill with us?"

Feeling giddy with relief, she mumbled a reply, barely knowing what she was saying. "Sounds like fun." She backed away, Jeffy already nodding into her shoulder.

"I could walk you home. He's looks a bit heavy for you."

"No!" She wasn't taking any chances that he had thought her nap comment a come on. "He's fine. I mean, I'm fine." She bent to pick up the sled's rope, long practice enabling her to leave Jeffy undisturbed in his perch. "We're fine. Bye."

As she turned toward home, she squeezed her eyes shut. She did not want to see if anyone had seen her making a fool of herself over this young man.

Back at home, she tucked Jeffy into bed and immediately dialed her sister at work.

"Okay, Cher. I'm ready. Fix me up with someone."

Her sister let out a whoop that no doubt went over well in the law office where she worked. That is, she worked there when she wasn't acting as the town matchmaker. "This is terrific, El. And I know just the guy. He's a teacher at the elementary school. New this year. Absolutely gorgeous. If I weren't madly in love already, I'd go after him myself."

A teacher. Like Jim. Stable, good with kids, just what she needed. She didn't know about the gorgeous stuff, but that wasn't important. Character and maturity were important, not stud-muffin good looks.

"Great. That's perfect." But then her sister asked the question Ellie knew would come.

"Not that I'm complaining or anything, but just last week you were saying you were fine on your own. Why the sudden change of heart?"

How could she explain to her sister her sudden attraction to a student? She couldn't. "I guess you were right. It's just time."

"Can't argue with that! I'll see what I can set up."

A week later, Ellie smoothed a nervous hand over her hair, fishing a paper streamer out of her curls. "Do I look alright?" The lady pirate costume seemed a bit over the top to her.

Cher smiled back at her. "You look terrific. Definitely the best looking English teacher pirate in the room."

Since the Mardi Gras carnival was a fundraising event sponsored by the school district, there were more than a few English teachers present. But knowing her sister's opinion of frumpy teachers, Ellie didn't find that comment too reassuring. It had been a long time since she dressed up for a date, and she had certainly never worn a halter top with a scarlet sash. She tugged at the striped fabric over her bosom, trying to make it cover more than it revealed.

"Do you think we should have made this meeting so public? Everyone I know is here."

"No, it's perfect. The teachers from all the schools in town have to show. So what's more natural than you and he talking together during the party?" Cher smacked her gum and grinned. "And, since the guy I have in mind for you is dressed like a pirate too, you have even more to talk about."

Ellie sighed. Cher's schemes for getting her friends together always involved these complicated plots. She knew she should appreciate her sister trying to ease her into this dating thing. But after seven days of feeling her knees go weak every time she thought of Tommy Blackburn, she was inclined to think desperate measures were required. She needed to get interested in a nice, mature guy and quick.

She scanned the men in the crowd, trying to guess which

one was the one her sister had picked for her. She caught a glimpse of a comfortable looking man wearing a lab coat. He looked her type, even if the costume was wrong.

"Do you know—" She cut off her question as she became aware of a single blue eye smiling in her direction. "Tommy!" Ellie took in the high black boots, the snowy white puffy- sleeved shirt, and the eye patch. "Oh, no!"

She could not believe the coincidence. What evil genie had made Tommy wear a costume that matched hers so exactly? She turned to ask Cher to get her pirate there quick, only to discover her sister melting into the crowd wearing a smug smile.

"Ellie." Tommy slid his gaze down her costume and back up. Despite her chagrin at discovering him there, she couldn't help the flush of pleasure she experienced at the approval in his grin.

"Tom. I didn't expect to see you here." She wished she had dressed as a southern belle. She could have used a fan to cool her flaming cheeks. "It's nice that you support your old school by coming to the fund raiser."

"Oh, I'm not that nice! I am here on my principal's orders." He flashed a grin every bit as wicked as his costume. "But I am sure going to thank Ms Patterson on Monday."

She puzzled over that remark while one of her yearbook students ran up. "Hey, Ms Pierce, how about a photo. Two pirates will look great in the Celebrations section of the yearbook." Tom quickly put an arm around her and pulled her close for a pose. She barely had a chance to paste a smile on her face before the camera flash.

"Great shot! Should I send one for your class bulletin board, Mr Blackburn?"

"That'd be great, Candy. Thanks." The girl ran off.

Ellie knew she wasn't dancing, but her head was definitely doing a reel. Candy, a very grown up senior, had called Tommy "Mr Blackburn." Like he was—no, it couldn't be.

"Mr Blackburn?"

"Well, that's my name." He looked down at her, brows arched questioningly. "I think students should call teachers Mr and Ms, don't you? Sort of a respect thing."

"You're a teacher?" She heard the disbelief in her voice, and clearly, so did he.

"Yeah. I teach at Mason Elementary." He nodded at the eager photographer. "Candy's little sister, Josie, is in my class. Cute kid, very bright."

"You're a teacher!" Her disbelief turned to joy. After all, there was nothing wrong with two twenty-something teachers liking each other, was there?

"Yes, I'm a teacher. Didn't you know?"

"No, I didn't." She shook her head, gold bangles slapping against her neck. "Somehow I still thought of you as, well, one of my students."

"I see." He turned to face her and clasped both of her hands in his. He looked into her eyes seriously "You know Ellie, I may be three or four years younger than you, but I am all grown up."

She looked him over. "Yep, something inside me has been telling me that." Of course, she wasn't quite ready to tell him the source of her information was her hormones.

Time enough for that come spring.

KEEPSAKE STORM

Susan D. Brooks

Victoria moved between the empty candlelit tables, making tiny, unnecessary adjustments to the placement of the crystal stemware. Tonight the Keepsake Café oozed romance with delicate white and gold china on hand-embroidered linen, red roses blooming in cut-crystal vases, and Vivaldi floating from discreet ceiling speakers. On each table rested the signature gift box bearing the evening's keepsake: a silver heart charm.

She felt a tingle of anticipation. This holiday could boost the café's reputation among the local residents, make it part of the neighborhood, not just part of the landscape.

But, there was one problem.

Victoria pushed aside white lace curtains and stared

through the frosted window. Snow fell thick and heavy as it had for several hours, drifting across the roads and wreaking havoc with traffic. According to the local news, many businesses planned to close early and send employees home before the roads became impassable. Another snowplow rumbled by, its flashing yellow lights a beacon for the long line of cars that followed. Victoria clenched her jaw in frustration. The people in those cars would not stop for a Valentine's Day dinner; they just wanted to get home. Her careful planning, expensive advertising, and countless hours spent choosing the menus would go to waste.

"Did you know it's George Washington Ferris' birthday?" Lauren, dinner chef and Victoria's business partner, came to stand beside her, peering over her friend's shoulder at the snow. "He's the guy who invented the Ferris Wheel."

"Trust you to know that, oh Queen of Trivia." Victoria teased.

"I can't help it." Lauren shrugged. "Stuff stays with me."

"I wonder if his wife combined the two holidays, like people do when a child is born on Christmas."

"Probably not. He lived in the 1800s. I don't think Valentine's Day was much of a holiday until the greeting card companies got hold of it." Lauren paused, then added, "Eric's parents never combined his birthday with Valentine's although my husband admits that he always bought his brother a card with hearts on it just to tease him."

"Really?" Victoria's fingers tightened on the curtains. "How amusing." The words came out terse, laced with irritation. Why did Lauren have to bring up her brother-in-law's name now?

"He said he was sorry." Lauren touched her arm.

"I know." Victoria offered her partner a weak smile and stifled a sigh. All her life holidays had meant working, seeing to customers' needs, first in her parents' historic bed and breakfast, now in her own elegant eatery.

After Lauren introduced Victoria to Eric two months ago, Victoria had dared to hope that this year might be different; that this time someone would be waiting with champagne and flowers when the café closed at eleven.

"I warned you that he's working long hours getting his business built up." Lauren reminded her.

"Yes, you did, but I didn't think that meant he would stand me up. Twice."

Lauren threw up her hands. "He had a new phone system installed in the shop on Saturday. It didn't work. Didn't he tell you that?"

"Well, yes, but—"

"Eric has plans for his future. To achieve those goals, he has to sometimes make sacrifices. You, of all people, should understand that. Think of what it took to open this place."

Victoria did understand, but her pride, shredded from numerous dead-end relationships, still demanded some stab at dignity. "Well, Lauren, who knows? Maybe one of these days we'll try again."

"You could at least talk to him instead of letting your answering machine do it for you."

Victoria nodded then shivered as the wind dashed freezing rain against the glass. "The storm's getting worse."

Lauren's impatient huff signaled annoyance, but she dropped the subject. "It doesn't look good for us, does it? The meat's thawed, marinated, and ready to cook. If we don't use it tonight, it's wasted. The salad greens will wilt, and the pastries you made this afternoon will be stale by tomorrow morning."

"We can donate whatever's edible—" Victoria paused as headlights from a passenger van flashed across the window. She watched it roll through the parking lot and stop a few feet from the front door.

"Get out," she whispered to the unseen driver. "Come inside where it's warm and there's good food." The doors of the vehicle popped open, and six people climbed out. "Yes!"

"A commuter van!" Lauren laughed. "They may not be couples in search of romance, but who cares? They'll be hungry. I'll get some fresh coffee brewing."

As Lauren disappeared into the kitchen, more cars began to turn off the road into the lot. A large, bearded man pushed open the door and entered. "I sure am glad you're open," he boomed, stomping the snow off his boots.

The other passengers crowded in behind him, tugging off coats and brushing snow out of their hair. One young woman in a suit remarked, "We're going to be here a while. The police just closed the road. Do you serve wine?"

Victoria stared at her a moment as she sorted all the information she'd just heard. "Yes, we have an extensive wine list."

Other voices piped up.

"I never knew you were here."

"What kind of name is Keepsake Café? Do you serve anything besides coffee? Isn't that what a café serves?"

"Can I get a beer?"

"Where's your TV?"

Victoria smiled and gestured toward the tables. "Yes, we have beer and a full menu. Please, seat yourselves and feel free to push tables together. One of our wait staff will be right over to get your drink order."

She walked quickly to the back room and alerted the four servers. "All right, people. I think things are about to get hectic. Just do the best you can."

As the servers rushed to grab menus and wine lists, more stranded motorists crowded through the doors.

Tables filled quickly. The dining room hummed with talk and laughter. Victoria said a silent prayer of thanks that the power hadn't gone out as she balanced a tray of appetizers, a bottle of wine, and wineglasses.

"Careful you don't exceed your maximum number of occupants." The deep voice came from beside her.

She looked up and found herself caught in the gaze of

steady hazel eyes. "Eric!" Her tray swayed dangerously. She blurted out the first thing that came to mind. "Happy birthday!"

"Thanks." He smiled tentatively. "I wasn't sure you'd be open."

"We came in early to get ready for dinner, and the storm hit so hard and fast we got stuck here." She tipped her head at the crowded room. "It's a good thing we did or they'd still be out in the cold."

Eric glanced at the people at the tables. "Me, too."

Why did he have to look so good in that bomber jacket? Why did his smile have to send tingles up her spine?

Victoria cleared her throat. "How come you're not at the garage?" She shifted the tray to the other hand.

"I did some work on Lauren's Jeep and took it out for a test drive. I, ah, thought I'd come by and talk to you. Instead, I've been sitting in traffic for three hours."

Victoria felt a sharp thrill at his admission. He was still interested. But what if he let her down again?

She shook off the feeling. She'd have to take a risk.

Eric surveyed the room and reached for the tray. "Looks like you could use some help. I waited tables after high school. I don't think I've forgotten how."

Victoria hesitated, pleased by the offer, but not sure she could accept. After all, it wasn't as if they were a couple, or even good friends. "I can't ask you to help."

"You didn't." He took the tray from her and winked. "I volunteered. Where does this go?"

Victoria pointed to a corner where an older couple held hands across a table. The woman said something to her companion who smiled and leaned over to kiss her. Eric watched them.

"That's how I want to be when I'm that age. They still look like honeymooners."

"Yes, they do, but they aren't. They celebrated their 43rd wedding anniversary here last month." She smiled at the memory.

"Good for them." Eric took a step toward the couple then added, "After this, I'll bring in some more firewood."

As the night went on, the customers continued to drink and eat, but boredom sifted through the room. Victoria wheeled out the large-screen television and turned the channel to a classic movie station. She opened the employees' break room with its small color TV to others who wanted to watch the hockey game. Someone produced a deck of cards, which led to a lively game of Spades while another group played charades.

When she ignored repeated messages from Lauren to take a break and have something to eat, Eric appeared and gently, but firmly, steered her into the kitchen. Victoria smiled to herself and marveled that, even after he left the room, his touch still lingered on her arm.

Outside, winds buffeted the building. The furnace hummed steadily, fighting to keep up with the falling temperatures. Victoria glanced at the stack of wood next to the hearth. At least if they lost power, there would still be some heat, thanks to Eric who brought several armloads in from the woodpile. She admitted to herself that it had been interesting watching his jacket stretch over his broad shoulders as he lifted the wood. Not to mention how his jeans molded to his thighs as he squatted to push the logs into position. Feeling her face get warm, she realized that the fireplace wasn't the only source of heat for her this night.

She spotted him by the front door, mopping up snow that had melted off people's shoes. No one asked him to do that; no one asked him to do any of the things he'd done. He simply saw a need and stepped in to take care of it. Gratitude washed over her along with a touch of remorse. Perhaps she had been too quick to anger over their cancelled dates. Maybe she could let him know somehow that she was willing to try again.

It took a moment for her to realize that he was staring back. He held up the mop, wriggled his eyebrows and mugged like Groucho Marx. Victoria laughed out loud. He really was cute.

Just after midnight, a glass of beer tipped over at table six, soaking the linen and dripping onto the floor. Victoria grabbed rags from the kitchen and hurried to clean it up. On the other side of the swinging kitchen door, she smacked into a warm, hard body. Knocked off balance, she sprawled on the floor. Looking up, she saw Eric staring back down at her, eyebrows knit in concern. "Are you all right? I'm so sorry." He reached out a hand and pulled her to her feet.

The kitchen door swung open again as Mattie, one of the servers, plowed through on her way back to her tables. Victoria stumbled against Eric, her hands braced on his flannel-clad chest. A faint smell of wood smoke mixed with a spicy after-shave. She drew in a deep breath. The combination was oddly sensuous.

His hands slid down her arms; he threaded his fingers through hers. "I still want to talk to you." His voice was soft, the words meant only for her to hear, but clear above the din of the crowded room.

Flustered, she ducked her head, wondering if anyone in the dining room watched. "We could meet in my office when things calm down a bit."

"All right. I'll be there."

Hours later, Victoria settled into the small office off the kitchen and began to sort through the night's receipts. The dining room had fallen quiet. Exhausted patrons stared numbly at the television or leaned back in chairs, the lucky ones managing to fall asleep. The older couple in the corner snuggled together on one side of the table now, not sleeping, but serene.

She thought of her king size bed and wondered when she would be able to get home.

"I thought you might need this." Eric set a steaming cup of cappuccino down on the desk in front of her.

"Thanks." Charmed by his thoughtfulness, she picked up the cup and wrapped her fingers around the smooth ceramic warmth.

Eric cleared his throat. "I, ah, need to apologize for last weekend."

"You said you had to work?"

"In a way." His words quickened. "I was about to close when this guy comes in and asks for me. Turns out he's with this auto parts store, and they're looking for a new car to sponsor. He saw me drag race this summer, and they're interested."

"Wow." Victoria's head snapped up.

"Isn't it amazing?" Eric laughed. "The money won't be much this first year, but I'll get free parts and oil and, well, it could become something big. Maybe one day I could turn the shop over to Lyle to run, and I could race full time."

"Eric, that's great." The excitement in his voice reminded her of how she felt working to open Keepsake Café.

"Yeah. You'll have to come to the track some time and watch." He paused, as if embarrassed. "That is, if you want to." He drew a deep breath. "Anyway, that was Friday. The same guy came back on Saturday, and I didn't expect him to. He had some forms for me to fill out, and it took a long time. The company installing the new phone system couldn't get it to work, and I couldn't call out. It was stupid. How could anyone be without a telephone these days? Monday morning I went out and got one of those cellular ones. Which," he added with an ironic smile, "is safe on a shelf in the shop. Anyway, I'm really sorry."

Victoria leaned back in her chair and studied him. Nothing in his behavior during the night had shown him to be thoughtless or unreliable. In fact, he'd worked as hard as her and seemed to find satisfaction in making the restaurant patrons happy. She recalled his fleeting smiles as they passed in the aisles, the glances across the room. He made her feel special, desirable.

She wanted more of that.

"Can we try again? Tomorrow night? Dinner?" He ducked his head, then glanced up at her.

"I'd like that." She smiled as his eyes lit up.

An odd, scraping sound interrupted them. Victoria glanced toward the window. At first, she thought there were more headlights, but the light was too faint, too general, for a vehicle's beam. She stood and looked out.

Sunlight. The storm was over.

People with snow brushes swiped at thick drifts on car hoods and trunks. Some vehicles already inched out of the parking lot toward the road where salt trucks rolled past. Eric moved up close behind her.

"Not much of a birthday for you, was it?" She looked up at him over her shoulder.

"It was better than I had hoped for because I got the chance to be here. With you." His eyes twinkled. "Even if you did work me to the point of collapse."

"I seem to recall that you volunteered." She half-turned toward him and put her hands on her hips. "I may have taken advantage of that, true, but I'm no dummy. I know good help when I see it."

Eric chuckled. "Maybe next year will be better."

"How could it be better?" She turned to face him. "This was a great Valentine's Day."

"Yeah, the Keepsake is a success."

"Well, yes, but that's not what I mean."

"No?" He raised his eyebrows.

"No." She tapped his chest with her finger. "Maybe when you pick me up for dinner tomorrow night, I'll explain it to you."

"The forecast is calling for more snow."

"Oh no." Victoria groaned and rolled her eyes.

"That's all right. By then all your customers will be safe at home." He grinned down at her. "We'll just stay here and lock the doors."

Victoria smiled. "And have a Keepsake storm of our very own."

HUNGRY FOR LOVE

Su Kopil

"Half my lunch is gone." Kate stared at her friend across the lunchroom table.

"Who would take half your lunch?" Janelle laughed.

"A kook, that's who. Look!" Kate held half a sandwich in a clear bag in one hand. "This is my pickled tuna on sourdough and this—" she picked up another baggie, "is peanut butter and jelly on white."

"At least, it was a considerate thief."

"Considerate?"

"Sure," said Janelle. "He left you half of his peanut butter and jelly."

"Ugh!" Kate dropped the sandwiches on the table and stuck her hand back in her brown lunch bag. "Ah," she smiled, triumphantly. "He didn't get my pickle." She withdrew a thin object wrapped in tinfoil. A piece of paper with blue writing on it was secured with a rubber band around the middle.

"Ooh, a note." Janelle sipped her diet cola. "This is getting exciting. What does it say?"

Kate threw her friend a withering look and unwound the note from her pickle. "Please accept my paltry offering as an apology. I realized my mistake after the first bite but couldn't resist the incredible taste sensation. Signed a Hungry Friend."

"Mmm, considerate and charming. Sounds like your thief needs a woman's touch at home." Janelle leaned forward, her gaze scanning the small lunchroom. "Who do you think it is?"

Kate shrugged and examined the remaining half of her sandwich before taking a bite.

"Burt in accounting?" Janelle nearly knocked over her soda in her excitement. "No, wait! I'll bet you it's Chet."

Kate choked on her tuna. "My new boss?"

"Your devastatingly handsome new boss. He transfers to our office and suddenly someone is eating your lunch. Fits perfectly."

"Ridiculous. Why would someone like Chet Johnson brown bag peanut butter and jelly when he could afford to eat at La Sage everyday with the rest of the suits?"

"I suppose."

Kate laughed at her friend's obvious disappointment.

"I've got to get back to work." Janelle picked up the remains of her lunch and tossed it in the trash. "Coming?"

"In a minute. You go ahead." Kate dropped the untouched peanut butter and jelly into the paper bag with the rest of her garbage.

What did the sandwich-napper write? She retrieved the crumpled note from the bag and smoothed it out, ignoring the pickle juice. Incredible taste sensation. A smile tickled her lips. Her thief was charming, and he did try to make up for his mistake.

Wait a minute! When had he become her thief? For all she knew, a woman could have stolen her lunch. No, that replacement sandwich definitely had man written all over it. Scrunching the note in her hand, she grabbed her lunch bag and tossed it into the trash. And that man was a thief, no two ways about it.

She arrived back at her cubicle to find her boss standing over her computer, searching through the papers on her desk. The angle afforded her an unobstructed view of his well-formed backside. Needing to tear her gaze away from the delectable picture he made, she glanced at her watch and realized she was ten minutes late.

"I'm sorry for being late, lunch—"

He waved her apology aside. "I was going to leave you a note." He straightened. "I've got to run out. Please cancel my sales meeting." Retrieving his briefcase from the floor, he stepped away from her desk. "In fact, don't schedule any afternoon appointments for the rest of the week. I'll be in and out of the office."

"Yes, Mr Johnson. Anything else?"

"No." He took a few steps before turning back again, a hint of a smile tugging at his lips. "Goodnight, Kate."

The fact that he made a point of acknowledging her warmed her heart. What if he really was her thief? "Goodnight, Mr Johnson."

At five fifteen she met Janelle in the lobby and together they walked through the parking lot to their cars.

"So did you find out who left you the note?" Janelle asked.

"No. I'd nearly forgotten all about it." It wasn't a lie. The last hour of work, she'd been too busy to think about her lunch thief. Janelle didn't have to know that the three hours before that she'd been consumed with curiosity.

"Well, I think I know who it is."

Kate frowned. "I thought you said it was Chet Johnson."

"No, you were right. Why would he steal someone else's lunch when he could just order in or eat out. It doesn't fit. But Brian, on the other hand...."

"Who?" she asked, somewhat irritated that for once Janelle agreed with her.

"Brian Olsen, in the mailroom. He asked you out once and you turned him down, now he's gun-shy. Peanut butter and jelly sounds right up his alley."

Brian Olsen had been the mailroom supervisor for two years and in that time they had gone out together as a group with other coworkers a few times. He was pleasant and nice to look at, but she thought of him more as a brother than a potential date.

"This whole thing is silly, Janelle. It was probably just a freak accident. Someone grabbed the wrong bag, and that's the end of it." Kate stopped at her car.

"Suit yourself." Janelle called over her shoulder. "But you better bring two sandwiches tomorrow, just in case."

On her way into the office the following morning, Kate spotted Brian waiting for the elevator. Upon seeing her, his usually pale skin turned a splotchy red. Could Janelle be right? Could Brian be her mystery thief?

"Good morning, Brian."

"Morning Kate," he mumbled.

"Are you going bowling in the office league Friday night?"

"Yes... no... I mean, maybe. Will you be there?"

The bright blotches were spreading at an alarming rate. Perhaps she should simply offer him the extra grilled chicken sandwich she brought and put an end to this charade. "I wasn't planning on it, but I—"

"Good... I mean... that's too bad." He patted his trouser pockets. "I think I left something in my car. Don't bother holding the elevator." Without another word, he hurried through the lobby and out the front door.

The elevator dinged and the doors slid open. Kate stepped inside and pushed the button. Brian's odd reaction could only mean one thing. He'd switched the sandwiches and was now too embarrassed to face her. No doubt that would be the end of it. Then why did her heart feel so heavy? She sighed, because, despite what she'd said to Janelle, she'd secretly hoped Chet, and her thief, were one and the same.

Kate spent the morning typing letters, sorting files, and watching Chet flit in and out of the office. Janelle was already sitting at the lunchroom table by the time Kate grabbed her lunch bag from the community fridge.

"It's about time you showed up. I've only got five minutes left, and I wanted to see if you got another note."

"Don't count on it." Kate smiled and told Janelle about her encounter with Brian.

"That's too bad. He's a nice guy."

"I know, but I'm just not interested that way about him." Kate dumped the contents of her bag onto the table and gasped. One sandwich was missing and in its place was a chocolate cupcake with another note wrapped around it.

"I guess Brian's got more guts than we gave him credit for." Janelle giggled. "What does it say?"

Kate unfolded the paper. "A sweet for a sweetheart of a girl. Your generosity humbles me."

"But he didn't take anything." Janelle picked up the untouched sandwich.

"Well, not exactly." Kate folded the note. "I brought an extra sandwich—just in case."

Janelle laughed out loud. "So much for a freak accident, huh? What are you going to bring tomorrow?"

"I hadn't thought about it. Actually, I planned on talking to Brian today."

"What's one more day? Bring your garlic cheese and tomato. You can tell Brian how you really feel tomorrow night at the lanes. Consider it his last meal." She giggled.

"I suppose I can wait until after work tomorrow."

Janelle scooped up her trash. "Enjoy your cupcake."

Kate finished her lunch and returned to work. With the last letter printed, she carried the papers needing Chet's signature into his office.

As usual his desk was neat and clean, papers stacked on the right side, pencils in one cup, pens in another. But the silver picture frame was new. She picked it up studying the young boy and pretty woman in the photo. Her heart sank. It never dawned on her that Chet Johnson could be married. The young boy in the photo, looking like a miniature Chet, was obviously his son, and the woman, his wife.

Kate hadn't noticed a wedding ring on his finger but a lot of men didn't wear them. She set the frame down, tamping out any last hope she may have had that Chet Johnson had been the one to leave her notes in her lunch.

The next day, true to his word, Chet left a pile of work for her while he scooted out of the office right before lunch. The computer screen blurred, and she rubbed her eyes, pushed back her chair, and stretched. How he managed to get any work done when he never seemed to stay in the office long was beyond her.

Grabbing her purse, she headed for the third floor. Upon entering the lunchroom her gaze was immediately drawn to a vase filled with gorgeous yellow roses sitting on top of the fridge. Two dozen gorgeous roses, to be exact, with an envelope attached addressed to "My Brown Bag Gourmet." She furtively glanced about the empty lunchroom, embarrassment heating her cheeks. Her fingers shaking, she withdrew the small card and read. "Roses pale in comparison to your beauty and generosity. Eight o'clock tonight at La Sage. Dinner is on me. Signed, a Hungry Friend."

She breathed in the roses sweet aroma. What was Brian thinking? Two dozen stunning roses. Dinner at La Sage. She shouldn't have let things go so far. It was her fault for not talking to him yesterday.

"I've got to find Brian," she spoke aloud. She turned to find one of the boys from the mailroom stroll in and drop change into the soda machine.

"Brian Olsen? He just left for the day."

"Oh, thank you." She carefully picked up the heavy vase. "Guess I'll have to catch him tonight at the lanes."

Kate pulled her car into the bowling alley parking lot at seven o'clock.

"I still don't see why I had to come." Janelle complained.

"Bring your garlic cheese and tomato. What could one more day hurt?" Kate glared at her friend.

"Point taken. Look, there's Brian's car."

"I see him. He's standing at the door. Looks like he's waiting for someone."

"Yeah, you!" Janelle laughed.

Ignoring her friend, Kate parked the car at the curb and jumped out. "Brian," she called.

"Kate?" He stared at her, his eyes wide. "I—I thought you weren't coming."

"We need to talk Brian."

"Now?" He glanced nervously around.

"Yes, now. I can't let this go any further. I tried to find you at work today, but they said you had left early." He wasn't looking at her. In fact, he looked scared to death. Better to just spit it out and get it over with for both their sakes. "The flowers are beautiful, Brian, but I can't accept them, and I can't go with you to La Sage tonight."

"Hi Brian." A girl with thick red hair pulled back into a ponytail joined them. "Who's going to La Sage? I hear they have incredible food." Her glance bounced from Brian to Kate to Brian.

"I'm sorry, Kate," Brian said. "I don't know what you're talking about. What flowers?"

"Did you rent our shoes yet, Brian? Remember last time, they didn't have my size, and I walked around looking like a clown all night?"

"Not yet, Trish."

"That's okay, hon." The red-head replied. "I'll go. See you inside."

"Hon?" Kate asked after Trish had gone. "Are you two dating?"

Brian glanced at his feet, his cheeks darkening. "I got the impression you weren't interested, so I—"

"So you really didn't send those flowers."

He shook his head. "I've no idea what flowers you're talking about."

Brian wasn't her Hungry Friend. Her heart beat faster. Could her thief be Chet Johnson, after all? No, he was married. Then who? Only one way to find out.

"I've got to run. Thanks, Brian. I hope you and Trish are very happy." She kissed him on the cheek, making him blush harder, and hurried back to her car.

"It's not Brian," she said, jumping behind the wheel.

"What? Who's that girl? What are you talking about?" asked Janelle.

"I'll explain later. Right now, I've got to change my clothes and get over to La Sage. I intend to find out just who my charming thief really is."

Kate arrived at La Sage to find a packed restaurant. Diners' faces blurred in the dim lighting. She followed the waiter to an empty table as the hum of conversation rose and fell around them. The smell of steak and garlic did little to quell her nervous stomach.

The waiter pulled out her chair and handed her a menu. "Your dinner companion will be back momentarily."

"Thank you," she glanced at the menu barely able to comprehend the words. What was she doing here? She must have been crazy to think something could come of a date with a man who steals sandwiches. She put down her menu and started to leave.

Then she saw him.

Chet Johnson. He walked toward her, a smile brightening his handsome features.

"Kate?"

"Mr Johnson?" Butterflies danced in her stomach.

"Call me Chet, please." He sat down across from her. "When I told the waiter my date would ask for a hungry friend, I never dared hope... dreamed it could be you."

"You mean you didn't know? But, the note said roses pale next to my beauty." Heat suffused her cheeks when she realized how she must sound.

He laughed. "I was speaking of your inner beauty though it certainly holds true in the other context. I only tried to make amends with the cupcake and then I saw you'd brought two sandwiches. I knew I had to meet the girl with such a generous heart and a talent for making incredible lunches."

It was her turn to laugh. "And what if I had been a man?"

"I would have requested a table that wasn't quite so intimate." He chuckled. "But I somehow doubted any of our male co-workers were the gourmet type."

"Are you disappointed?" The words were out of her mouth before she could stop them.

"Not even close. And you?"

"That depends."

He arched a brow.

"Aren't you married?"

"Divorced." He smiled.

The butterflies stopped dancing, and a warm glow filled her. "But, I'm still not sure I understand. Why is someone like you, I mean, someone who can afford..."

"Stealing other people's lunch?" He finished for her. "The first day, I'd grabbed your bag by accident, thinking it was mine. What with the new job and house hunting—" He shrugged. "I want my son to have a home when he comes for visits."

"Visits?"

"Troy comes every other weekend." His gaze sought hers. "Perhaps you've seen his picture on my desk?"

"Yes, the one with his mother. He looks just like you." She smiled.

"It's the only picture I could find until I finish unpacking."

"But what about this meal and the flowers? You shouldn't have spent the money." Kate said.

"Actually, I'm celebrating two things tonight. The deal on the house Troy and I picked out went through. We can move in next weekend."

"Congratulations! What else are you celebrating?"

He lifted his wineglass in a toast.

Kate followed suit, aware of the mischievous sparkle in his blue eyes.

"To finding a woman who can satisfy my hunger." He grinned.

She giggled. "And to a man who stole more than my pickled tuna."

Their glasses clinked, and Kate found his warm laughter filling her heart.

ONCE IN A BLUE MOON

Carolee Joy

Amanda stood at the upstairs window of her childhood bedroom. Even from here, memories of what she had given up made her heart ache. The ethereal light of a full moon streamed in and glinted off custom ice skates occupying a corner of the white desk. Championship ribbons adorned pictures of her with her former pairs partner. Figure skating trophies gleamed in the moonlight, mocking her.

From the poster bed, her daughter's breath rose and fell with the soft, even sound of a child sleeping. This room held the ghosts of so many childhood dreams. Did Katie feel them while she slept?

Amanda pressed her forehead against the frosted pane. A block away, skaters circled around and around the outdoor rink, their bodies no more than shadowy shapes against the glimmery, white ice. What would have happened if....

"Every night you stand there watching. When are you going to stop dwelling and start doing?" Her mother's voice gently chided from the door.

"Shhh." Amanda whirled and pressed a finger to her lips. "You'll wake Katie, and I don't have the energy to read even one more bedtime story."

"Then answer my question." Her mother gave her an understanding smile and a quick hug. "When are you going to be out there twirling around?"

Amanda sighed. When, indeed. Ever since Bryan's desertion, the simple work of daily living was all she could deal with, which was why she had moved home with her four-year-old daughter.

"Maybe the next blue moon," she joked, knowing there wouldn't be another one this year.

Her mother picked up the skates by their silvery laces. "Then I'll watch Katie. Dress warmly. It's a little colder tonight, what with the moon being so full. And nice and blue."

"But—" Amanda's thoughts raced. She absolutely did not want to go out there with those other skaters. Skating would do nothing more than remind her of all she had lost for a man who later walked away from their daughter and their marriage. The rink was where Bryan had proposed to her just five years ago. The last time she ever skated. The night she turned her back on Joe, her partner since she'd first laced up a pair of skates.

"It's time, Amanda." Mother's voice became more insistent. "You've loved skating since you were Katie's age. I'll never understand why you gave it up. Go, you might even meet some old friends there."

She doubted it, but maybe if she went to the rink, she could put those old regrets to rest. Sighing, she gave into the determined gleam in her mother's eyes.

A short time later, she stood at the edge of the old

practice rink. Her misgivings returned as she realized there was no way she could enter the warming shack without breaking down.

Kids chased each other in games of tag. A few couples drifted around the ice, mittened hands clasped tightly.

Tears welled in her eyes. She couldn't do this, she just couldn't. Then the loudspeakers swelled with a song she remembered from skating pairs with Joe. The music flowed through her and made her tension slide away. Her feet practically twitched with a need to be on the ice.

Sitting on the snowbank, she traded her boots for skates The next thing she knew she was slowly gliding over the smooth surface. Legs spread, arms stretching wide, she threw her head back, caught a snowflake on her tongue and embraced the night.

The next song made her accelerate in time with the music. She moved faster into a loop, then spun into a crescendo for a dramatic finale. She slowed from a double axle to the sound of applause coming from the dozen other skaters at the edge of the rink. Embarrassment heated her cheeks at the thought of all these strangers watching her take over the rink. Then she blushed with the realization that the man gliding up to her like a phantom was the one she hadn't been able to stop thinking about since she returned to her hometown.

Smiling, he slid his arm around her waist. "May I? The moon is just the right shade of bright."

"Joe!" She couldn't deny the happiness welling up inside at seeing him, looking as delicious as sin and wonderfully familiar. A moment later, he led her across the ice in a well-known dance. Caught up in the magic after a few strains, thoughts of what might have been faded away and possibilities took their place. Being here with him suddenly seemed more right than the regrets she'd harbored since their bitter break-up the night of the Winter Festival competition five years ago.

"I'm glad you're back." He smiled down at her.

"Me, too." She shot him a quick glance. Did he remember all the times they'd circled the rink? Holding hands, they'd laughed and teased about how the full moon made it impossible to find a dark place to steal a kiss before the caretaker came storming across the ice to break-up the innocent intimacy. Tonight, brilliance sparkled across the rink, turning it into the reflection of a million diamonds.

Joe's arm around her as they circled the rink felt better than nice, it felt right, like coming home to a warm fire. Their breath mixed in a frosty plume. Caught up in a kaleidoscope of shared memories, Amanda's heart raced. Did he regret her leaving? Or blame her for throwing away their chance to go to the national competitions?

If Bryan hadn't been so jealous, she and Joe could have continued skating together. She dismissed the thought as soon as it occurred. He wouldn't hear of it, and she had been forced to choose. And how could she wish for things to be different when now she had Katie?

"I have a daughter," she said softly and waited for his reaction.

"I hope you're teaching her to skate. Maybe she'll be an angel on ice like her mother. I've missed you, Amanda."

"I've missed you, too," she whispered.

His gaze searched her face as he pulled her closer. "I think you should know I'm not interested in taking up where we left off."

Her heart skipped several beats. What was he trying to say? Could they be more than friends, or had she been wishing for the impossible?

"I want a new beginning. For both of us."

"Me, too," she said, at last realizing the real reason she'd come home. Not just for Katie, not because she didn't have other choices. She wanted to start over with Joe.

As his lips brushed hers in a soft kiss filled with promises, she knew a second chance like this only came along once in a blue moon.

THE PERFECT PAIR

Betsy Norman

"That baker man sure has some great buns." Lida nudged my attention to the sculpted posterior of Paul, the apron-clad proprietor of Gillies' Bakery.

I ignored her innuendo and manufactured a bright grin when Paul turned around and spotted us. "He sure does. Very cinnamon-y, too."

"Good morning ladies! How are my favorite customers?" Paul smiled, looking as delectable as his sweet rolls with a bit of icing along his jaw.

"Just peachy," Lida piped in. She postured coquettishly against the display glass. My subtle elbow to the ribcage straightened her spine. "I mean—Emmie is ready to order."

"Will that be the usual?" He winked at me and revealed a hidden treat with a come-hither glint in his eye. "Or could I tempt you into trying my new pastry?"

"Oooo... And just what is this masterful confection?" I asked.

"It's a pecan puff. Light and flaky, with lots of cinnamon. Your favorite, right?" He held one up to my lips, teasing. "Mine, too. Here, try it."

I couldn't resist his offer and took a slow, mouth-watering bite. "Mmmm, de-lish. I'll take one to go."

"I hoped you'd like it. Here's an extra for your friend."

He plopped them into the bag and gave it to me, brushing hands. His looked strong from hours of kneading firm dough and made me tingle at the contact. I started for the door, but Lida lagged behind.

"By the way," Lida leaned back over the counter toward Paul and slipped a business card out of her purse to dangle it above the "free dozen" fishbowl. "I believe you were asking for one of these."

"Thanks." Paul took her card and pocketed it. I saw the chagrin on his face at having me witness the exchange. "Look forward to seeing you tomorrow, ladies." He quickly shifted back into a grin, waving.

"Bye!" We called in unison.

I was devastated. I thought for sure that the attraction was mutual between Paul and me. Yet, here he was, asking for Lida's phone number.

"The extra is for you, Lida. Don't you want a bite?" I offered the luscious puff half-heartedly.

"Of that? No way! Those things are so bad for you, Emmie." Her husky giggle scraped over my ears when she recanted saucily. "Though I wouldn't mind taking a nip out of him. MmmMm!"

Lida's covetous remark jarred me. She knew how I felt about Paul. "Sex pot. Must every man be a meal to you?" I snapped.

She ran a quick finger over the sticky icing. "At least men don't have any calories."

Ouch.

Lida's pert reminder stung. For the first time I resented my runway model thin friend. My hourglass figure held a lot more sand than hers did, but our friendship always seemed to counterbalance her obsession with weight and appearance. Realization struck home that she was a much better physical match for my baker man. They made the perfect pair. I stuffed the pastry back into the bag and picked up the pace of our walk.

"I'm sorry, Emmie."

I slanted her a resigned look. "Oh, Lida. It's not that."

"Then what? The business card?" She hedged and waved a hand in dismissal. "That was nothing. We go in there every morning so you can moon over him, not me. Besides, the two of you were practically in each other's arms over that pecan puff!"

"We were not! Besides, who's to say he doesn't already have a girlfriend, or isn't interested in—someone else?"

"Oh, please, why would he flirt with you so much? Since when did you become so insecure? Is this the same lady who seduced a conductor into a date by composing risqué librettos?"

"That was just a lark, and a long time ago. I'm ready for something a little more substantial now." It was too bad my heart was set on someone who obviously wanted my best friend's phone number, and not mine. "He flirts with all the customers to sell more buns." I tried to be flippant to disguise my growing heartache.

"Not a chance. He flirts with you because you're stunning with chestnut hair that doesn't require a root job every six weeks, porcelain skin without makeup, naturally long nails—and about a dozen other features I'd kill to have been born with."

"But I'm no match for your size five, and I never will be. It wasn't my business card he was after." Lida's checklist of my alleged assets sounded superficial to me, but so did moping over dress sizes. I didn't want this damaging our friendship.

We reached the intersection where we ended our walk and headed to work. Lida gave me a much-needed hug and a cheer-up smile before undulating off on her stilettos. I turned down the street to the Music Muse, where I double as manager and tutor.

Maybe Lida was right. He did seem very animated whenever we came in. I just couldn't understand why it was her card he wanted and not mine. Maybe her svelte appearance was more appealing to him. I set the morning's bakery bag aside. The bitter taste of reality had ruined my treat.

I decided to quit stopping in at the bakery. My sneakers would just have to speed right on by the open door siren of cinnamon icing and smiling blue eyes.

"I'm sorry I'm late! I overslept!" The next morning, I pretended to huff and puff down the street toward Lida. I stopped short when I saw her lounging in front of Gillies' Bakery with Paul. She was giggling into his ear, and the two of them acted like they were making plans. Lida hush-hushed Paul when I approached. Their greetings were warm and open, despite the secretive glances exchanged.

"No problem, I already packed your breakfast. Couldn't start the day right knowing you went without." Paul held the small white bag out for me.

"Sure, thanks. Just let me grab some change—"

"Don't bother, Emmie." Paul shot Lida a glance. "Just tryin' to score points."

He interrupted my purse rummaging with a soft touch. I stifled the shiver it caused.

"One day I'll call 'em in, but not today. You're late, remember?"

Too late, I guess.

The points he was scoring were for Lida's benefit. I

should've known all along. Trudging off to work with a heavy heart, I lied to Lida and told her my hours had changed and that I'd have to skip our walks from now on. That would give her the opportunity to get closer to Paul and me to lick my wounds in private.

"Emmie!" Ralph, the part-timer, called into the back where I was carefully unpacking an order of flute cases a few days later. "Some guy here with a box of baked goods looking for you. You gonna share?"

My hands froze on the instruments. It couldn't be him! My heartstrings began tripping a staccato beat on the off chance it was Paul.

"You can have them, Ralph. I'm trying to cut down on sweets." I couldn't set myself up for disappointment. I decided to stay hidden in the storeroom.

"I don't see any reason for you to. You look great to me." I jumped at the warm baritone of Paul's voice filling the claustrophobic quarters, so flustered a flute case juggled right out of my hands.

"What—what are you doing here?" I quickly scampered to recover the case and stuff it onto a shelf. It gave me an excuse to stay down on my knees, which were too weak to stand.

"Special Delivery. You won this week's free dozen." He bandied the box of buns for proof.

"But how? I've never put a business card in that jar."

"Well..." He dimpled into a broad grin. "Lida gave one to me. I sorta cheated the drawing a bit this time."

"Lida gave you my business card?" My assumption had been so wrong.

"I asked her for it so I could find out where you work and surprise you."

"And here I thought you and she—I owe her an apology." I started to blush.

"Nah. She knows the score. But she does miss her

walkin' buddy. Promise you'll start visiting the bakery again each morning?" He held out his hand to help me up and added softly, "I miss you, too. Very much."

"You do?" My resolve to stay clear of him began to crumble at the low entreaty accompanying his touch.

"You bet I do. I planned on coming here to ask you out to dinner."

"Really? I guess I find that hard to believe. Lida is much better suited, you being so well built, and her trim shape." I stammered over the embarrassing confession of ill-conceived logic. "You two make a much better looking pair."

"Says who? Your friend is pretty and all, but her bony little figure just couldn't stand up to my kind of lovin'. I'm sorry, Darlin', but a man who kneads his fists in dough all day long likes the feel of something soft and firm in his hands." He stroked the back of a knuckle against my jaw. "Wanna know what I think?"

"What?"

"I think you've got the type of curves this baker man has grown awfully fond of. With a beautiful face to match." He leaned down from his towering height and gave a floury soft brush of lips to my cheek. His breath—a mixture of cinnamon and nutmeg—lingered near my temple.

"I think we're the perfect pair."

"I think you're right."

WHEN HEARTS HEAL

Susan D. Brooks

"Hey, Mom? You seen Gunther?"

Celeste cast a quick look over her right shoulder, not sure she heard correctly. Her eight-year-old son sat cross-legged on the back seat of the Jeep, gnawing his lower lip.

Her foot stomped on the brake of the Wrangler and brought the vehicle to a screeching halt. She threw the car into neutral and jerked up the parking brake. After a quick glance at the floorboards, she turned to glare at her son.

"Why is Gunther here?" she demanded.

A smile curled the corners of Scott's mouth, revealing the dimples he'd inherited from his father. He ducked his head. "I couldn't leave him home alone for a whole weekend."

"He can take care of himself just fine." Celeste opened

the door and stepped out onto the empty, narrow road. "He shouldn't be loose in the car. I could have stepped on him, Scott."

She peered into the back seat, spying Gunther's aquarium. "That explains why you didn't want to sit in the front today. How did you sneak this into the Jeep without me noticing?"

"I put it in my duffel bag." Her son's voice held a note of triumph.

"Now it all makes sense. I thought you wanted that huge old canvas thing to put toys in. Ah, there you are!"

Gunther, a slender ribbon garter snake, peered back at Celeste over the first aid kit stored under the driver's seat. She grabbed the small reptile and laid it gently in her son's waiting hands. "Please, please put him in his cage. He could have been hurt."

"He likes to crawl around."

"I know, honey, but this isn't a good place to let him roam." Celeste got back behind the wheel and buckled her seat belt. "Don't let him out at Aunt Karen's. Someone might kill him. A lot of people don't understand having a snake for a pet," she admonished, putting the Jeep in gear.

In the rear view mirror Celeste watched Scott lean down to put Gunther back in his aquarium home. When he sat back up, he asked, "Is Uncle Nathan going to be there?"

Celeste stiffened at the mention of her brother-in-law. Nathan had been a big part of their lives before an accident took her husband's life. For eight years, Nathan had spent most of his leave from the Marine Corps at their rural Maryland home, captivating her son and husband with tales of his experiences in the Corps. When he returned to duty, his letters to the family arrived often, the gifts to Scott frequent and imaginative.

Yet for all Nathan's devotion to David and Scott, he kept Celeste at arm's length. He was always pleasant, always helpful, but he never sought her company and left the room whenever they were alone together. When she asked David about the odd behavior, he shrugged it off.

"He's a Marine. He's just used to being with guys."

"That's a lame explanation," she sniffed, not bothering to hide her bruised feelings. "He's nicer to the checkout clerks at the Stop 'n Shop."

"Don't let it bother you," he said, pulling her into his arms. "I'm crazy about you and that's what matters."

Celeste had pushed the problem to the back of her mind, but decided to sit down with her brother-in-law and try to get him to talk to her. The opportunity never came. David died on the first evening of Nathan's next visit, throwing her world into a torment of loneliness and grief. Being strong for Scott took all she had, there was little left to worry about her silent brother-in-law.

Nathan visited just once after David's death. Arriving unannounced on a dark winter day, he dropped a bag of Christmas presents by the door and had a cup of mulled cider while he played with his overexcited nephew. Nathan spoke briefly about his decision to leave the Marine Corps, indicating that he wanted to start his own business. Her surprised questions went unanswered as he grabbed his coat and almost ran out the door. He hadn't been back since.

"Yes, honey, Uncle Nathan will be at your aunt's house, but I don't know how much time he'll spend there. There's a big Civil War reenactment this weekend. You know how he is about that."

"Yeah, he's an ar-art-artill—" Scott's voice rose with excitement.

"Artillerist. I suppose that sounds exciting, but it's dumb. Grown up people playing soldier." The moment the words left her lips, she regretted them.

"It's not dumb. Dad used to do it. You did, too." Her son's words, faintly accusing, floated over the whir of the engine.

Heaviness fell across Celeste's shoulders. She glanced in

the rear view mirror. Scott's hazel eyes reflected back at her.

"I did third-person living history, that's different. I wasn't pretending to be someone I'm not. I was educating the public." Her words, however, lacked conviction.

"It's the same thing." A challenging tone edged Scott's voice. "The soldiers teach, too. They just wear uniforms and shoot guns."

He sank back into the seat, eyes downcast. More mumbled words followed, but Celeste chose to ignore them.

She drew a deep breath and let it out slowly. Scott echoed his father's sentiments with surprising accuracy, but without David's playfulness. She recalled mock fights she and her husband had, debating the merits of first person versus third person living history.

"You can't be someone you're not," she'd insist. "All you can do is show people how things were. You can't really give them the experience of it."

"Yes, you can, and the public loves it." His smile turned mischievous. "You don't think Colonial Williamsburg is a good idea?"

Celeste would roll her eyes, explain that Colonial Williamsburg was not the same thing at all, and they'd go round and round until they agreed to disagree. Then they would fall into each other's arms, all other thoughts lost in a wave of love.

Scott's involvement in the hobby remained the one hurdle they never got over. Celeste took Scott to occasional living history demonstrations, but she refused to let him attend any battle reenactments until he turned eight, the age he had reached officially a week ago. David thought her silly, but she worried that their sensitive son would react adversely to the sight of people being shot, even if it was just pretend.

And, since the accident, she had another reason: Scott began having nightmares about Civil War soldiers, dreaming that he watched them kill his father again and again.

Although he hadn't had one of the dreams in over six months, she worried that seeing someone dressed in blue or gray would trigger their return.

Celeste knew, as only a mother does, how deep the wound was that cut into her son. The sepia-toned picture of David, standing stiff and proud in a Civil War uniform next to his reproduction Napoleon cannon, hung on the wall over Scott's bed. The glass protecting the print was smudged from kisses Scott didn't think Celeste knew about. When she once suggested replacing the photo with one of the three of them together, he shook his head. "This is how he looked that day," he said softly.

Celeste shook herself out of the bittersweet daydreams. A feeling of bewilderment washed over her as she wondered if she'd made the wrong choice by insulating her son from the past.

Well, this isn't the time to worry about that.

"All right, buddy. I know when to surrender. But I expect liberal terms and a complete cessation of hostilities."

The light tone of her voice and the unexpected use of military surrender policies brought the expected response: Scott giggled. He turned to look out the window and dropped the conversation.

Forty five minutes later, Celeste drove past George Washington's Headquarters on Braddock Street in Winchester, Virginia, for the third time. She pulled over to the curb and smoothed the directions to her sister-in-law's house over her knee. Scott frowned and twisted to look over his shoulder. "Aunt Karen lives that way."

"Not anymore. She and Frank bought a new house."

"A new house? Does this one have a pool, too?"

Celeste nodded. "Yes, Water Boy. A heated one. But it's only May. They might not have it filled yet. Besides," she added, glancing at her watch, "they'll be having dinner soon. We will, too, if I ever find the place."

"I brought my swim trunks. Aunt Karen always has the

pool open when I come. It's plenty warm."

"All right, but no pouting if things don't work out."

"I don't pout anymore, Mom. I'm eight, remember?"

Karen rushed out onto the wide porch that extended the length of the house, arms waving madly overhead. "Scott! Celeste!"

Celeste grinned at the sight of her sister-in-law. Red hair flying behind her, the trim, petite female that flew toward them looked more like a thirty-year old than a woman about to turn fifty. Face flushed, eyes glittering with excitement, she charged the Jeep, pulled the door open, and hesitated. A mother of two boys, now grown, she was ever mindful of being too intimate without the permission of the child.

Scott undid his seatbelt and threw open his arms. Happiness lit Karen's face as the two embraced. Celeste watched, shocked by the display of affection although she knew that Karen was Scott's favorite aunt. He rarely let anyone touch him anymore.

Karen released Scott, leaving one arm around his shoulders. Her gaze met Celeste's. "I'm glad you came."

"Me, too. It's good to see you again." She smiled, affection for this loving woman warming her heart. Phone calls just did not take the place of a personal visit.

"We wanted to wait until you were ready." Karen tipped her head to one side. "The family can be overwhelming when they're all together, and they still talk about David a lot." She ruffled Scott's hair. "You'll hear lots of stories about the things he did when he was your age, I'm sure. Now, let me get one of the boys to carry your luggage."

"Hi, Aunt Celeste! Hi, Scott." Lee, Karen's oldest son, emerged from the front door at a run, a basketball under his arm. "Mom, see you later. Going to shoot hoops at Joey's."

Celeste's greeting was lost in Karen's demand that he be back in time for dinner. He trotted up the street, dribbling the ball, the soft thwang sharp in the quiet countryside.

"Grant's still here. He can bring in your suitcases." As she turned to enter the house, a small red pickup rolled around the corner of the garage. Grant waved as he pulled out of the driveway.

Karen's hands went to her hips. "For crying out loud. They might just as well have gone away to college for all the time they spend here—"

"I'm still capable of carrying heavy loads. Just have to tie my shoe." The deep voice came from inside the house. Celeste's throat tightened at the familiar sound. Nathan stepped onto the front porch and smiled first at Celeste, then at Scott. "Hey, buddy! I haven't seen you in a long time."

Scott launched himself at his uncle who knelt down and wrapped the boy in his arms. Celeste stared at the tall, lanky man. With his head turned away, dressed in those jeans and red flannel shirt, he could have been her husband back from the dead. She could feel Karen's eyes on her, watching for a reaction.

"Mom didn't think you'd be here." Scott's muffled voice floated out from his uncle's shoulder.

Nathan's blue eyes widened as he looked up at her. "Why?"

"There's a big reenactment—" Celeste shrugged.

Nathan looked back at his nephew.

"Yes, I'll be going to that for a little while tomorrow. I thought you might want to come with me. After all, you're eight now. That was the deal, wasn't it?"

Both turned and looked to Celeste, who stared back. Astonished that Nathan remembered David's promise, she opened her mouth to speak, closed her mouth, swallowed and finally stammered, "I don't know. This is a family reunion. I want Scott to see his relatives."

Nathan nodded. "I agree with that. I'm just going to go for a few hours. I think he should go with me." He rose to his feet and looked into her eyes. "The guys have been asking about him. They want to see David's son."

Karen, silent until now, jumped in. "Let's give Celeste some time to think about it. Inside, everyone. And Nathan, don't forget the bags."

Scott ran ahead to the Jeep. "I'll help!"

"I don't want you to get the wrong impression." Nathan touched Celeste's arm. "I just want to spend some time with him. Reenactments meant a lot to David."

"I'll think about it." Celeste turned away, certain she would find a way to say no later.

As Karen led her through the two-story Colonial home, Celeste made the appropriate admiring remarks, but her thoughts remained with Scott and Nathan.

I want them to spend time together. But do I want them to do it at a reenactment? What if Scott starts having nightmares again?

"This is your room." Karen stopped before a closed door. "I hope you like it." With a flourish, she swung open the door and held out her hand for Celeste to enter.

"Karen, it's lovely." Celeste glanced around the room. Done in shades of green with touches of rose, it had a distinctly early American feel, a look she adored.

"I decorated it myself."

"You did great. Where will Scott sleep?"

"I have a room all ready for him next door to yours. Come on, let's go downstairs. Want a beer?"

"That sounds good."

On the way down the stairs, they ran into Scott and Nathan on their way up with the suitcases. Scott carried the aquarium under one arm like a football. Thoughtfully, or under his uncle's direction, he had it wrapped in his jacket. If not for the shape, Celeste wouldn't have recognized it.

"Scott, your room is the first one on the right. Your mom and I will be in the sunroom. Come down when you're settled." Karen continued down the steps.

Celeste started to follow her when Nathan laid a hand on her arm. He leaned toward her and said in a low voice, "I'll make sure Gunther stays hidden."

"Thanks. He's really no trouble, and Heaven knows he's not dangerous, but most people don't understand snakes and sometimes Scott forgets to put the screen back on—"

"I'll make sure he remembers. Karen's got cats now."

"Cats? Oh no." Her stress level jumped another notch. This would not be a good time for Scott to lose a beloved pet. "Remind Scott to keep his door shut. And Nathan?"

He turned, his eyes questioning. She expected him to step away, to keep distance between them as he always had, but he just smiled and waited for her to speak. A wave of emotions washed over her: confusion, gratefulness, and wonder. She swallowed.

"Thanks." Celeste felt her cheeks burn as she hurried down the stairs to catch up with Karen.

In a spacious sunroom off the back of the house, Celeste looked out over the deck and pool. Beyond were the green shadows of the mountains, rising to the south. A soft glow from the town brightened the evening sky to the east. Karen handed her a frosty mug of pale gold beer. "Forty three acres. What do you think?"

"It's beautiful. Peaceful."

"Which is amazing when you think this was once part of a battlefield."

"A battlefield?" Celeste stared at Karen.

"Uh-huh. One of the battles for Winchester during the Civil War took place here. I forget which one. I think there were three big ones, but the city changed hands constantly."

"I'm surprised you could buy it."

"Because of the preservationists? That's why we bought it. Developers were after it, too, but the owners didn't want to sell to them. We had the money, so…." She shrugged and took a sip of beer.

"It's wonderful you could do that. I'll bet a lot of people are relieved."

"After this weekend, we're donating the land." Karen looked down into her mug.

"You are?"

Karen nodded. "All but the two acres surrounding the house."

Nathan and Scott entered the room. Scott ran to the window and exclaimed over the pool.

"It's heated," Karen said. "You can go in if your mom says it's all right."

At Celeste's nod, he yelled, "All right!"

Punching the air with his right hand, he whirled to race upstairs for his swimsuit when Karen stopped him.

"Scott, can you wait a minute? I have something I want to tell you and your mother."

She put her mug down on a table and folded her hands in front of her. "Scott, Celeste. Nathan, Frank, and I want to do something in David's memory. We thought since he loved reenacting so much we'd tie his name to something significant."

Karen looked at Scott. "Honey, we are donating forty one acres to the local historical society in your father's name. In return, they've erected a small memorial to him." She pointed to a corner of their yard. "There, just outside the fence. It's still on sacred ground but not intrusive to the landscape. The dedication is tomorrow morning." Karen drew a deep breath and let it out. "What do you think?"

"This is the family party you brought me down here for?" Celeste said the first thing that came into her mind.

Karen nodded, cheeks turning red.

Celeste glanced at Scott, whose eyes misted as he looked out over the land. She knew how she should feel, knew the response Karen wanted, but all she felt was empty and just a bit angry. How could she celebrate the very thing that killed her husband?

She fiddled with the mug, hoping the appropriate reaction would come. Scott saved her.

"Wow! A memorial to Dad? Cool! He'd like that, wouldn't he, Mom? What's it look like?"

Karen threw a nervous glance at Celeste and turned to answer Scott's question. Nathan moved to Celeste's side. "You all right?"

"This is a bit of a shock." She gulped her beer.

"Let's go outside." Nathan took her elbow and guided her through the double doors onto the wide cement patio. A chorus of crickets chirped in the tall grass as fireflies darted in and out of a fragrant lilac bush.

She shook her head. "I'm having trouble with this."

"We thought you might."

"A monument to the very thing that killed him?"

Nathan shook his head. "To the very thing he loved. The military tradition goes way back in this family. His bad heart kept him from being part of that, but the reenactment group made him feel that he could at least experience something of what our ancestors went through." He hesitated. "Celeste, reenacting didn't kill him. He had a heart attack and drove off the road."

She whirled, angry that he brought it up. "I know that, but if he wasn't hauling that stupid cannon he wouldn't have lost control of the truck."

"The autopsy report indicated a massive heart attack. The doctor said it would have been fatal anyway."

"We don't know that for sure. The official cause of death was drowning. He was trapped under water in the cab of that stupid truck for half an hour."

"I know. I was there, remember?"

Celeste's hand flew to her mouth. "Oh, God, Nathan, I'm sorry. I'm so sorry. I know you were there. I know you tried all you could to save him."

Her anger disappeared, replaced with remorse at her thoughtlessness, but Nathan appeared unaffected.

"You still miss him." His eyes, filled with understanding, searched her face.

The words made her think.

"Of course," she replied. "Sometimes, but lately it's been easier. What we had is here," she tapped her heart, "forever. But it's done. My life has moved on. It's just being here with you and Karen sort of brought it all back."

"I know what you mean. For months after the accident, I'd look for him at reenactments, I'd pick up the phone to call him then remember he wasn't there." Nathan crossed his arms over his chest and looked down at his feet. "I haven't done that in a long time." He lifted his gaze to her and smiled. "We're healing."

"Yes." Relief swept through her as she realized that this would not be a maudlin weekend, but a joyful celebration of David's life and love of history. "And I'm glad."

"Me, too."

"Mom!" Scott appeared in the doorway wearing his swim trunks. "Here!" He tossed his towel to Celeste as he passed and hurled himself into the pool. Cool water sprayed Celeste and Nathan. Scott surfaced, laughing.

"All right, buddy," Nathan teased, pointing a finger at the boy. "I'll remember that." He tugged at the shirt, pulling the wet knit fabric away from his skin. "Good thing I wear the same size as Frank."

"You didn't bring any clothes with you?" Celeste asked.

"Nah, I just live on the other side of town."

"Oh, that's right. Scott mentioned that."

"I bought an old farmhouse with six acres. I always lived in apartments and bachelors' quarters when I was in the Corps. I want trees and grass, maybe a horse or two."

"Are you still working for that roofing contractor?" Celeste glanced at Scott as he paddled from one end of the pool to the other.

"Actually, I bought him out and expanded the business. We install vinyl siding, too." He waved his hand at the house. "I did this one."

"Really?" Celeste looked up at the silhouetted house.

"You like doing that sort of work?"

"Sure do. Being outside, doing physical labor, being my own boss." He nodded. "It suits me."

"Are you getting a lot of contracts?"

"I had to hire two employees last year, and I need one more." He shifted his feet and turned to watch Scott execute a near-perfect dive. "Karen told me the company you work for is shutting down."

"Production stops in December, but they're shifting all the accounting functions to corporate headquarters before Labor Day." She shrugged "I'll find something else. One thing the world always needs is bookkeepers."

"As a matter of fact, I need one. Would you consider working for me?"

"For you?" Celeste stared at him for several seconds, then rubbed her tired eyes. The idea to relocate had never occurred to her. Could she? What about Scott? She blurted the first words that came into her mind. "I don't live in Winchester."

"You could always move here." The corners of his mouth twitched. "I'm sure you could stay with Frank and Karen until you found a place of your own."

"I, ah, well..." she stammered, digesting the surprising offer.

"Nathan, Frank's truck broke down." Karen stood in the doorway leading to the kitchen, waving a cordless phone. "Could you go get him? He's on Route 7, just outside of Berryville."

Nathan glanced at his watch. "Tell him I'll be there within thirty minutes."

"This is the third time this month. Nobody at the garage knows what's wrong, nobody at the dealer knows, nobody knows. Frank, he'll be there within a half hour." Karen's voice faded as she went back into the house.

"I caught you off guard, I know." Nathan dug his keys out of a pocket. "Think about it, and we'll talk more later. Okay?"

"Sure." The consent came automatically, but so much had to be considered first. She and David talked several times about moving to Winchester, but they never took the steps necessary to make it a reality. She'd have to sell their house, pack all their things, find new doctors, a new bank, a new grocery store. She looked at Scott, jumping off the side of the pool. He'd have to leave his friends, but he'd be with family.

Nathan moved toward the driveway then turned and, walking backward, called, "It would be good for Scott.".

Celeste thought of the eager hugs and frequent laughter from her son since their arrival. Yes, the move would be good for Scott.

"What would be good for me? If you marry Uncle Nathan?"

Celeste jumped at the sound of her son's voice beside her. He stood, a puddle forming around his feet, arms wrapped around his waist, shivering. She threw the towel around him and hugged him to her.

"Marry your Uncle Nathan?" she laughed, "Where did you get that idea?"

"Then, what would be good for me?" he repeated, watching Nathan until he got into his truck and drove away.

"Your uncle offered me a job with his company." She watched for a reaction, but his expression remained impassive. "We'd have to move to Winchester if I take it."

"Oh."

"Would you want to move here?"

"I don't know." Scott's eyes held a hint of wariness.

"Why not? We'd be with family and, hey," Celeste added, hoping to keep the conversation from becoming too serious, "look at the pool you'd have to use whenever you want." She pretended to frown. "Well, maybe not in February."

"I'd miss my friends."

"True. And I'd miss mine. But we'd make new ones."

Scott looked down at the ground and ran his toe along the edge of the patio. "I can't feel Dad here."

Celeste nodded and brushed his hair back with her fingers.

"You know?" He looked up at her. "Sometimes at home I come down the stairs, and I swear he's there. I think he's going to grab me and tickle me like he used to. You ever feel that way?"

"I have, honey, many times. Not as much lately, though."

"I'd feel like I'm leaving him if we moved. But, I guess you'll overrule me if you want to come here."

"Overrule?" He'd never used that word before.

"That's what Tommy Lake's parents did. They asked him if he wanted to go, he said no, and now he's living in Boston." Scott made a face. "He sent me a letter saying he hates it."

"Honey, this isn't just my decision or just your decision. We think about it, talk about it, then we make a decision together."

His chin quivered, the corners turned down. "I don't want to move. Maybe someday, but not now."

"Then we won't."

"Really?" A wide smile lit his face.

"Of course not. You have a vote in this, too."

He pushed the towel away and jumped back into the water.

Celeste plunked down on a green canvas patio chair and leaned back, hearing Scott's splashing while looking into the indigo sky. A crescent moon shimmered on the eastern horizon as stars winked above. She lifted the mug for a sip, then watched as beads of sweat rolled down the glass and over her wedding ring.

Her absolute, certain response to her son's question returned to haunt her, and she found disappointment pushing in through the cracks in her mood. In all honesty, a move to Winchester intrigued her. A change would be good for them, she thought, but Scott seemed dead set against it, and he should have a say in their future.

Shouldn't he?

Yes. Absolutely.

She set the mug down with more force than necessary on a glass-top table. Just because she was the adult didn't mean that her life was more important. Her son's happiness meant more to her than her own.

Yet, the more she thought about Winchester and working for Nathan, the better she liked the idea.

But Scott should have a stable life in an environment that's familiar to him. At least, that's what the school counselor said last year during the annual conference.

Then why was her traitorous mind already at work devising ways to turn Scott's "no" to a "yes"?

"Dinner's going to be late." Karen slid into the seat next to Celeste's and stretched out her legs. "I'll bet Scott is starving."

"Me, too," Celeste admitted.

Karen folded her hands over her stomach, glanced at the pool, then asked in a light, airy voice, "Have you had any interesting conversations with Nathan? I saw you two talking out here."

"And here I thought the offer was spontaneous!" Celeste laughed. "Was the job your idea?"

"Actually, it was all Nathan's doing, but I confess, I encouraged him." Karen leaned over and placed her hand over Celeste's. "And I did it for the most selfish reason, too. I want you and Scott here with us."

"I'm flattered."

"It's not flattery. I miss you. You were a big part of my life, you know. I feel like you walked out on us."

"You do? Oh, Karen, I'm sorry," Celeste stammered. "These last two years have been hard for me."

"Is that why we've only seen you twice?"

"Twice?" Celeste echoed, brushing her hair back from her face, trying to remember the past 24 months. "I didn't realize—"

"That's just what I told Nathan." Karen waved a manicured hand. "I told him that you didn't care any less for us just because David's dead. I figured you just had to sort things out and get your new life up and running."

"I'm sorry. I've just not... been myself. This time has been very difficult."

"Well, it's done. Now we can go on." Karen leaned back in the chair and crossed her legs at the ankle.

"You have my promise that Scott and I will be around a lot more in the future."

Frank and Nathan returned an hour and a half later. Celeste stood at the stove, stirring a batch of spaghetti sauce while Karen put a loaf of Italian bread into the oven then began to slice tomatoes for a salad.

"There she is!" Frank hollered as he entered the kitchen and spied Celeste. He dropped his jacket on the counter then enveloped her in his massive arms, holding her tight against an equally large chest. "We've missed you!"

Karen handed him a fresh beer as he looked into the stainless steel pot and sniffed appreciatively. "Mmmmmm. Smells good." He released Celeste and caught his wife in a hug, giving her a quick kiss.

"Hope there's a lot because I'm hungry," announced Nathan.

"Me, too," chirped Scott from the doorway. He ran for Frank and grabbed his uncle around the waist.

Like Nathan earlier, Frank got down on his knees to take the boy in his arms. Wordlessly, he buried his face in his nephew's neck then quickly pushed him to arm's length, frowning. "Hey, for a minute I thought you were Scott."

"I am," Scott giggled.

"Nah, you can't be. Scott is a little kid. You're big."

"I've grown up." His thin shoulders straightened. "I'm eight."

"You're mighty scrawny, whoever you are. Better feed you. Go on into the dining room."

Nathan grabbed Scott as he passed, picked him up, and flipped him upside down over his shoulder. "I'll take him in."

Scott's laughter rang through the house as the two disappeared through a doorway into the next room.

"So, when are you moving here?" Frank fished a strand of spaghetti from a pot on the stove and dropped it in his mouth.

"Does everyone know about this?" Celeste retorted, exasperated, but pleased at the same time.

"Hey, it took me two months to entice Nathan's bookkeeper away from him, and at a higher salary, too."

"Frank." Karen glared at her husband.

"What? She wasn't right for that company, and she's perfect for me. Within a week, she had that computer system up and running." He plucked a tomato from the cutting board and tossed it into his mouth. "Nathan doesn't even have a computer."

"Honey, go find out what Nathan and Scott want to drink, please." She pushed him firmly toward the door.

"Frank hired Nathan's bookkeeper?" Celeste heard a whoosh of water as Karen emptied the pasta into a colander. "Was Nathan mad?"

"No. She may have that computer running, but she's useless when it comes to running the office. Nathan needs someone who can basically do everything, from purchasing to customer service, not just the books. He needs you. Here's a bowl for the sauce."

"I don't think he's going to get me." Celeste made a face. "Scott doesn't like the idea of moving here."

"We'll work on him." Karen's determined tone made Celeste smile. "He'll change his mind when he finds out that Nathan wants to be his—"

Celeste looked up as the words abruptly stopped. Her sister-in-law stared back at her, wide-eyed, hand clamped over her mouth. "Be his what?"

"Friend."

"He already is." A suspicion too outlandish to be true took form in Celeste's mind. She laid the wooden spoon on a ceramic rest, turned to Karen, and folded her arms across her chest. "What's going on here?"

Karen lowered her chin and looked up at Celeste through her eyelashes. "We just wanted to help Nathan."

"Help Nathan do what?"

Karen winced. "Find someone."

"He needs your help to find a bookkeeper?"

"Not just that."

The muffled words puzzled Celeste further. "Karen—"

"I'm just trying to help my brother."

"That's commendable, but what's that got to do with me?"

"A lot." Karen chewed on her lower lip then reached for the refrigerator door handle. "He's in love with you."

Time skipped a beat. In that swift moment, Celeste's mind whipped into a vortex where no logical thought could prevail. Nathan? In love with her?

"That's absurd. Until today I didn't think he could stand the sight of me."

"Probably because he didn't know how to act around you. He's felt this way for years." Karen drew a tub of margarine from the shelf and shut the door. "That's why he went into the Marines when you and David got married."

"I don't believe it. How could he hide it all this time?" Celeste watched bubbles rise to the surface of the sauce and pop leaving a string of small, orange dots across the pocket of her lavender silk blouse. She felt the same pressure grow in her chest, certain that her emotions would burst through her skin and drain her of feeling.

"Oh, Nathan would never let you know." Karen reached into the cupboard under the sink and pulled out a box of stain remover wipes. She handed one to Celeste. "He's a great guy."

Celeste fingered the damp square of synthetic fabric. "These are the same as baby wipes, you know. And those cost less." Her voice, distant and flat, seemed to come from someone else. What was she talking about? Who cared about wipes?

Karen turned off the burner and led Celeste to a high stool at the breakfast bar. "Sit."

"Did David know?" Celeste climbed onto the chair and placed both forearms on the counter, feeling the smooth, cool tiles against her skin.

"I think he suspected, but he never said anything." Karen tipped her head to one side. "David was an expert at hiding his thoughts and emotions, as I'm sure you know."

"Yes, I know. He got better, but... Karen, what should I do?"

"How do you feel about Nathan?"

"Ah." She felt a rush of color on her face. "I—well. If you asked me yesterday, I would have said he's just David's handsome brother, but today, oh, I don't know."

"Hmm." Karen's eyes narrowed speculatively. "He's marvelous with Scott."

Celeste managed a weak smile. "He's always been great with Scott."

"No one is asking anything from you. You're not even supposed to know any of this. You're here to have a good time. Besides," Karen added with a wink, "it's supposed to be flattering when a handsome man is interested in you."

Celeste giggled. "It is." She looked into her sister-in-law's eyes, but in her mind saw Nathan's.

Karen laughed, gave her a quick hug, and called the men

to help set the table.

After dinner, everyone settled in front of the television to watch a movie. Karen and Frank's sons returned home, grabbed plates of pasta, and sprawled on the floor, trading good-natured jibes with their parents and Nathan. Scott slouched on the couch, yawning between giggles.

Celeste watched for a few minutes until restlessness sent her wandering into the back yard.

As fireflies flickered in the dark, she made her way to the monument, still covered with a white canvas tarp until the unveiling tomorrow. She leaned her elbows on top of the split rail fence and looked out across the silvered fields. A barn owl swept forth from a treetop, swooping across the clearing, the flight call distinct above nocturnal calls. A quiet calm stole into Celeste's heart.

This should be shared with someone.

Nathan.

As if on cue, whispered footsteps in the grass warned of someone's approach.

Nathan stepped to her side. The faint scent of his cologne mingled with the smell of new-mown grass. She glanced up at him, admiring the strong line of his jaw, the classic cut of his forehead and nose. He stood, staring into the darkness for several minutes. Finally, he sighed. "My sister has a big mouth."

"I'm glad she does." When Nathan didn't immediately respond, Celeste started to regret her impulsive answer. Was Karen wrong? People's feelings often changed. Had he stopped loving her?

"Celeste?" He cleared his throat, still not looking at her. "I don't want you to feel like you have to say anything. I mean, yes, I'm in love with you, but don't let that ruin tomorrow."

"What?"

"I don't want you to feel awkward with me because of how I feel. I promise I won't do anything or say anything to make you uncomfortable. I just want to be near you."

"You don't make me uncomfortable." She touched his hand. "I always thought I made you feel that way."

"Me?"

His surprise tickled her.

"Yes, you. Always disappearing when it was just me and you in a room. Barely speaking when I was around."

"Oh, yeah." He chuckled softly. "I guess I did that, huh?"

"Uh huh."

"I was glad you and David were happy together, but sometimes it was hard to watch."

"At least now I understand."

Nathan shifted his feet, causing his hip to bump against Celeste's. She felt a jolt of electricity shoot down her leg. Her thoughts turned physical, leaping far beyond the unintentional touch.

My gosh, I'm acting like a school girl. She smiled. *And it feels nice.*

"You don't have to answer this, but—do you think maybe you might someday feel something for me?" The question rushed from his lips. "Not now, but someday when you're ready."

"What's wrong with now?" Celeste peered at him, wishing for daylight to better see the look on his face. His soft gasp spoke volumes, but didn't reveal every line, every light in his eyes.

Strong arms caught her to him. Gentle lips pressed against hers, tentative then with growing desire. Celeste wrapped her arms around his neck, pulling him closer. She sank into a satin world of heat and honey.

A burst of laughter from the house broke the spell. Celeste pulled away first, stepping back out of his embrace.

"No." Nathan caught her hand in his. "Don't leave."

"I have a son to put to bed. It's getting late."

"Karen will see to him."

Celeste hesitated, uncertain what should come next. She

didn't want to go inside, but worried that Scott might miss her. "All right, a few minutes more." She leaned against his chest and marveled that the darkness could look even more inviting from within his arms.

"Have you decided about Scott coming to the reenactment tomorrow?" Nathan's voice broke into her thoughts. "It will be held right here," he nodded at the meadow beyond the fence, "so he can come back any time you want."

"I'm just not comfortable with the idea. He can watch the soldiers from here."

Nathan shifted his feet, his lips tightened in a line. "I'll be with him every minute, Celeste. I promise you he'll be safe. Scott loves it, you know."

"Scott doesn't know. He's never been."

"Yes, he has."

"With you and David?" Her throat tightened.

He nodded.

"Why are you telling me now?" Celeste gripped the top of the fence, using it as a focal point for her spinning thoughts.

"Because at the ceremony tomorrow, Scott might remember, and I don't want you to find out in front of a television camera. Right now, he doesn't have any recollections. Before you arrived at the hospital that day he'd thrown up a mental block. Karen, Frank, and I thought it would be best if you didn't know. The doctor said it was good that he didn't remember, it would help him heal, but I see no point in hiding the truth anymore."

Celeste gaped at Nathan. "You're telling me Scott was there that day?" She threw up a hand. "No, Karen and Frank had him at their house."

"They were at the reenactment, too."

Celeste curled her fingers around the rough wood of the fence. She had to ask. "Was he in the accident?"

"No."

"But he saw it?"

"Yes. He was with Karen and Frank, right behind us."

"Who's 'us?'"

"Me and David, a couple other reenactors who were riding with me in the back of the pickup. We got flipped out when the truck turned over."

Celeste rubbed her forehead. "That's where the nightmares came from. For a long time he dreamed that Civil War soldiers were killing his father by holding him under water."

"I'm sorry." His head dropped to his chest. "I thought as long as Scott didn't remember, it would do no harm to keep it from you."

She could hear tears in his voice and understood how difficult it was for him to confess his part in the deception.

"It's not your fault. It's not anyone's fault," she whispered then turned and escaped into the house.

Upstairs in her room, Celeste sank down on the bed and covered her face with her hands. She should have been there that day. David had asked her to come, and she'd said yes, but a last minute call from the volunteer coordinator at the Historic Bowman House, changed her mind. They needed more guides, she was told, could she help? Of course, she'd answered.

So, David had taken Scott with him in her place.

Anguish pierced her heart as she thought of the pale, puffy-eyed boy who clung to her side during his father's funeral. Did he truly not remember? He'd said nothing for three days, then the bad dreams began and continued for almost two years.

She brushed her hair back off her forehead and lay back across the mattress. Did she really know now what happened that day? Did the accident happen as Nathan said? Something deep inside told her, yes, he'd told her the truth. He'd just left out one giant detail.

Tears welled in her eyes. She started to brush them away,

but more followed, and she let them come.

She cried for David and his lost future, for Scott and his lonely Father's Days, for herself because life had moved ahead without her.

Or had it?

Wiping her eyes with the sleeve of her blouse, she waited for the next inevitable wave of despair, but this time, it didn't come. This time, the future beckoned and hope dangled from the fingers of a man very much alive and so different than David.

Her marriage had been forged in passion, but anchored more in familiarity. She'd known David for seven years before they got married and even then, the decision to say yes came hard. Celeste loved him, but knew his restless spirit would keep him wandering, maybe all his life. She wanted children and a home to replace the one she'd lost when her parents died in an automobile accident her senior year of high school. With no other family living, she'd felt adrift, lost; a feeling she never wanted to experience again.

David wanted to explore.

Never quite sure what to do with his life, he flitted from one job to another in various cities, trying different careers and locations, discarding them as soon as he grew bored.

She'd never been comfortable with his vagabond ways, yet had been drawn to David for that very reason. He was so restless, so exciting, so comfortable wherever he was, unlike her who hated to go further away than an hour's drive from Hagerstown.

Now those days were done. Something new reached toward her. All she had to do was reach back.

Celeste sat up and rubbed her temples.

Through the open window came the sound of a door opening and the voices of Frank and Nathan. Hushed and muffled somewhat by the drone of the television, Celeste couldn't understand their words. Until Nathan said, "I'm not giving up. I can't let her go."

"She's worth fighting for," Frank agreed. "So's the boy. But she needs to get back into the world. Scott told me she doesn't do living history anymore. Never thought I'd see that happen."

"I know what you mean. Scott said they haven't even been to Harper's Ferry, and you know how she loves that place. He wanted to go there for his birthday and climb up to Maryland Heights, but he thought it would upset her, so he didn't ask."

"She's attached a stigma to Civil War history, still blaming the hobby for David's death, not his bad heart."

Celeste bit her lip. She'd heard those words many times, but this time she listened. In the driveway, Nathan's truck roar to life. She slipped from her room and went downstairs to talk to Karen.

The next morning, Celeste rose and showered early. The household stirred to life as she pinned up her hair and laid out the Civil War era clothes borrowed from Karen the night before. Years of practice enabled her to dress herself in the awkward clothing, and by the time she pinned a tatted lace collar to the neckline, the aroma of hazelnut coffee filtered under her door.

Celeste, needing a larger size shoe than Karen, debated over which shoes to wear when Scott burst into the room. She looked up in time to see his eyes widen, his mouth form an "o" of surprise.

"Well? What do you think?" Celeste pirouetted before her son.

"Awesome," he hollered, "Then it's true? We're really going to the reenactment?"

"Hey," Celeste teased, putting her hands on her hips, "I wanted to tell you. Did Aunt Karen give it away?"

"She told Uncle Nathan, and he told me."

"Nathan's here already?" A tingle danced up the back of her neck.

Oh, stop, Celeste. The man is nothing to you.

At least, not yet, a tiny voice in her head whispered.

"Yeah, he came real early." Scott darted a look at her out of the corner of his eye. "He's wearing his uniform."

He'd look handsome in gray, she thought. Another tingle, but this time the feeling affected a much different part of her anatomy.

Focus, girl, focus.

She grinned at her son. "Anyway, yes, we're really going. Happy birthday a little late."

His hug nearly cracked a rib, but she held on to him just as tight. He grinned up at her.

"When? Uncle Nathan said some of the other boys in the regiment would teach me to play drums. Do you think I can learn in one day? Maybe I should take lessons. Uncle Frank found a uniform for me to wear. It's going to be a little small, but that will make it auth—authtic—" He winced as he stumbled over the word.

"Authentic. Yes, soldiers' uniforms rarely fit, but don't forget, buddy, we have the memorial dedication to go through first."

Scott's face fell. "I have to go? You couldn't go without me?"

"It's for your dad, honey. I think you should be there. Don't you want to go?"

Scott's shoulders slumped. He walked to the window and pulled aside the curtain. When he didn't answer, Celeste repeated the question.

He shrugged. "I don't know."

"I was counting on getting through it together."

"What if I start crying?" He turned to her, his face a mask of sadness.

"What if you do?"

He shifted his feet and stuffed his hands in his pockets. "He's been dead for two years. Shouldn't I not be sad anymore?"

"Scott, there's no time limit on being sad." Crossing the room, she sat on the edge of the bed and peered into her son's face. "Sometimes I wish I did have a calendar that I could point to and say, 'There, that's the day it will stop hurting', but sadness isn't like that. I will always miss your dad. And, that's all right."

She waited, heart aching, as a myriad of emotions crossed her son's face: sorrow, understanding, and finally, acceptance.

"All right, Mom." He drew a shaky breath. "I'll go with you." Scott took a step toward the door. "Can I wear the uniform, though, and stay an extra long time at the reenactment?"

She thought of the relatives invited over for the party and looked in her son's hopeful eyes. "You can stay as long as your Uncle Nathan does."

Scott enveloped her in a quick hug then quirked up one eyebrow. "But you said all the relatives want to see me."

"They'll see you at the dedication. If they want to see you again, I'll show them your school picture."

She could hear her son's laughter all the way down the hall.

By nine thirty am, the back yard of Frank and Karen's house was filled with friends, family, preservation society members, and the media. Celeste drew smiles and approving nods as she moved through the crowd toward a small knot of men and women dressed in clothing typical of the Civil War era. Nathan, talking to Frank, caught sight of her and did a double take, his mouth falling open. She laughed until she noticed Scott, wearing a gray kepi, a wool jacket with sleeves several inches above his wrists, and pale blue trousers worn through at the knees. A drum rested on the ground between his feet. Standing close to Nathan's side, he stared wide-eyed at video cameras.

"Celeste," Karen touched her arm. "Would you mind talking to the media? Just a few words?"

"Oh, sure. I don't mind." She nodded toward Nathan and Scott. "Heaven only knows what they're getting out of my son and his uncle."

"A lot of blank looks," Karen answered, her eyes twinkling with amusement. "That's why they asked me if you'd answer a few questions."

Having experience with the media from her years as a reenactress, Celeste stepped confidently to her son's side. She laid one hand on his shoulder and smiled at the four men and one woman with press badges swinging from their belts and pockets.

"You the widow? You getting anything out of this?" asked one as he fiddled with his microphone.

Celeste's smile never faltered. Turning slightly away from the man with the rude question, she announced, "Good morning. I am Celeste Kinsley. I'd be happy to answer any questions you may have about my husband."

For several minutes she spoke of David's life and his love of history and reenacting. When the focus turned to Karen and Frank's land donation, Scott pulled his mother a few steps away.

"Mom, how many times are they going to ask me the same thing?" He pushed the brim of his kepi up off his forehead with the end of his drumsticks. "Every one of them asked me if I remembered my dad. Geesh, it's only been two years. Of course I remember him. Would they forget their dads?"

"Of course not, honey. These people have a job to do, and this is a human-interest story. They're looking for a reaction. Unfortunately, they all want the reaction for their television station."

"That's kinda what Uncle Nathan said they'd do."

"You talked to him about this?"

"Yeah, for a long time before you got up this morning. We talked about a lot of stuff. Even Gunther."

"Oh, I'm glad, because—" Celeste paused as she caught

a movement inside her son's jacket. "What's that?"

He cast a glance around and lowered his voice. "Gunther."

"Take him back." Celeste pointed to the house.

"I can't. Aunt Karen wants the bedroom doors open so she can show everyone the house. I hid the tank, but what if one of the cats finds it with Gunther still in it?" He ran a hand gently over his chest. "He'll be happier out here."

"Ladies and gentlemen, may I have your attention, please." Frank's voice rose above the hum of conversation. "If everyone would come over here we'll get started."

"You keep him hidden," Celeste warned, "I don't want anything to happen to him."

"He's a snake, Mom. He already knows what he needs to know to survive."

Before she could digest this extraordinary answer, he ducked away, joining three other young boys by the fence nearest the monument.

"Ready?" Nathan appeared at her side and offered his arm. "I haven't had a chance to tell you that you look beautiful."

For the first time, she noticed his ragged butternut uniform, patched, stained, and missing two buttons. A day's growth of whiskers shadowed his chin. "I wish I could say the same about you."

He laughed as they joined Karen, Frank, and numerous official-looking people Nathan told her were from the historical society and the city government.

For the first twenty minutes, everything moved quickly, speeches kept short and to the point. Scott stood ramrod stiff beside his new friends, twitching occasionally from what Celeste surmised were tickles from Gunther.

Finally, Frank nodded to Nathan. Nathan squeezed Celeste's hand and stepped to the front of the crowd.

"Today is a special day for me," he began. "My brother, David, would have loved all this, but he sure would have hated playing the part of the dead guy."

Celeste drew in a sharp breath, but laughter from the other reenactors stirred a memory: David hated to play wounded or dead during a battle, remaining standing even when overwhelmed by blue forces. Nathan used to tease him about it, but David didn't care.

Nathan's gaze caught and held hers as he continued, his words bonding together into a relay of image and emotion. Pale sadness looped through her, lodging and growing in her heart. She let the feeling extend to every cell in her body, expanding until it burst in a bright array of joy and release. Tears wet her lashes, but the aching loneliness had fled.

Scott fell in with the other drummers, tapping out a simple beat as they marched past the memorial. They turned toward the crowd where one camera operator stood, focused on the young faces. A high-pitched scream from one of the city clerks startled everyone.

"Snake!" Her shaking finger pointed at Scott. "It's going to kill him!"

People began to back away, compacting the crowd, pushing Celeste back, out of her son's sight.

"It's a pet!" Nathan's voice pierced the air.

Celeste shoved bodies aside, calling Scott's name. She caught sight of him just as he drew the snake from his shirt. The reptile slipped from his hands, falling to the ground. By the subsequent ripple of quick-footed hops through the throng of people, Celeste realized that Gunther was headed for freedom.

She swallowed her disappointment and made her way between the twittering guests. She knelt in front of Scott. He made no move to go after Gunther, but stared dully along the path his pet had taken. His hat gone, hair sweaty and sticking out at odd angles, he looked helpless and small.

"Honey?"

"I let him go, Mom," he whispered, "I let go of him." His suddenly old eyes sought hers. "It was time."

My God, he's not talking about his snake.

With one shaking hand, she smoothed back his hair. "That was a very big decision to make."

"Yeah." He managed a wan smile. "It hurts, though."

"Of course it does."

"Mom?" Scott wiped sweat from his forehead with his sleeve. "It would be okay if you took that job with Uncle Nathan."

"But we'd have to move here, and I know that's not what you want." Celeste watched her son's face, waiting for a sign that he regretted his words. Instead, he lifted his chin and looked into her eyes.

"I don't need to live there anymore." He patted her shoulder. "I think it would be a good move for both of us."

The first notes of "Do They Miss Me At Home?", a sentimental Confederate ballad, drifted across the landscape. Celeste looked toward the band.

"David's favorite song," she murmured, more to herself than to Scott.

"Well, it ain't mine." Her son sniffed. "I like 'The Invalid Corps' and 'The Battle Hymn of the Republic.'"

"Those are Union songs." Celeste gasped and mimed a swoon, her hand thrown across her forehead. "And you a Reb drummer boy. What will the family think?"

"Why, ma'am, we'll think he's a right smart youngster." Nathan stood over them, in his hands an artillery sponge-rammer used to swab and load ordinance into the big guns. "Them Yanks do have some fine music."

Scott giggled as Nathan offered a hand to help Celeste back to her feet.

"You'd best join the other drummers. Looks like we've got a battle comin'." Nathan nodded to the fields beyond the fence where troops in formation moved over the sloping fields. Scott's eyes widened with anticipation. With a little wave at Celeste, he ran off to meet up with his new friends.

Nathan gave Celeste a brief smile then turned away,

hesitated, and turned back. "I'll look after him."

"You knew he was going to do this."

"With the snake? It was his idea. Of course, I didn't think he'd free him during the ceremony, but apparently Gunther had a glimpse of freedom and that was that." He chuckled. "At least people will remember the day they dedicated the David Kinsley memorial. Maybe it will become an anecdote on a battlefield tour."

Celeste laughed softly. "I know I'll never forget how everyone panicked at the sight of that bitty snake."

"Now all the other drummer boys will want one. Their mothers will be cursing you for months to come." He looked into the fields to the east. "I have to go. The battle."

"Yes, yes. Go. Have fun."

"You don't want to join us? They're a great bunch of people."

"No. I'll be here."

"For how long?" Nathan stepped closer, leaning toward her, promoting intimate conversation.

Celeste understood that they no longer discussed the reenactment. She looked into his eyes and made her decision. "For as long as it takes to get the office running well. It may take some time, you know."

"Maybe years," came his hoarse response. "What about Scott?"

"His heart has healed, thanks to you. He'll love it down here."

Nathan stared down at her in silence, eyes seeking something she knew he would no longer find. A sudden, brilliant smile assured her of his success.

Nathan turned, tossed the sponge-rammer over the fence, and effortlessly climbed over behind it. Friends joined him, slapping him on the back, pushing him toward the artillery battery already formed on a slight ridge. Celeste watched him go, staring hard, waiting for the clue that would prove her wrong, but she couldn't find it. All traces of David were gone; only Nathan was left.

Quiet joy filled her soul, and she let the elation lift her up, reveling in the discovery that when hearts heal, they expand. New love mingles with past love, allowing room for more and more.

A bugle blared nearby, startling her. Muskets popped in the distance and the thunder of artillery shook the ground. Scott and Nathan were out there together, forging a new tradition. In the next second, Celeste hurtled over the fence, giving the startled crowd a flash of lace-edged drawers.

This time, she'd be part of the fun.

She caught sight of Nathan's astonished smile over the wheel of the big gun. With one hand she blew him a playful kiss and, laughing, ran across the fields to join the other ladies.

HIDDEN FIRE

Carolee Joy

Shella bounced down the front porch steps to get the morning paper and furtively glanced down the street. Just as she reached the terrace, a black and white van cruised past. She stifled the impulse to glance at her watch, knowing he was right on schedule. The driver laid on the horn and gave her a jaunty wave and a smile. As always, she felt a little flutter of pleasure. Dark hair, moustache, he was so handsome. He seemed nice, too. At least as far as she could tell just seeing him drive by every morning. Smiling, she picked up the newspaper and turned to find her next door neighbor watching with undisguised interest.

"Subtle, isn't he?" Grady caught her attention as he bent to retrieve his own paper.

"Depends on who you're comparing him to." Irritated,

Shella frowned. He was a fine one to talk. Ever since he'd moved into the small frame house next to hers a few months ago, Grady managed to find increasingly creative excuses to stop by, borrowing everything from laundry soap to a cup of motor oil until she felt like the neighborhood stop and shop.

She tossed the paper onto the passenger seat of her compact car and climbed in behind the wheel as he walked up. "Sorry, I can't stay and visit, but even though it's summer, some of us have to work."

Grady grinned, the sudden flash of perfect white teeth momentarily transforming his rather ordinary face. "Don't worry. I'll more than make up for the time off when school starts." He paused. "It's Friday, Shella. Working late? Or would you like to see that new movie with me?"

It wasn't her turn to stay late at the store, but Shella hesitated, hunting for a reasonable excuse to say no without hurting his feelings. After all, Grady was nice enough, and a good neighbor, even though his persistent friendliness sometimes grated on her. "Not this time, okay?"

He shrugged good-naturedly. "No problem. There's always next Friday."

Next Friday. Shella repeated the words to herself on the drive to The Waxahachie Electronic Wizard, the TV, audio, and electronic store where she worked as purchasing manager. No matter how many times she told Grady no, he never seemed to mind. Or give up. As if it wasn't any big deal one way or another. After two years of casual dating following her divorce, Shella had decided she was no longer willing to settle for anything less than spontaneous combustion in her next relationship. Which definitely put Grady out of the picture.

Monday morning, the man in the van slowed down to a crawl and gave Shella a wink and a smile as he drove by. Then he honked. Startled, she dropped the paper and bent to retrieve it as Grady's huge hand scooped up the wind scattered pages.

"I'll bet he eats garlic bagels for breakfast," he said with mock gravity.

Shella couldn't help but smile at his effort to amuse her with his daily dose of wisdom.

On Wednesday, Grady said, "He's probably got wives in six states."

Shella laughed.

Rain poured down on Thursday. Shella glanced toward the sidewalk, expecting her paper to be soaked. But when she opened the front door, her paper had been wedged between the screen and oak door. Fresh washed air blew her shoulder length hair as the van slowly passed her house. Like every day for the past several weeks, he honked. From his screened-in porch, Grady raised his coffee mug to her in silent salute.

Friday morning, hoping to avoid Grady's weekly query, Shella left for work early, thus missing his invitation but also the stranger in the van. Occasionally, she saw the black and white van around town, and she wondered if they would ever really meet. Waxahachie, Texas boasted a small town's friendly atmosphere, but its high concentration of restored Victorian homes and close proximity to Dallas made it a prime tourist escape as well as the location for occasional movie sets.

She sighed. Most likely, the sexy stranger flirted with lots of women. It was foolish to make a big deal of his interest.

Late morning, Shella was out on the floor while the sales manager went to an early lunch. She flipped idly through the compact discs, searching for a favorite she might have overlooked when suddenly a man's voice spoke in her ear.

"This is a good one," he said.

Leaning close and reaching in front of her, he held up a CD from a rock group Shella had never heard of.

Startled, she glanced up and sharply drew in a breath as her eyes locked with the unmistakable brown ones of the man in the van. "What are you doing here?" she stammered.

He crossed his arms over his chest, drawing her attention to finely developed muscles beneath his tailored shirt while his eyes danced with laughter. "Is that your idea of a sales technique?"

Quickly collecting her poise, she smiled. "Okay, how may I help you?"

"By having lunch with me, pretty lady."

His open smile took the brazenness from the words and heat rose in her face. No one had ever called her that. Not even Grady. Especially not Grady.

He thrust out his hand and clasped hers in a strong grip. "Tom Mattson. The sales manager told me you were the one I needed, Shella."

Didn't she wish! Ordinarily, she would never consider dining with someone she didn't really know. Or one who was so overly familiar. Somehow after the past few weeks of seeing him drive by her house every day, she felt as if he were already a friend. Or at least a neighbor. And if that stuffy sales manager thought it was okay, well, it must be. With his return and quick nod of approval, she collected her purse and walked with Tom to the sandwich shop next door.

She was only halfway through her iced tea when he lowered the boom.

From the leather portfolio he carried, he extracted several color brochures of various lighting fixtures and bulbs. "Lucky break for me that your store is in my territory. Take a look at these, and tell me how many you'd like to order for The Wizard. I guarantee we can beat any price in Texas. And for you," he gave her a heart-stopping wink she now knew to be as fake as a vinyl handbag, "I'd make a special deal."

Feeling like an idiot for completely misreading him, Shella managed to get through the "business" lunch. Wouldn't Grady laugh if he knew what a hopeless romantic she was?

Later that evening, Shella returned home to a darkened house. Locking her car, she sighed. Usually such a welcome refuge, now the snug frame house seemed to mock her solitariness. Maybe she should have accepted Grady's invitation. Spending the evening with her friendly neighbor at the movies had to be better than wallowing in her own foolish gullibility. What had made her think Tom was more than a friendly flirt?

She glanced over at Grady's. His house sat silent and dark as well. Most likely, he found someone else to escort to the movies. Why did her stomach seen to plummet with disappointment at the thought?

"Hey, neighbor." Grady's voice welcomed her from the shadows of his porch.

Shella slowed her footsteps, then with a burst of purpose, strode to her neighbor's and plunked down next to him on the cushioned swing. "Mind if I join you?"

"It's what I've been hoping for."

She jerked her head toward him, suspecting he was teasing her, but his expression was serious and sincere.

"Had lunch with the Van Man today." She pushed off the swing with the toe of her shoe.

"Really? What happened?" His tone was cautious.

She gave him a rueful laugh. "Nothing. He just wanted to get in my purchase orders." At his questioning look, she continued. "He's a lighting contractor."

Grady's laugh rang out, warm and strong. "Guess that's his loss."

A feeling of warmth and acceptance crept over her. "Yeah, I guess it is." She stole a glance at the man with whom she'd shared coffee, smiles, and weed killer. No one would ever call Grady O'Connor handsome, but his steadfast calm and unwavering interest in her well being appealed to her. Not to mention his warm blue gaze and the honest affection she saw in his expression. "It's a good night for the movies."

His hand closed around hers, and suddenly it felt as right as sitting next to him in the old-fashioned wicker swing did. "I was beginning to think I'd never hear you say that."

She hadn't thought she'd ever admit it, either, but as a blaze rushed through her when he brushed the softest of kisses on her lips she wondered why it had taken her so long to figure out that Grady was just the kind of man she wanted after all. Solid. Sincere. And after all, where there was heat, there had to be a fire.

PAPER HEARTS

Betsy Norman

If Billy Peterson eats one more purple crayon... Moira's clenched fists hit the countertop with a soft thud.

"Miss Brannon?" An insistent tug at her skirt forced Moira to ungrit her teeth, turn around and smile.

"Yes, Courtney?"

"Aren't you supposed to count to ten when you're mad?"

Moira hung her head. To have one of her kindergartners regurgitate her own rules should make her proud, but having one do so because they'd noticed her mood, didn't.

"Yes, that's right, sweetheart. That's just what I was doing, and I'm much better now, thank you." She kneeled next to the little girl and gave her a reassuring pat on the back. "Have you finished your picture?"

"No." Courtney fiddled with the construction paper in her hands. "I can't color the rest of the hearts. Billy stole my purple crayon. He stole *all* the purple crayons," she pouted.

Moira drew a long breath and silently counted. One, two, three…"Well, then, we'll just have to have another talk with Billy, won't we?" She gave Courtney a terse smile and retrieved a purple crayon from her secret supply drawer, then told her to go color far, far away from Billy Peterson.

Moira kneaded the tense knot in her brow. Her headache had nothing to do with crayon eating little boys, really, but everything to do with parent-teacher conferences tomorrow.

The bell rang, and she clapped her hands. "Clean-up! Clean-up!" Moira chirped the motivational song to engage all the youngsters to participate. They scrambled amongst the litter of toys to see who could pick up the most.

"Remember, children, no school tomorrow, but Monday is the big Valentine's pageant. Don't forget to finish your parent's corsages!" Moira packed the kids up in their coats and hats, making sure each had their backpacks, and waved goodbye.

One straggler remained.

Moira felt her chest tighten at the sight of a mopey, freckled frown. In the midst of all the animated, eager children in her classroom, Annie McClanahan was the only one who remained isolated, hovering just outside of the other's play, afraid to join.

The conference with Annie's father was the one she dreaded most. Moira knew he was divorced and because of his job transfer, Annie had to switch schools. Two months had passed, and the little girl still hadn't adjusted to her new surroundings. Moira had made sure to emphasize this point in her letter requesting a parent-teacher appointment. She gave him the last time slot, so as to utilize more than just the routine fifteen minutes to discuss his daughter's aversion to school.

Moira knelt down next to the little redhead and began buttoning her coat. "Ready for your big debut, Annie?"

"No," she said. Moira wondered if the single word could sound any smaller.

"And why not? You know all your lines. You're my best narrator ever." She'd hoped giving the little girl an important role would draw her out of her shell.

"Billy says my corsage is ugly!" Annie blurted out.

"What does Billy know but what flavor crayon he likes best? Besides, I think he likes you." Moira tried to cheer her up. "Let's see your corsage, and let me decide if it's ugly or not."

"I tried to make it pretty for Daddy, and show him how much I love him." Annie reluctantly handed Moira her creation. It looked like a bouquet chock full of hearts. Red, pink, big, small—but no purple ones, of course.

"It's beautiful. One of the prettiest I've seen. I'm sure your dad will love it as much as he loves you." Moira encouraged her with a hug and smiled when it was returned. She felt so close to this lonely child.

It was a struggle being shy, and Moira knew the feeling all too well. She hadn't dated in months. The easy excuse was to tell herself that her schedule was hectic with the school curriculum, but in truth, Moira was too timid to show return interest in anyone who asked her out.

But the small chin dropped again. "If he can come," Annie said. "I better go get on my bus." Off she darted, holding the valentine bouquet tightly to her chest.

Moira's heart broke. There was something desperately wrong with her new student and Moira meant to make things right.

Conferences went swiftly the following afternoon. She had an exceptionally bright class this year and delighted in the parents' eager responses to her good reports. Moira made sure to extract a promise from Mrs Peterson to wean Billy off of purple crayons pronto.

The last meeting was scheduled for 7:45 PM. It was already after eight o'clock and there was no sign of Patrick McClanahan. Moira paced the classroom, giving him five more minutes. And five more minutes after that. She finally sighed in resignation and packed up her student folders before grabbing her coat.

"I'm sorry I'm late." A harried looking man in jeans and T-shirt puffed through the door. "Oh, no. Too late?"

"Mr McClanahan?" Moira asked. She had expected a three-piece suit type. A self-absorbed career climber. Not an exuberant, blue-eyed and handsome thirty-something. She took a deep breath. "The janitor is about to lock the doors."

"I know, I slipped in, and he jangled his keys at me. Can we still talk about Annie tonight?"

He sounded concerned, which was a good sign. Moira nodded. "But they do have to close the school."

"How about the coffee shop?" he asked. He looked so expectant and genuine. She had to give him a chance. But to go out for coffee with a good-looking, single man?

She'd do it for Annie. "All right, Mr McClanahan. I'll meet you there."

"Great." His relief was evident. "Thank you so much, Mrs Brannon."

"Miss Brannon, but since you're over four feet tall, you may call me Moira."

"Only if you call me Patrick." They both laughed, and he escorted her out of the building and to her car.

Moira applied fresh lipstick and powder in the rear-view mirror at a stop sign. No use looking washed out under bright lights, even if it was just a parent-teacher conference, she told herself. When she pulled into the lot, Patrick waited for her, ready to hold the door.

He paid for two coffees at the counter and led her to a table. Moira couldn't help but question his appearance. She thought he was the Director of Operations at the local industrial equipment plant. The transfer and late hours would attest to his position, but his attire told a different story.

He must have read her mind. "You're probably wondering where my briefcase is." He dusted off one knee revealed through the hole in his jeans before sitting down.

Moira frowned. Maybe this had something do with Annie's introversion. Had he lost his job? "Well, yes, actually. Annie always talks about how you have to work so late."

"It disappoints her, but it won't for long." He sighed. "I've told her that to keep it a surprise, but I guess my absence is harder on her than I realized. Your letter really opened my eyes."

"What surprise?"

"I'm building a playroom in the basement. She stays at the sitter's house extra hours so I can work downstairs without her knowing. I wanted to get it done in time for Valentine's Day. She had one at our old house, so I thought—"

"You thought you'd try and make her feel more at home here, too." How like Annie he is, Moira thought, to try and do something extra special out of love. "But her behavior in school—she's having trouble joining in and making friends."

"She's always been shy, but the playroom helps. She can invite friends over and they have their own little world. One on one, she develops playmates and begins to feel more comfortable and confident in the classroom. This tool really helped when she began preschool."

His understanding of Annie's needs turned Moira's perceptions upside-down. She'd thought him the stereotypical workaholic father, ignoring his child in lieu of getting ahead. He proved her so wrong. "What an excellent idea. How did you ever come up with it?"

Patrick shrugged, a small grin surfacing. "I was a shy kid, too. Dad built me a fort in the backyard that was the envy of the neighborhood. It helped me fit in."

"And you thought a playroom would help Annie, too."

"Uh-huh. I finished up the wallpaper this evening. Rows of colored hearts, her favorite. That's why I was so late." He scrubbed self-consciously at the dried paste on his clothes. "Next week she can hand out invitations for a tea party to get things going."

"Oh, a tea party. I used to love those as a little girl. For a single father, you're rather ingenious when it comes to making friends for your daughter."

"Yeah, well, at least one of us will make a few in this new town. Maybe next I should build a fort?"

"Oh," Moira laughed, ducking her head to hide a blush. "I don't think you'll have any trouble. Once all the mothers meet you—" she stopped herself, realizing what she was about to say. "You'll be invited to all their little girl's tea parties too, I'm sure." She knew a few divorced moms who flirted shamelessly. Patrick would have to beat the more enthusiastic ones off with a stick.

He shrugged. "I guess in that way, I'm more like Annie. I prefer one on one to begin with." His intense look made Moira shiver.

After their talk, she thought about Patrick all weekend long, wishing she could be the other half of that one on one. She daydreamed about Annie in her playroom and the good-hearted man who built it. The three of them seated around a miniature table and porcelain tea set, sharing cookies and pretend tea.

Monday morning, eighteen excited kindergartners wiggled through dress rehearsal and the letter "V-for-Valentine" lessons. Hoping to see Patrick at the pageant that night, Moira was as anxious as they were.

When the time came, the children performed their lines and sang off-tune love serenades to a room full of proud parents. Annie's narration was perfect and delivered with a beaming smile. Patrick sat in the front row with his corsage pinned boldly on the lapel of a pinstriped suit.

Afterwards, during refreshments, Moira wasn't surprised to see Annie passing out invitations to her classmates and their parents. She and Patrick came over and handed one to Moira, too.

"Miss Brannon, will you come to my tea party? Daddy built me a special playroom." Her radiant face told Moira everything Patrick said was true. "With paper hearts and everything."

"Oh, Annie, I'd love to." Moira smiled at Patrick, both acknowledging the obvious change in the girl's attitude. She bent down to whisper to Annie. "Is Billy coming?"

"Yes." The girl grinned beneath her freckles and ran off to join Courtney.

"I was hoping you'd come, Moira." Patrick asked, his blue eyes bright with anticipation. "I don't have time to build a fort, but I think you're more the tea party type, anyway."

"Will there be real pretend tea and cookies?"

"Of course, every little girl's dream. Afterwards, maybe the three of us could go to dinner?"

Now he was talking grown-up girl dreams, one on one with a handsome dad and his darling daughter. "I can hardly wait." Moira smiled.

Maybe being shy wasn't so bad after all.

FVTVRE DESIGNS

Susan D. Brooks

The invitation arrived at Singular Look Bridal Designs by special messenger at 8:01 Monday morning, before owner Chloe Bauer had even turned on her sewing machines.

Encased in a crisp ivory parchment envelope, the announcement listed the time, date, and place where Trixie Lowe, Chloe's most demanding and wealthy client, would finally marry her beau.

"The pleasure of your presence is requested... Patricia Marie Lowe to Cameron Marc King IV...."

The card left Chloe's fingers, fluttering to her desk where it lay, pale and stiff on top of the latest fabric samples.

Cameron King. And Trixie.

For a moment, she stopped breathing, her heart stopped beating, her mind refused to produce a single thought other than: Cameron's getting married.

She snatched up the invitation, crumpled it into a ball, and tossed it into the wastebasket. She wouldn't go. No way. This was a joke. A joke Cameron would enjoy at her expense, if she let him. After all, although she was a successful businesswoman, she wasn't married. As he'd predicted.

Tommy, her current boyfriend, eased into her mind, pushing Cameron aside. A warm rush of affection washed over her. She might not be married, but she was involved. Very happily involved.

Chloe pulled the parchment out of the trash and smoothed the paper flat to study it again. The invitation came from Trixie, of course; Chloe had been expecting one. Designing, sewing, and fitting the perfect wedding gown took hours of close contact, and friendships sometimes formed between the client and designer. While Chloe didn't consider Trixie a close friend, she enjoyed her company and appreciated her excellent eye for style.

As most brides did, Trixie spoke often of her fiancé, Marc, and Chloe, after years of listening to such chatter, paid little attention. If Trixie mentioned his last name, she never heard it.

And Chloe understood about the name now. Cameron, the fourth generation male with that name, switched to his middle name when heading off to attend college at his father's alma mater. Only his parents, a few close buddies, and Chloe still called him Cameron after his freshman year.

Evidently, Trixie did not know of the connection between Chloe and Cameron. One afternoon while having the gown's neckline adjusted, Trixie had mentioned that her groom had an ex-fiancée, but never said a name. She had spoken without jealousy, but with a kind of bewilderment that any woman would let Marc slip out of her grasp.

Knowing Cameron, he wouldn't have told Trixie any details. He'd keep the knowledge to himself, loath to admit that any woman turned him down in lieu of a career.

Crossing the room, Chloe gazed through a doorway into her dressmaker's showroom. Bolts of cloth, racks of trim, and rows of buttons lined the walls leaving the center of the room open for fittings. Plush couches and chairs in shades of green and mauve formed a circle around the gleaming hard wood platform where the brides modeled their gowns. Custom wedding dresses demanded a great deal of space, so much fabric, so much excitement and, therefore, so many family members and friends along for the show.

Chloe learned early in her career to cater to the rest of the wedding party, particularly the mother of the bride. More often than not, they would decide to have a custom dress created, too, so they could strut and twirl on that platform.

On the far wall hung the ivory silk creation finished just two days ago: Trixie's wedding dress. Chloe considered the one-of-a-kind gown to be the best she'd ever made. Adorned with a scant amount of seed pearls at the hem and neckline, the sheath-style dress took on unexpected curves when draped across the tall, lithe body of Trixie Lowe.

"Daydreaming?" Rebecca, Chloe's assistant, spoke softly from the cutting table where she had laid a pattern marked with adjustments.

"We've been invited to Trixie's wedding." Chloe turned and held up the card.

"That's nice, although it's a little short notice," Rebecca commented.

"I thought I'd be out of town this weekend. When I mentioned the trip was cancelled, she insisted that I go."

"I think you should go," her assistant mused. "I mean, how often do you get to go to The Palmer House? Lots of gourmet food, name-brand booze, and a real band for dancing."

"She's marrying Cameron." Chloe watched for her friend's reaction.

"What?" Rebecca's mouth fell open as the marker

dropped from her finger to the floor. She scrambled to retrieve it, then looked wide-eyed at her boss. "Your Cameron?"

"Not MY Cameron, thank you very much. Not for a long time."

"But she always called her guy Marc."

"He started using his middle name when he went away to the university. In high school everyone called him 'The Fourth'. He hated it." Chloe shook her head in bewilderment. "There's hundreds of men with the name Marc in Chicago. It never occurred to me that her Marc was Cameron."

"Are you going to go?" Rebecca slowly returned to her stool, eyes still on Chloe.

"Yes. I'll just go to the ceremony with Tommy."

"He'll be disappointed," Rebecca warned. "He loves wedding receptions."

"I'll make it up to him somehow." Chloe smiled. Happy-go-lucky Tommy loved social events and so did Chloe when she went with him. Adept on the dance floor, he also excelled at the art of conversation and could draw people out. Being with Tommy was anything but dull.

"You think he'll pop the question again?" Rebecca quirked an eyebrow.

"Yes," Chloe sighed, thinking of the hope in his eyes each time he mentioned marriage. "He does at every wedding."

"I think you should put him out of his misery and say yes." Rebecca turned back to the project on the cutting table. "There are worse things than being married to the sexiest carpet cleaner in Illinois."

"I haven't said no," Chloe reminded her. "I'm just not ready to commit."

"Baloney." Rebecca sniffed in disgust. "You're going to let a wonderful man get away because you can't believe marriage is a partnership, not a prison."

Although the words stung, Chloe had to acknowledge

their truth, at least in part. Fearing that she would become isolated and dependent like her mother, Chloe went overboard in the other direction.

Her father's death and the subsequent revelation that he had accumulated massive gambling-related debts nearly destroyed her mother emotionally.

So much for trust, she'd thought bitterly as the For Sale sign went up on her mother's home.

Chloe used her savings account to put a down payment on a condominium for her mom and used monthly receipts from her store to whittle down the mountain of obligations. Her mother, now enrolled in chef's school, worked part-time in a grocery store and appeared to blossom. She told Chloe that for the first time in years, she felt free to enjoy life, despite the burden of debt.

Chloe vowed that she would never allow that kind of dependence to happen to her. She'd make her own way, handle her own affairs. That, she concluded, was how to create a secure future.

The morning passed quickly. Rebecca and the two seamstress trainees kept three sewing machines humming. Rich fabric slid under needles, emerging in raw dresses for a large wedding at the end of summer. Chloe forced herself to concentrate on the business at hand, but, while convincing a mother-of-the-groom that white may not be an appropriate color for her dress, memories of Cameron intruded.

Their wedding was to have been a major social event, too. Her daily planner had bulged with ideas about everything from invitations to what color napkins would be used at the reception. Swept along in the excitement, Chloe lost sight of what marriage meant until Cameron, unhappy with his dry cleaner, badgered her to find another for him, one where they'd get the starch right. Other suggestions about grocery stores, pharmacies, and auto repair shops dragged her focus away from the ceremony to the reality of the years to follow.

Cameron expected her to take over all the housekeeping chores and attend to his personal needs. Could she find happiness worrying about someone else's laundry or in finding a way to keep lettuce from turning brown? Maybe, she'd decided, if such chores made up only part of her life. But she also needed a reason to get up each day, some personal goal to work toward. Without one, her future looked empty and unsatisfying.

When Chloe admitted as much to Cameron and told him that she'd taken a position with a dressmaker to learn the business, he became infuriated.

"Without my consent? Without my opinion at all?" he demanded.

"This is for me, Cameron. I have to have a creative outlet."

"Then decorate the house I bought in Lake Forest," he snapped, "or volunteer at the museum."

"I'd rather do this," she replied simply. "Eventually, I'll have my own business."

His jaw twitched as he ground his teeth. "Think this through, Chloe."

"It won't cost you a thing—"

"Oh, it's not that." His voice, low and angry, stung her. "Don't you get it? I can't marry a seamstress."

"What's wrong with being a seamstress?"

"I don't want you to work at all." He crossed his arms and waited. "I certainly don't want you working in some sweatshop."

"You want control of my life," she accused him, her voice filled with dismay. Within seconds, his good looks, smooth talk, and elegant manners fell away like leaves off a tree in autumn.

"Nonsense," he sniffed unconvincingly. "I want you to stay home and raise our children."

"You've always made decisions for me and," she added,

amazed, "I let you. What was I thinking?"

"Make your choice, Chloe. You can't have a career and marry me, too."

Chloe thought of her mother, a stay-at-home mom with unfulfilled dreams, trapped by the expectations of others. She would not let that happen to herself.

Slowly, she tugged off the diamond ring and handed it to Cameron. He stuffed it in his pocket.

"I'll find a woman who'll appreciate what I have to offer." His scowl turned to a sneer. "And my investment firm will make me rich. We'll see how well you do sewing for a living."

"I'll do fine, Cameron. All I really want to do is make dresses. The money will come. If not...." She shrugged. "At least I'll love what I'm doing."

"Maybe so, but you'll do it as a single woman." He left and never contacted her again.

One year ago, she'd met Tommy when he came to the store to clean the carpets. An undeniable physical attraction brought them together, but common interests deepened their relationship. Unlike Cameron, he never gave ultimatums, never made plans without her consent, and asked her opinion on everything. He was a sparkling change in her stale social world, and she cherished their friendship.

But now Tommy wanted more, and she owed him an answer.

Before lunch, Chloe, helping a customer in the showroom, spotted one of the apprentices waving frantically to her from the sewing room doorway. As soon as she could, Chloe rushed to see what had happened.

"I can't fix it anymore." Rebecca, surrounded with small machine parts, sat on the floor, looking perplexed.

"It's really dead this time, huh?" Chloe slumped into her desk chair, staring at the skeleton of the industrial sewing machine. She rubbed her temples, wishing away the sudden headache.

For two months, Rebecca had been able to glue, patch, and coax the parts into working again, but the inevitable had finally happened. No more repairs. Chloe would need a whole new machine. She thought briefly of the $5,000.00 check she'd given one of her father's creditors the night before, but knew that wishing for it back would get her nowhere. Another six months and those debts would be paid off. In the meantime, she'd have to juggle.

"We can't do without, not with six weddings coming up." She chewed the inside of her lip. "The material for the McKay bridesmaids dresses can wait another week. Hopefully, Trixie will pay us for her dress when she picks it up today." Chloe stood and paced the length of the room. "I'll go to Magner's Sewing and Vacuum. Mr Magner knows me. He'll let me put a deposit down and take the machine with me today, but it won't fit in my car." She reached for the phone. "I'll have Tommy take me."

Promptly at noon, Chloe heard Tommy's ancient pickup wheeze to a halt in front of the shop. She glanced up in time to see him bounce out of the passenger side door, the broken driver's door having been roped shut for a month.

He breezed through the front door, his perpetual good mood spreading out from him like ripples on a wind-touched pond. Female customers watched, returning his smile, admiring his trim physique and handsome, boyish face.

Tommy worked for his father in the family's carpet cleaning business and seemed to find satisfaction in whatever he did, but Chloe knew of his secret longing. Once, when one of her clients married a park ranger, Tommy had sighed and admitted that he'd love to work outside, landscaping maybe. When she suggested that he pursue his dream, he just shook his head.

"No, Dad's health isn't so good right now. His eyes, you

know. He needs my help for at least another year." He shrugged. "After that my brother's taking over, and I'll see what he needs first."

Tommy agreed to look into landscaping courses at the community college, but said nothing more about it. Chloe didn't press the issue, admiring his loyalty, but wondering at the same time what would happen when his dad retired.

"Hey, Sunshine!" He crossed the room and leaned down to kiss her. "Ready to go?"

"Almost." She grabbed her purse from under the desk. "Thanks for taking me. I'd never get the machine in my car."

"No problem." He caught sight of Trixie's dress hanging on the rack. "She hasn't picked it up yet?"

"She said she'd be by sometime this afternoon." She waved to Rebecca as they headed out the door.

When they returned to the shop, Rebecca waited at the front door of the shop.

"Cameron was here." Rebecca shot a sidelong glance at Tommy.

"Cameron?" A feeling of dread crept up her spine. "Why? What did he say?"

"He came in with Trixie and accused us—uh—you of sabotaging their wedding."

Tommy's frown prompted Chloe to send him into the back with the new machine. "Just put it on the table, hon. Thanks."

As he carted the big box to the back room, she turned to Rebecca. "Start from the beginning."

"Trixie came in to get her dress. She saw Gail McKay's gown and liked it better. When I told her we couldn't possibly redo her gown, she left and came back with Cameron." Rebecca looked down at her hands. "She told him that since he wanted her to have the dress made here, he should make sure she gets what she wants."

"Ah." Chloe exhaled a deep breath. "That's what

happened. So, now she wants a cathedral train?" She reached for the gown. "I guess I could fashion something from the shoulders—"

"She wants it edged with Flemish bobbin lace," Rebecca added. "She said she'd pay an extra $2,000.00. Cameron just grinned and said he'd pay whatever it took to make her happy."

"Forget Cameron. Our concern is this dress." She held the dress up and looked at the back. "Did she leave a deposit or pay what she promised?"

"No."

"Then we can't do it." Chloe shook her head. "We couldn't do it anyway. No one can get Flemish bobbin lace in two days."

"She said she won't take the dress without it."

"She has to take it," Chloe stammered as she heard a clunk as Tommy settled the new machine on its stand. "She signed the agreement. And what else would she wear? The wedding's in four days."

"That's what I told her, but Cameron said she has a backup dress and if we couldn't do this one the way she wants he'll take us to court for breach of contract."

"That's ridiculous." Chloe felt her face flush with anger. "And why is Cameron involved in this anyway?"

He's trying to get back at me, she realized.

"I don't know." Tears welled in Rebecca's eyes. "Can he do anything to us?"

"Of course not." The illogic of the demand for alterations at this late date stunned Chloe. Cameron's threats infuriated her. No one could expect such extensive changes to be made so quickly, at least no one with a modicum of sense.

Tommy walked up to Chloe and slipped his arm around her waist. "What time should I pick you up? Mom's expecting us at seven. She's making lasagna."

"I can't go," she said slowly, looking at Rebecca. "I have some work to do."

"Not again." Tommy's face fell. "Dad was looking forward to seeing you. He wanted to win at Canasta again."

"Give him and your mother my apologies. I'll come another time." Chloe hated to say those words. She loved going to the Osterweis home with Tommy where she became immersed in a loving, caring atmosphere. Of course, as much of that came from Tommy as from his parents. "I'll call you later tonight."

"Dad says you work too hard, and he's right." Tommy's impatient words surprised Chloe. "Just once I'd like to be more important than your customers."

"But you are. I only have to finish this—"

"Chloe, I know it takes hard work and sacrifice to be successful in business, but relationships need attention, too." He tugged his keys from his pocket. "I'll talk to you later."

Chloe watched him leave, regret heavy in her heart. She took two steps after him then stopped. Was he right? Were the clients more important than him? Or anyone else for that matter?

She let her shoulders slump. Of course he wasn't right, but she couldn't worry about that now. She'd call him later and patch things up. Right now, she needed to save her business; she needed money; she needed to work on that dress.

Trixie sent her chauffeur to pick up the gown on Friday. In a note, she assured Chloe that if the dress met her expectations, she'd pay in full before the ceremony.

You're darned right you will, Chloe thought as she folded the cathedral train into the garment bag. Attached at the shoulders and waist, the net and lace train would appear to float along the floor behind Trixie all the way up the aisle. Silently, she prayed that Gail McKay wouldn't come in for a peek at her gown. More of the rare lace wouldn't be delivered until next week.

"Stunning," Rebecca admitted. "I think this is your best."

"And it will be my last if she doesn't pay her bill," Chloe answered, watching the limousine drive away, the dress spread across the back seat.

Outside the church, Chloe climbed up the numerous steps and into the cool vestibule. Summer gripped the city, causing the male guests to unbutton suit coats and tug uncomfortably at neckties. Tommy wore the same gray wool suit he always wore but seemed impervious to the heat.

"You know," he said, "I wouldn't let anything happen to you or the shop."

"What?" His words caught Chloe off guard.

"All that debt you're paying off? I could help with that. You wouldn't be so strapped for cash."

"Oh, Tommy, that's so sweet, but my mother would die of humiliation if she thought you even knew about it." She ducked her head. "I only told you because it worried me so much at first."

"Thanks."

She looked up at him, puzzled.

"It takes trust to tell someone family secrets." He shrugged. "Like I told you about dad and what a lousy businessman he is. He's a great guy but doesn't know beans about making money. I hope he did a good job here," Tommy continued as they made their way through a throng of well-dressed people.

"Here?" Chloe automatically looked down. "He cleans hardwood floors, too?"

"No, he had to repair the runner. You know, the white carpet they roll out before the bride walks down the aisle."

"Oh."

"He's been doing the work for this church for years. And hey, I didn't tell you—Dad did some work yesterday for a Chicago Cubs pep rally. He got to meet Sammy Sosa."

Chloe tried to look impressed.

"He hit sixty-three home runs last season," Tommy told

her, his eyes lighting up.

They stepped to the doorway of the sanctuary and stopped.

"Hi, Brian." Chloe smiled at an usher, one of Cameron's old friends. He blinked in surprise.

"Chloe? What are you doing here?" He glanced around as if looking for someone.

"The bride invited me. Don't worry, Cameron knows I'm here. At least, I think he does. But put us on the bride's side in the back."

Brian took a step and gestured toward a gleaming oak pew. Chloe slid in first, smoothing her short Armani skirt over her thighs.

Tommy sank down beside her and eyed her legs appreciatively. "Did I tell you that you look great? I'm glad you didn't wear one of those long numbers. As it is, I don't see your legs enough."

Chloe smiled at him, pleased with the comment. He often told her that she looked nice, but never had he been so specific. "I'm glad you're not mad at me anymore."

"I was never really angry, babe, just discouraged." He leaned back against the wooden bench. Before Chloe could formulate an answer, a voice interrupted.

"Miss Bauer?" An older woman stood at the end of the pew. "Would you come with me, please?"

Puzzled, Chloe nodded. She followed her down a set of stairs and into a room bustling with activity. In the center of the hubbub, Trixie, wearing the gown Chloe had designed, struck poses for her wedding party to admire. She caught sight of Chloe and preened.

"It's beautiful. Absolutely perfect," Trixie gushed amid a chorus of agreement. "I so wanted everything to be perfect." One manicured hand waved to a counter. "There's your check."

"Thank you." Chloe glanced at the amount expecting to see the full amount, but found it was $2,000.00 short. "Ah, I know this isn't the time or place, but—"

"Oh, don't worry. Cameron will pay the rest when we come back from Europe."

Chloe stared at the check as the bridal party moved toward the door. Trixie accepted her bouquet from the maid of honor. How could Trixie be so cavalier about the money after Chloe had worked so hard to give her what she wanted?

"You look lovely," one of the maids cooed.

"Yes, don't I?" Trixie beamed.

Chloe watched the three flower girls, two ring bearers, ten bridesmaids, and the maid of honor make their way up the aisle to the haunting tune of the Pachebel Canon.

"Quite a parade," Tommy whispered. He shifted to get a better look.

"Indeed it is," she agreed. "Trixie actually wanted more attendants, and her fiancé said no."

Which makes perfect sense now that I know who the groom is, thought Chloe. *He probably told her what color underpants they could wear, too.*

The organist paused and changed music, playing the opening bars to "Trumpet Voluntary".

Following the direction of the bride's mother, everyone stood as the white runner rolled open down the center aisle.

A ripple ran through the crowd.

Trixie, walking alone holding a huge bouquet of pink lilies, moved out of the vestibule, smiling serenely.

"Sweetheart," Tommy leaned toward her, and Chloe waited for the proposal. "I'm real proud of you. That dress is a work of art."

"Thank you," Chloe whispered, pleased at his remark. He squeezed her hand and returned his attention to the ceremony.

Unexpectedly, several guests laughed out loud. Trixie's cheeks blushed red.

"Hey, way to go!"

"My stars! Is that supposed to be here?"

Chloe felt a chill settle in her veins as she strained to see past the crowd to the bride. Frantic thoughts tumbled through her mind. The gown had been perfect.

"Tommy, what's going on?" she demanded, tugging at his arm.

"I'll be darned." He looked stunned.

"What? What?"

"I think Dad made a mistake."

Chloe caught a glimpse of Trixie between the shoulders and heads of the startled guests. Pale and strained, she fought for composure as she reached Cameron's side. His face, although tight with tension, revealed nothing. The best man, next to him, grinned from ear to ear.

The ceremony began. Chloe's thoughts wandered as the minutes passed. She listened to the minister, heard the faint responses, then realized she was waiting for Tommy to ask her to marry him.

I'm going to say yes, she told herself with surprise. *Why? What's different?*

Before she could sort out her thoughts, the organist began to play the recessional music. Chloe leaned over to see Trixie's dress, certain a seam had come apart, but as the couple came toward her, the gown looked fine. Then she looked down at the floor.

Emblazoned on the carpet runner, done in the cheerful red, white, and blue of the Chicago Cubs team colors, were the words, "GO TEAM!" punctuated with the familiar logo.

She gasped, then clapped a hand over her mouth to stifle a laugh.

"Looks like there was a mix-up." Tommy gazed at the floor, wide-eyed.

"Oh my gosh. What could have happened?" Chloe stared at the runner, half amused, half horrified.

"Well, all I know for sure is that there was a pep rally yesterday for the Cubs, and they had a runner to be cleaned."

He frowned. "This church had a runner that had to be mended before it could be used for a wedding." His eyebrows arched up as he looked at her. "I wonder if the pep rally had a nice white carpet?"

Guests now followed the retreating wedding party out of the sanctuary.

"This is great. We should have done this at our wedding," said a distinguished-looking, white-haired man.

"Over my dead body," responded his wife. "Now, if you wanted the White Sox, I'd go along with it."

"I think it's the ultimate in tacky," observed a woman in a blue chiffon dress.

"I wonder if the reception will be done with a Cubs theme, too," mused a young woman sidling out of the pew wearing jeans and a red satin blouse.

"It's cool," said a young boy eagerly scanning the length of the aisle. The woman behind him rolled her eyes and gently nudged him toward the front door.

Tommy chuckled and winked at the youngster who smiled back. Chloe felt a rush of love for this man who took things so easily in stride. If something like this happened at his wedding, he'd laugh and enjoy the joke.

Then she realized that he hadn't asked her to marry him. Chloe's palms became clammy as disappointment washed over her.

Has he changed his mind? Is he losing interest?

She reached into her purse for an aspirin.

In the receiving line, Trixie air-kissed Chloe's cheek. "Thank you for coming," she chirped and passed her along to the groom.

"I'm surprised you came." Cameron limply shook her hand.

"Wouldn't miss it for the world," she answered and turned to introduce Tommy. "Tommy Osterweis, this is Cameron—"

"Osterweis?" Cameron injected. "The carpet cleaning family?"

"The same," admitted Tommy, offering his hand.

"That was your family that did that in there?" Cameron's voice shook with indignation.

"My father made a mistake, and I apologize." Tommy let his arm drop to his side. "I'll find a way to make it up to you. Maybe clean the carpeting in your home for free?"

"I wouldn't let you or your idiot father touch my driveway much less my carpet," snapped Cameron.

"Cameron! Stop it right now." The rebuke came from his father, standing to his right. "It's just a rug."

Cameron glowered, but said no more as Chloe and Tommy finished greeting the members of the wedding party.

As they stepped out into the late afternoon sunshine, Mr King III called to Chloe. She turned and waited as he caught up to them. From his pocket, he pulled a piece of paper.

"Trixie told me that Cameron didn't pay for the last minute alterations on the dress as he promised." He handed Chloe a check. "That should take care of the bill and any inconvenience it may have caused." He smiled and walked back inside the church.

Chloe looked at the check. "$3,000.00!" Relief washed over her.

Tommy grinned and, taking her by the elbow, led her a little away from the crowd. "I've got something to say."

"Yes?" Chloe held her breath. At last, he was going to ask the question so that she could say yes!

"I've accepted a job with Landscapes Unlimited." He held up his hand. "It's just mowing and trimming at first, but I'll learn. I'll go to college and study, then I'll become one of their landscape architects."

She'd wanted him to follow his dream, but did that mean he no longer wanted her to share in it? "That's great, Tommy. Working outdoors is what you've wanted to do."

She smiled, proud of him for taking the first step toward his goal.

"So, now. Let's go eat." Tommy pulled her toward the parking lot.

"No." Chloe dug in her heels. Now that she'd made up her mind, she wasn't going to let him go so easily. "I've got something to say, too."

"What?" He stopped and smiled.

"I've decided to marry you."

"Oh?" One eyebrow shot up. "But I haven't asked."

"This time, I'm asking you." She waited, watching his eyes, his mouth, but they gave no clue to his thoughts.

"Why?" he finally asked. "Why now? Because of my new job?"

"No, of course not," she stammered, "because I love you."

"I never doubted that." He tilted his head, waiting.

"And because," she said slowly, "I've noticed that security doesn't come from things you have. It comes from trusting. Trusting you, myself, God, family. You see?"

"Yes, sweetheart, I've always seen." He gathered her into his arms and smiled down at her. "I'm glad you finally do, too."

She pulled his head down for a kiss, relishing the heat that jumped between them. When she finally broke the kiss, she glanced back to where the bridal party and guests were throwing birdseed at the departing couple. "So, is that a yes?"

He laughed. "Yes, that's a yes!"

"I want a big wedding."

Tommy nodded. "Fine."

"But let's make sure the white carpet is in tip top shape before the ceremony."

"Aw, I was going to ask if we could use turf instead." He laughed at the face she made. "All right, all right. How about if we use a Chicago Bulls theme? Michael Jordan could be the ring bearer—"

"He's retired," Chloe reminded him.

"Oh, I'm sure he'd do it if Dad offers to clean his carpets."

"I'd tell you to be serious, but I think you are!" Chloe swatted at him playfully.

"No," he said smiling, "the only think I'm serious about is you. And the future we'll design together."

ONE KISS

Carolee Joy

"How could you do this?" Amber stared at the shattered remains of the ceramic angel she'd discovered shoved aside in a corner of the bookcase. Shards jabbed through the paper towel into her trembling hand.

When her husband didn't reply, she repeated the question, this time with tears stinging her eyes.

"You want me to help around here, Amber? Then don't get on my case when I do. I broke it when I was cleaning and forgot to tell you. At least I saved the pieces." Kirk sat up from the couch and rubbed his face.

"They were your wedding present to me," she said softly, setting the pieces of the boy angel next to the remaining figure of the girl.

"Yeah, well, they spend more time kissing than we have lately," he retorted. Scowling, he plucked his truck keys off the shelf near the door on his way to the garage.

"If you didn't stay out in the yard until dark, then fall asleep in the recliner every night, maybe we'd be kissing, too!"

For a moment, his shoulders slumped, making her wish she could recall the hasty words. Kirk worked hard, and lately had been pulling ten-hour shifts at the plant. But that didn't give him the right to ignore her when he got home. She didn't want to seem like a spoiled brat, but she'd been putting in extra time at the hospital and still did her best to make their home a welcoming place to return to each day.

They had agreed early on in their marriage that housework should be an equal opportunity event, but lately, she'd taken over more and more of the burden in the hope that they'd have extra time to spend together.

It hadn't worked out that way. Kirk seemed content to let her handle things in the house while he puttered aimlessly in the yard, until one night she'd finally exploded from resentment and exhaustion. Sure, she'd like a pretty back yard, but it would have to wait. Keeping the house clean and the laundry done was all they could expect right now. He'd grudgingly agreed to pitch in with the weekly cleaning.

And now he'd done this.

"It's just a piece of glass. If it meant so much to you, then how come it took you a month to notice?"

She gasped. He hadn't even bothered to tell her? How dare he! "Don't you understand? It's irreparable this time." The wings had broken off once before, and Kirk had managed to glue it so that only a close examination revealed the imperfection. Tears trembled on her lashes, but she fought to contain them. "Last time you were able to fix it."

"Yeah, well, it held together better than we have." Turning on his heel, he stalked out of the house. The door slammed shut behind him.

Why had he become so angry? Was this a typical fight for a married couple, or were things worse than she'd suspected?

She held the girl angel in her hand and traced a finger over the angel's pearly robe up to her puckered lips, determined not to let the tears fall until she knew he was really gone. Even then, she held them in with sheer stubbornness.

If he cared so little about being with her, or taking care of their marriage, why should she get so upset or try so hard? If he could just stomp off without a backward glance, then she could, too.

She packed a small suitcase, gently placed the ceramic figure in it, and went to spend the night with her sister.

Monica greeted her with a hug, a sympathetic ear, and a cup of hot chocolate. Then told her she was being unrealistic.

"I don't know what you expect of the man, Amber. He's working like a drudge to pay for the house you both couldn't wait to have."

"So am I!" she retorted. "At least I don't expect it to be like a hotel complete with maid and room service." Why couldn't Kirk understand it took a lot of hard work to make a house a home? Why didn't Monica?

Her sister squeezed her shoulders. "I'm on your side, always. I just know you're miserable right now. And I'm betting Kirk is, too."

Amber went to bed wondering if that were really true. He could at least call, or come and get her. He must know where she was, for heaven's sake. She just needed a little consideration and understanding.

She rolled onto her side and hugged the pillow. She needed a kiss.

One kiss, that's all it would take to bring them back together. She was so sorry she'd made a big deal about the angels. She picked up the figurine she'd tucked under the pillow and stroked the pearly shimmer. Again, she ran a finger over the angel's kissing mouth. How like her it was, ready to kiss and make up, and no one there to do it with. How sad they both were, waiting for something they might never again experience.

When she awoke, bright light from an early morning sun streamed through the lace curtains of Monica's guest bedroom. Startled, she bolted upright, sending the angel to the hardwood floor and shattering it into a dozen pieces.

Oh, no! The last symbol of hers and Kirk's marriage destroyed. Panic welled up inside her. But as sunshine reflected off the iridescent pieces, she realized what a fool she was.

Kirk had given her the angels to commemorate their first kiss because he was as sentimental as she was. She loved him with all her heart. He loved her. She'd been fussing at him about the housework, while he worked like a field hand in the yard on some back breaking project he didn't want to trouble her with.

What did it matter if there were dust bunnies under the bed? Or dirty dishes in the sink after a long day? So what if he fell asleep in the recliner or worked in the yard all evening? Even if he was too tired to do things with her, at least he was home. If she tried a little harder to spend time with him, she was certain he would try harder, too.

They had each other, or at least she hoped they did. Flinging the covers aside, she scrambled from the bed, careful to avoid the shattered angel. She cleaned up the mess, then took a shower and raided Monica's closet for a pretty sundress.

If she had to run begging Kirk to forgive her, she wanted to make sure he found it easy to say yes.

An hour later, she stood in the drive of their modest bungalow. A small truck blocked the entrance to the garage. The back gate stood open. Two strange men pushed wheel barrels of dirt toward her back yard.

What was Kirk up to?

She found him, dirty, sweaty, and looking like the answer to her prayers, putting the finishing touches on the most amazing rose garden she'd ever seen.

"Kirk!"

At the sound of her voice, he turned, grinned ruefully, and wiped a grimy hand across his forehead.

"Your sister promised to detain you until this afternoon."

"I left while she was at the grocery store. I guess she thought I'd sleep till noon."

"Obviously, you didn't," he said, a low rumble of laughter in his voice.

She cast her gaze downwards. "I barely slept at all. I missed you."

"I missed you, too."

His warm voice surrounded her with hope for a new beginning. "Can you forgive me?" she whispered.

"That depends."

Her gaze flew up to meet his, but she found his eyes dancing with suppressed laughter. "On what?"

"If you'll forgive me for picking a fight. It took every bit of strength I have to walk out last night, and I hope you like this. I've been planning it for months and didn't know how I could finish it without you finding out. If it's not what you wanted...." He spread his hands as if he didn't know what he'd do.

"Oh, Kirk." She breathed in the heady scent of roses. Dainty pink blooms climbed a trellis. Clusters of American beauties ranging from pink to red to sun-kissed yellow clustered in front of the platform where the framework for a gazebo stood. A four-foot tall pair of kissing angels, their marble likeness exactly like the small ceramic figures she'd loved, held court over it all. "What is all this?"

He grinned with a mixture of self-assurance and diffidence that shot straight to her heart. "Besides the time I put in here after supper, I've been sneaking out to work in the yard every night after you fell asleep. Happy Anniversary, sweetheart. I wanted to surprise you."

Tears filled her eyes, but this time it was with happiness. "I'm overwhelmed. Especially since it's not our anniversary for another six months."

"I beg to differ with you."

At her puzzled expression, he bent and brushed his lips lightly against hers.

"Our first kiss. In the rose gardens at the botanical park."

Heedless of the workmen, the dirt and everything else except for the happiness soaring through her, she threw herself into his arms and raised her face. As her lips met his, she knew this was another kiss she would never forget. Even if they did encounter a few thorns every once in a while.

PROM QUEEN

Tami D. Cowden

Sara stared at her reflection as she smoothed the shiny fabric of her gown over her waist. The silvery satin shimmered in the soft glow of her bedroom lamp. *It's too dressy,* she thought guiltily. *I should have chosen something plain.*

Sara wished she'd been asked to do anything other than be a chaperone for the high school prom. But Jillian had volunteered her for the task. And the truth was, most kids didn't want their parents at the prom.

For that matter, most parents didn't want to go to their kids' prom.

Of course, in Louisville, most parents had gone to their own prom.

Not Sara. When her class had its prom, she was six

months pregnant with Jillian. A new school policy had allowed her to stay in school and graduate. Still, in those days, pregnant girls most definitely did not go to the prom.

Even if attending in a maternity gown would have been thinkable, she wouldn't have had an escort. Jillian's father had taken another girl. When push had come to shove, he'd shown himself to be a boy, not the man he'd pretended to be.

Her first reaction when her daughter told her that she'd "volunteered" had been excitement. Finally, "The Prom." She had missed out on lots of things by being a teen mother. Hard earned wisdom and harder work had enabled her to get her current good job, nice home, and terrific daughter, but sometimes the little things made her wistful. The beautiful dress, limousine ride, and wrist corsage had been the least of teenage wonders her pregnancy forced her to miss. Funny how the absence of those shiny memories still caused pangs.

Sara took herself to task. Imagine, thirty-five years old, and giddy at the notion of going to a high school dance. She wouldn't dance, she'd reminded herself firmly. Her job was to keep the punch unspiked and the young couples out of deserted classrooms.

Now, smiling wryly at herself in the mirror, she acknowledged that she was the perfect choice for chaperone, after all. A reminder to teenagers that young love has consequences.

"Mom, the limo is here!" Jillian poked her head into her mother's bedroom. "Wow! You look great. I knew that color was perfect for you." The slim girl glided into Sara's room, her own pale rose taffeta rustling softly. She slipped her arm around her mother, and the two smiled at their reflections.

"I'm afraid your friends will think I'm trying to be younger than I am. I don't exactly look matronly." A frown creased Sara's brow

"No, not matronly." Cocking her head, and pursing her lips, Jillian appeared to ponder the issue. "Elegant." She nodded. "You look very elegant. That gray is just the color of your eyes."

With a pout, the girl continued, "I wish my hair was black like yours, instead of this mousy brown. I should have dyed it," she added darkly.

Sara smiled at the description of her daughter's glorious chestnut hair. This old mother-daughter argument calmed Sara as compliments had not. "Come on, little mouse. Let's go to the ball."

"Right. Hey, Mom, maybe you'll meet Prince Charming tonight."

"Ooh, maybe. And maybe they'll crown me Prom Queen, too." Laughing, Sara accompanied her daughter to the waiting limousine. Jillian and her girlfriends had abandoned tradition and come as a group rather than with boys. They'd even pitched in for a limousine. Sara followed in her own car.

Arriving at the dance, Sara busied herself with her duties while the girls vanished into the crowd. She arranged refreshments, encouraged shy youngsters to pair up for dances, and stood conspicuously nearby whenever high spirits threatened to overtake good manners.

After an hour of such activity, Sara sat down at one of the bistro tables. Looking around, she felt a small sigh of satisfaction. Even as a chaperone, she was having fun. The decorations were beautiful, and the kids all looked so grown up. Still, she couldn't help her wistful glances toward the dance floor. A run of Seventies disco tunes made her feet tap with remembrance.

"Excuse me, Ms Walker, what do you say we show these kids how to do the hustle?"

Turning with surprise, she gaped at the grinning face of Mike Powers, the widowed father of one of Jillian's friends. Like her, he sported a chaperone's ribbon. Heat rose in her cheeks. She'd noticed Mike at the girls' varsity basketball games. It had been a long time since just seeing a good looking man made her feel tingly inside, but there was something about Mike's rugged masculinity that made her want to forget all her hard earned knowledge of men.

Whoa, Sara. You are not a teenager anymore. "Oh, I don't think chaperones should dance."

His brows raised above deep brown eyes. "On the contrary, we should set a good example for all these wallflowers hiding behind the refreshment table." He nodded toward the sizable crowd hovering near the snacks.

Sara smiled timidly but shook her head. "I don't think I remember how." She blushed and pretended a fascination with the cup of punch in front of her.

"It's like riding a bike." He slipped into the chair beside her. "Besides, you'd be doing me a big favor. I never danced at a prom before."

She chanced a look into his eyes at that. "You didn't go to your prom?"

"Nah. I had to quit school. Actually, my oldest was born a few days after the prom." He shrugged. "He's in college now."

Sara nodded her understanding. "You didn't chaperone his prom," she said after a moment of silence.

A crack of laughter greeted this question. "No way! He'd have been mortified." Tilting his head, and cocking one eye at Sara, he continued. "Tina, well, she was all fired up for me to come tonight." His grin returned. "Now I understand."

She stared at him blankly for a moment, and then the light dawned.

"Oh!" Speechless, she looked wildly around for her daughter. Spotting Jillian with Tina, both avidly watching their respective parents, she started up from the table. A warm strong hand on her wrist stopped her.

Mike's smooth deep tone rolled over her. "I don't know about you, but I am kind of grateful to the girls."

She sat down again.

Taking a sip of punch, he gave her a look that reached

into her soul. "Sort of breaks the ice. Gets us past that awkward stage." Waving a hand at the foil stars and moons dangling above the dance floor, he added, "Look at this. The night is full of stars, we're dressed to the nines, and romantic music is playing. Am I a great date, or what?"

The band burst into "YMCA" just as he finished his speech. Sara dissolved into giggles. "Or what, I'd say."

They sat in companionable silence, smiling across the crepe paper decorated table. After a few minutes, Mike tried again, "I'd really like to dance with you, Sara."

"I'm not sure we should give the girls the satisfaction." Her voice was prim and steady, but she felt an excitement she had forgotten.

"Maybe not. But don't you think our duty requires us to makes sure no one gets too serious out there?" She followed his gaze to the dance floor. The frenetic sound of the Village People's signature tune ended. A slow tune brought the teen couples together.

Pursing her lips, she nodded with mock solemnity. "Well, if you think it's our duty—" She took his proffered hand and followed him to the dance floor. Nobly, they ignored the squeals of delight from their daughters.

She glided though the rest of the evening in a glow of happiness. Finally, when the last of the high schoolers trailed home, Sara and Mike walked out of the building hand in hand. Sara stopped short when a limousine pulled to the curb next to them.

"Don't worry. Jillian took the gang in your car." Mike smiled. "I thought my prom queen should have a suitable conveyance." He winked as he added, "Tina and Jillian liked the idea."

After a moment's hesitation, Sara allowed Mike to hand her into the limo. As he slid in beside her, she thought about the scolding she would give her daughter about the evils of matchmaking. But while the driver took the long way home, through the park and past the lake, Sara and Mike talked. His teasing smiles and lingering glances promised more than a single evening's conversation. By the time the long white car pulled up in front of her house, Sara's lecture for Jillian more closely resembled a thank-you note than a scolding.

A short while later, Sara quietly stepped inside her house, still warm from Mike's gentle good-night kiss. Walking up the stairs, she smiled. The prom might be the highlight of a high school romance, but for her and Mike, it was the beginning.

LETTING GO

Su Kopil

"I want a divorce, Kurt."

Holly didn't mean for it to come out that way—so abrupt, so cold. The silence on the other end of the phone caused her to hesitate. She bit her lip, choking back the impulse to shout, *I love you. I'll wait forever.*

Instead her friend Phil's voice echoed in her mind, *It's time to let go. Move on.*

Phil had been her rock through those first horrible months after her miscarriage. She'd cried on his shoulder, not Kurt's. And he'd remained at her side, gently prodding and pushing, reminding her she had a life to lead despite the loss of her baby and the withdrawal of her husband.

"Kurt?" Her fingers clutched the receiver. "I want you to pick up the rest of your things. No more excuses."

Three times he'd promised to get the rest of his clothes. She'd even packed them in boxes for him. Three times he failed to show up. Just like he failed to accept they would never hold their daughter, Katie, in their arms. Instead of staying home so they could comfort each other, he'd gone out every night, some nights not bothering to come home at all. Finally, six months after her miscarriage, she'd asked for a separation.

"Will you?" She heard a hiss of air as though he'd been holding his breath.

"If that's what you want. I'll be there in twenty minutes."

"No! Not tonight."

The phone clicked in her ear. Too late, he'd hung up.

She glanced at the grandfather clock in the foyer, a wedding present from her parents. Seven-ten. She hit redial. On the third ring Kurt's machine picked up. She paused at the sound of his voice on the recording. What could she say? *Not tonight, I have a date?*

Phil was due to arrive in less than an hour. After months of friendship, he'd finally told her he'd like to move their relationship forward, assuring her it was time. Holly liked Phil. She didn't want to disappoint him after all he'd done for her so she'd agreed to dinner and a movie.

But now, laying the receiver back in the cradle, she hoped he'd be late.

Her palms felt moist. Holly wiped them on a bath towel before patting her short hair into place one last time. Maybe Kurt wouldn't come. After all, why should she believe him now? She hadn't been able to depend on him in a long time. Not since Katie.

At first, she'd understood. He needed time to grieve in his own way. But as the months slipped by, the distance between them became an abyss—unbridgeable.

Holly caught her breath at the sound of a loud knock. *Please don't let it be Kurt.*

Pulling open the door, her heart fluttered the same as it did six years ago when a co-worker first introduced them.

He'd changed little since then. Perhaps a few more lines across his forehead and around his mouth, but for her they only added character to his handsome face.

"Kurt, I—" She stopped when his scowl eased into a faint smile and stepped back.

He entered the foyer still looking at her.

She suddenly felt self-conscious in the short blue dress she'd bought. Her palms started sweating again. She glanced out the window.

"What's the occasion, Holly?" Kurt took a step toward her, a sparkle in his eye. "Hot date?"

She knew that teasing tone. Did he think she'd dressed up for him, that her asking for a divorce had all been a ruse? Without thinking she blurted out, "Yes."

He fell back as though she'd punched him. "Didn't waste any time, did you?" His brown eyes darkened.

"It's been six months." She couldn't help the defensive tone. "How long did you expect me to wait?"

His body stiffened. Without answering, he strode down the hallway.

She hurried after him.

"Not there." As though he were a stranger, she directed him away from the bedroom they had once shared so intimately,

He stopped. Waiting.

The bright hallway light picked up red glints in his chestnut hair. She wondered how many times they'd kissed here. She watched his eyes shift to her lips and wondered if he was thinking the same thing.

"I put your things in here." She gestured to the closed door next to the bathroom.

He hesitated ever so slightly before pushing the door open.

She heard the sharp intake of his breath.

"What have you done?"

She moved behind him, the familiar ache constricting her

throat. She watched as he took in the partly disassembled crib his parents had bought and the cartons packed with unused baby clothes and toys.

He bent down, retrieving a plush teddy bear that had fallen out of an overstuffed box. His hand absently stroked the soft material before he let the toy slip back to the floor.

"Why?" His questioning gaze mirrored the pain in her heart.

"Because it's time." She glanced at the empty shelves and bunny wallpaper. "I can't live in the past anymore, Kurt. I have to go on with my life."

"Just like that you can forget?"

"No." Tears pricked beneath her eyelids. She blinked them away. How could he ask such a thing? Losing their baby in her seventh month had been the hardest thing she'd ever had to face.

"I'll never forget. Every moment is etched in my heart. I've simply learned to accept what's happened."

Kurt turned toward the window.

Holly felt an overwhelming sorrow. She never stopped believing—hoping—their marriage could be happy like it was before Katie. Until now. Kurt would never be the same man she married just as she would never be the same woman. But deep in her heart, she knew it could be better—stronger, if only he would give it a chance.

"We can't bring the past back," she whispered, wishing she could hold him. Wishing that together they could find a way to ease the pain in their hearts. "We can only go on from here."

The doorbell rang.

Kurt moved away from the window.

Their gazes locked.

Holly backed toward the hall. "My date. I have to go. Your things are in the corner." She pointed. "Can you—?"

"I'll let myself out."

She nodded.

"Holly?"

She glanced back, frail wings of hope fluttering once more in her chest.

His lips parted, but he shook his head.

The bell sounded again. She hurried down the hallway.

Phil, handsome as ever, proved to be a charming and thoughtful date, everything a woman could want, yet, all Holly could think about was the pain in Kurt's eyes. Even before they reached the restaurant, she knew the date had been a mistake. Despite what Phil thought, she wasn't ready.

She asked him to drive her home, hoping he'd understand. As he pulled down her street, she apologized again.

The corners of his mouth lifted in an understanding smile. "It's okay. I shouldn't have rushed you."

She said goodnight and stepped out of the car. That's when she saw Kurt's blue pickup in her driveway. He should have been gone by now. Why was he still here?

She found her husband where she'd left him. Kurt sat on the floor with a screwdriver in his hand. Pieces of the disassembled crib lay scattered about him. The teddy bear had disappeared, and the cartons were sealed with tape.

"Hi."

She stared at him, unsure what to say or where to begin. "My date—I didn't feel well."

"I'm glad."

Her eyes widened.

"I mean, I'm glad you're home."

The anger was gone from his eyes, but the pain remained, along with a soft glow. He put the screwdriver down and stood up.

She started to speak, but he shook his head, and she stopped.

"I'm sorry for the way I behaved. Your date—the thought of losing you—made me realize I've been running away from you, away from the pain, when I should have been running to you. But I never stopped loving you." Kurt took her hands in his. "Can you forgive me? Please say you'll give me—us another chance."

Hope beat harder in her chest, spreading a gloriously giddy feeling inside of her. She nodded, afraid that if she spoke the tears might flow and never stop.

He held out his hand and she moved into his arms. The tension, the fear, even a bit of the pain, ebbed away in the comfort and strength of his embrace.

"I can't change the past." His gaze swept over the nursery then back to her. "I know that now, but I'm ready to let it go."

FLAVOR OF THE DAY

Carolee Joy

What did the guys mean, he wasn't the passionate type?
Carey waited for the light to turn green and thought about the
bet his buddies had going on over which one of them was the
most romantic. Certainly he had one of the more "sensitive
guy" types of occupations. He owned and operated an ice
cream shop! Wasn't that a touchy feely kind of business?

Too bad he'd had such lousy luck in the Valentine's
coupon draw, getting the one for a late night run for ice
cream. What a dumb idea Jack had this time, anyway. His
best friend was always coming up with some strange
competition between the circle of former college buddies,
but this time he'd gone so far off he was miles beyond the
end zone into uncharted turf.

But maybe Carey could salvage it. Instead of just taking

Elissa out for ice cream, which for her would be no big deal, he'd take her to that fancy Italian restaurant where he'd proposed to her. The one where they made the flaming desserts. A little Bananas Foster, and they'd see who was the most passionate.

Except didn't Bananas Foster have rum in it? Not a good idea for a lady in Elissa's condition. Seemed like the best desserts always had alcohol in them. Maybe that was the secret to their flavor, their wide appeal.

Secret ingredient.

The light changed, but Carey didn't respond until the guy behind him honked several times.

Ignoring the other driver's impatience, he slowly made the turn, running through the possibilities of what he could add to his sauce. No doubt about it, time to do a little experimenting. He HAD to come up with something memorable for the Valentine's Day sundaes he planned to serve at the shop if he wanted to outdo last year's rousing success.

He forgot about the romance competition, the coupon, and about his wife, in his race to the kitchen.

Much later, elbow deep in sugar, butter, and flavorings, he didn't know Elissa stood watching him until she spoke.

"It didn't seem like a big thing to ask for."

Carey looked up from the chocolate sauce he was cooking. Elissa's lower lip trembled, and his gut tumbled and twisted. No, of course it wasn't much to ask. But the next thing he knew, her beautiful blue eyes would be swimming with tears, and he would feel like the biggest heel in the world, simply because he had forgotten to bring in her favorite flavor of ice cream from his truck. After an evening in the unseasonably warm Texas heat, it would be curdled pink mush. Nasty stuff.

"I'm sorry, sweetheart. I was anxious to get this new flavor adjusted, and I just, well, I forgot." He gestured at the array of liqueur bottles lining the kitchen counter. No sense in telling her the ice cream had sat in the truck while he'd met the guys for a few beers. Then he'd have to confess about the romantic coupons.

"The ice cream guru forgets the ice cream. Can't you see the irony in that?" With one hand pressed into the small of her back, the other resting lightly on her swollen belly in the gesture that filled Carey with pride, Elissa was the picture of injured dignity.

He hurried to fill the silence before he sawed off the limb he was out on. "Shouldn't you be in bed?"

Elissa bit her lip before she replied. "Shouldn't you?"

He adjusted the heat under the pan and stirred the sauce, inhaling the deep chocolatey aroma, the faint hint of hazelnut. Ah, now that was the way chocolate sauce was supposed to smell. Now for the taste. He had the spoon halfway to his lips, when he noticed her wounded expression. Uh, oh, there were the tears.

She cried a lot lately. Although part of him wanted to just think it was the hormones, maybe the guys were right.

He had the poetic soul of a flounder.

Despite being concerned the chocolate sauce would scorch, Carey set the spoon down and hurried to press a kiss to her cheek. A tear rolled down her face.

"Come on, Elissa, you should sit." Gently, he guided her over to a rattan and chrome chair and eased her down to the cushioned surface.

"Is that all you're going to say?"

What else was there? "I told you I'm sorry. I mean it, sweetheart, I feel like a heel." He knelt before her and took her hand.

Elissa dabbed at her eyes with a crumpled tissue. "I thought maybe you forgot on purpose. Because—because I look like a beached whale!"

"Nah." He smoothed his hand over her stomach, encased in one of the tent dresses she seemed to live in. "You just look pregnant. Very pregnant."

She dissolved into tears.

Now what? "Elissa, honey, are you okay?"

"Noooooo." She absently rubbed one hand against the small of her back. "Maybe. I don't know."

Of all nights for him to forget her favorite ice cream, when she was wallowing in waffle land, as he liked to call these periods of moody indecision which she seemed to be having more and more frequently.

He rubbed the back of her hand with his thumb. "Why don't you go back to bed? I'll finish up in here and be there before you can blink those beautiful baby blues of yours."

Elissa took a deep breath. "Carey, I don't want to be a pain. But I had my heart set on that ice cream. I've been craving it all day, and you promised to get it, or I would have gone myself."

"You know the doctor doesn't want you to go out alone." He glanced at the clock. Midnight. All the nearest stores carrying her favorite flavor of chocolate covered cherry would be closed. It made no sense to go tearing around town for ice cream when he owned an ice cream store, for peanut's sake.

Carey, you've got as much romance in your heart as one of your industrial sized freezers. He could still hear the guys chuckle as he accepted his romantic coupon. *Since you still haven't figured out how to make Elissa's favorite flavor, you need this more than Jack does.* The guys had practically gargled their beer, they'd been laughing so hard.

He patted his shirt pocket. Romance, he'd show them, and make amends with Elissa all at the same time. Instead of going to the grocery store like anyone could do, he'd go down to the shop and MAKE her some for her very own. That would be an even better treat than the Bananas Foster.

Never mind that he didn't have a recipe for chocolate covered cherry. Forget that he'd been trying to come up with one for months. He could wing it. And if Elissa was asleep when he got back, well, it would keep until morning. As long as he didn't forget and leave it in the truck again.

"Honey, I'm going back to the shop to make your ice cream."

She squeezed his hand. "That's sweet, but you'll be gone for hours."

He shook his head. "You can eat it soft-set if you want. Go back to bed, and this time I'll wake you when I get home." He rose, went to the stove and turned off the heat. The chocolate sauce was scorched, anyway.

Elissa's nose twitched. "Leave me here alone with that awful smell? I'm not up to that. And I miss you, Carey, you've been gone all day." Bracing one hand on the table, she levered herself up.

For a brief, exciting moment, he thought he was home free. She'd go back to bed, he could stir up another batch of sauce, and get the ice cream tomorrow.

She gathered up her purse and headed for the door. "Let's go."

Carey's spirits sagged. No getting out of the midnight run now. Not that he didn't want to be with her. He did. But as her due date loomed ever closer, he worried more and more about being stuck on the freeway while she delivered their baby.

Wasn't it better to have her with him, though? He really didn't like the idea of leaving her here all alone in the middle of the night. He bent and gave her a light kiss. "Okay, sweetheart, let's go."

Carey drove slowly, taking the road bumps easy and keeping an eye on his wife until Elissa sighed with exasperation.

"I wish you'd stop looking at me as if you think I might hatch at any moment."

"Sorry." Gee, what was a guy supposed to do? If he disappeared into his thoughts, she'd complain he wasn't paying any attention to her. But he could kind of see her point. He wasn't exactly giving her a tender, loving look.

More like she was a grenade, and he wasn't sure if the pin had been pulled or not. He unclenched his hands from around the steering wheel and resolved to be more discreet with his anxiety.

Although it wasn't easy watching the road and casting furtive glances at her, a short time later they were at the shop. Elissa made herself comfortable at a high-back chair in the corner of the kitchen while Carey turned on the rest of the lights and poured her a glass of milk.

He rubbed his hands together. "Okay, one chocolate covered cherry ice cream, coming up." Gathering the ingredients together, he began mixing and blending, tasting occasionally and giving little samples to Elissa to see if he'd mastered the flavor yet.

She waved away a spoonful of what he hoped was the final blend. "Enough! I'm sorry, but I can't take even one more bite." She eased down from the stool and ran a hand over her distended belly.

Immediately, Carey was by her side. "Are you okay?"

She rose on tiptoe to kiss his cheek, but shrugged off the hand he placed on her elbow. "Fine, fine. Think I'll just lie down in one of the booths for a few minutes." She yawned. "I think my stomach is a little upset, all those rich flavors. But it's very good," she hastened to assure him. "And you are wonderful."

Carey watched her waddle into the dining area and slide into a black vinyl booth. She had to push the table a little more toward the other side, but otherwise seemed okay. He returned his attention to the ice cream concoction.

A knock resounded on the back door.

"Mr Lyons? Everything okay in there?" Hank, the night watchman for the shopping center, called out.

Carey hurried to answer the summons before Elissa tried to pry herself out of the booth. He checked through the peephole and swung the door wide. "How's it going, Hank? Just trying to come up with a new flavor."

"Need a taste tester?" Grinning, Hank stepped inside and closed the door.

"Yeah, I think Elissa's had too much of a good thing." He motioned to where his wife lay curled up, well, somewhat curled up, in the booth.

She groaned.

"Hey, there Mrs Lyons." Hank greeted her on his way into the kitchen.

"Hello, Hank," Elissa's voice was weak. Sleepy probably. A twinge of anxiety zinged through Carey but disappeared when Hank raved over the new flavor.

"Whatcha going to call this one?"

"Elissa's Favorite, I guess."

Hank made smacking noises. "Um, hmm. Bet you can think of something more original."

"Midnight Rendezvous at the Ice Cream Shop? Clandestine Concoction?" Carey sealed the carton and placed it in the deep freeze.

"How about Elissa's in labor?" This time her voice was louder and followed by a sharp cry of pain.

Carey dropped a blending spoon onto the floor and rushed to the dining room. Elissa, on her back on the booth seat, propped herself on her elbows. Her breath came in short gasps.

No, not here. This wasn't possible. She still had a week until her due date, and he'd always heard that first babies came later not earlier.

"Are you sure? Maybe it's just false labor again." She'd had her share of that sending them to the hospital two times in the past two weeks only to be sent home.

"Carey," she positively glared at him. "I'm being torn in two here. Don't try to tell me what I'm feeling!"

The look on her face dispelled any further doubts he had. *Oh, my God.* He extended his hand. "Hold on, Honey. I'll get you to the hospital."

Squeezing her eyes shut, she bit her lip and held her

breath. Carey's heart stopped. Then she let the breath out slowly.

"No time," she panted.

Just then her water broke, dripped over the edge of the bench seat and soaked his tennis shoes. Oh, no. This was what the Lamaze classes had warned could happen. But just because the water broke, didn't mean the birth was imminent. Sometimes it could still take hours.

Not for them, he realized as Elissa's face contorted with pain again. Less than a minute since the last one. No way would they make it to the hospital. His worse fears would be realized about birthing their baby on the side of the road. Or having to watch helplessly as she struggled beside him while he drove. At least here, he could do something.

But what? His mind blanked. He swallowed nervously. Call for an ambulance. Hank could do that.

"Hank!" He hollered, sending the middle-aged man scurrying. "Call 911! Quick!"

He heard the back door slam and shoved the booth away from the table. At least that gave her a little more room. Maybe he should put her on the floor. Before he could make any kind of decision beyond removing her drenched undergarments, however, Elissa shrieked in agony.

"Breathe, sweetheart! Breathe!" Putting his arm around her shoulders, he spoke calmly. At least he thought he was calm until Elissa's eyes showed the reflection of his own fear.

"I am breathing!" she snapped.

"Okay, okay. I'll get some towels. Boil some hot water. Hank!" he hollered again, only then realizing the older man had disappeared. Great. Now how was he going to help her and call the ambulance at the same time? He'd need something to cut the cord with. Wait! Was he supposed to do that in a case like this? Or just wrap up the baby and wait until they got to the hospital?

"I'll be right back!" He rushed off to the kitchen, racing

back to Elissa the instant he heard her cry out again.

"Two scoops, please," she panted.

Carey looked down at the ice cream scoop he'd snatched up in the kitchen. Oops. He hurried off again, this time returning with clean towels, a sterilized knife, and the worse case of panic he'd ever had in his life.

"Carey, Carey, Carey," Elissa panted. The baby was well and truly on the way out now. The first dark tufts of hair on the infant's head became visible.

He held her hand and wiped her forehead. "You can do it, sweetheart." He just wasn't sure he could. What was he supposed to be doing now?

She groaned with the effort of pushing out the baby. Just let it emerge naturally is what the childbirth instructor had told them.

Yeah right. He wished more than anything he could reach in there and pull the child out and end his darling wife's pain.

Flashing red lights flooded the store front. Someone beat on the glass door.

Carey gestured wildly, but no way was he going to leave his wife's side now.

Why was the fire truck here?

Elissa screamed as the baby's head emerged. The shoulders and tiny body quickly followed, accompanied by the sound of breaking glass.

What the hell?

"We have a girl!" Carey shouted.

A paramedic and several firemen burst into the store as Carey gathered up the infant, placed her in Elissa's arms and covered the baby with a large towel

Tentatively, she reached up and stroked a finger down the infant's plump cheek. "Oh, Carey, she's so beautiful," she whispered, collapsing back against the vinyl seat.

Tears filling his eyes, he clasped his wife's hand while the paramedic tended to the final details of the birth. "So is her mother," he whispered, his voice choked with tears.

"What are you going to name her?" Hank stood at the door, his face wreathed in a huge smile. "Rocky Road?"

"Whatever we decide, it won't be Hankette. Where the hell did you go?" Carey tried to be exasperated with the night watchman, but realizing he had been the one to call for help, and ecstatic over the sight of his baby, he couldn't think of a good reason to be.

Hank shrugged. "Had to call from somewhere. Guessed my car was as good a place as any to phone the dispatcher."

A few minutes later, Carey sat beside Elissa and their daughter in the ambulance on the way to the hospital where her doctor and the pediatrician would meet them.

Her face weary but happy, she smiled up at him, letting her fingers curl against the pocket of his shirt. Something crinkled against her hand. Oh, no. He'd forgotten all about the coupon!

"What's this?" She withdrew the piece of paper that was his "romance" coupon. "Late Night Run For Ice Cream? What's that supposed to mean?"

He leaned down and kissed her. "Just a little bet the guys have going." He felt the tips of his ears grow warm. "We were having a little contest to see who would give their lady the most romantic Valentine's evening."

She lightly touched his face. "You get my vote."

Bringing her hand to his lips, he kissed her fingertips. "How do you figure that? I can't even remember to bring your favorite ice cream in before it melts. And making it for you, well, look what that got us."

She stroked her finger over the baby's downy head. "Yes, just look." She gave him a dazzling smile. "Carey...."

Her expression became soft, and his heart nearly burst with love for her.

"Anyone can bring home ice cream. Or go out for it. A few can even concoct some. But delivering your own child, now that's romantic!"

ANYTHING BUT STANDARD

Susan D. Brooks

Officer Marlene Frye reached over the receptionist's desk and accepted the clipboard holding the blank medical forms. *I do not want to be here; I do not want to be here. I'd rather get the flu than this flu shot.*

"Fill in the boxes marked with an 'X' and return them to me." The receptionist flashed a quick smile. "Don't worry, the doctor's gentle. The chief got his shot this morning, and he said he didn't feel a thing; it's just standard procedure."

Marlene forced a smile, wondering if her boss, Police Chief Hank Covell, ever felt anything. She accepted a pen and sank down into one of the overstuffed burgundy chairs by the picture window. Mechanically, she began to fill out the forms: name, address, date of birth, name of employer.

Her pen stopped, paused over the last block, then wrote "City of Hadley Ford."

Hadley Ford, Maryland; not Dallas, Texas. A sudden death, a newly widowed sister unable to cope alone with four school-age children, and whoosh! A new home, a new job, and a new life for Marlene. Living in a house with four kids took some adjustment; for instance, privacy was a thing of the past. But each evening when she arrived home, instead of the echo of emptiness, a chorus of eager voices rose in greeting. Instead of standing at the kitchen counter wolfing down a microwave meal, she now sat down at a large oak table and ate a well balanced meal as she listened to tales of too much homework, demanding teachers, and wacky friends. And residing in the same house with Katrina again reawakened memories long buried; good memories of being part of a family.

She wished, however, that her job brought the same satisfaction. Chief Covell both annoyed and intrigued her. He connected well with the people of the community, but his relationship with her stayed remote, unfathomable. When she tried to draw him into conversation, he listened politely and made no comment. Even Marlene's suggestions regarding police procedures received the same response.

They never spoke of personal matters or spent time together after work, something unheard of in her last job where meeting at a local barbecue joint after their shift was routine. Once or twice Hank teased her about something she'd done and she had laughed, thinking that it was the breakthrough, but nothing changed. After she stated that she liked hazelnut coffee, he put a cup on her desk each Monday morning, but brushed aside her thanks.

"It will help keep you alert," he'd say curtly.

Many times she thought that if she had to do it again, she would refuse her sister's suggestion that she interview for her husband's job.

"But I have a job in Dallas," Marlene protested when

Katrina first brought up the idea. "And how could I take Phil's old job? I'd feel—funny."

Katrina appeared not to hear her concerns. "He would have loved it. He always wanted you to move up here so the kids would grow up knowing their Aunt Marlene." With a wistful smile she added, "Phil adored you, you know."

"But this town is so small. A two-person police force. There isn't enough to keep me busy."

"You told me you're tired of Dallas, that there's too much violence. Hadley Ford is just what you need." Her sister drew a shaky breath. "You're just what we need."

Marlene's heart melted. For Katrina to admit that she faced a situation too tough to handle startled and humbled Marlene, rendering her arguments impotent. She agreed to meet with the chief of police, a lanky six-footer with curly brown hair and somber gray eyes.

"I'm seeing you today because I was told to interview you immediately for this opening." He studied her across the top of a steel desk, the surface worn and scratched.

"I know." Instantly defensive, Marlene lifted her chin. "And I'm here because Katrina asked me to talk with you about this opening."

His eyebrows shot up in surprise. Apparently, that was not the answer he expected. Had he thought she begged for an interview? She almost smiled.

"I just meant that the town councilors let me bypass the interview application process." Chief Covell's voice held a hint of amusement.

"Oh." Marlene felt a flush rise from her neck and spread over her face.

"Why would you want to come here? The only advancement is my job, and I plan to hold on to it for a long time."

"I'm not looking for promotion," she assured him. "I like being on patrol."

"I don't want someone to come in and leave a year later.

We're looking for someone who'll stay for a while."

"My sister is going to need me for a long time. I plan to make my home here." She straightened her shoulders. "I can do this job."

Covell sighed and acknowledged that point. "That isn't the question. Your resumé and references are impressive."

"Is it because I'm a woman?"

He jerked back as if she had hit him. "Of course not."

"Then what is it?"

He opened his mouth to speak, shut it, then said, "Nothing. The job is yours if you want it."

Marlene forced her thoughts back to the present. She let her gaze drift to the picture window and the row of Victorian houses that lined the avenue, their delicate details burnished in golden sunlight. Behind them, the tree-covered Catoctin Mountains wound their way north. She smiled. Such a beautiful place and peaceful, too. Violence here consisted of an occasional stolen bike, a stray dog howling in someone's back yard. Who would have thought such heaven still existed on earth?

Even here in the doctor's office, a sense of welcome flowed between people. She studied two teenage boys slouched in chairs next to the front door, absorbed in magazines about deer hunting. According to the receptionist, one had a broken leg from skateboarding; the other was the high school's track star suffering from an infected ingrown toenail that wouldn't heal. Both greeted Marlene respectfully, with smiles. In Dallas, they may have been gang members, insolent, menacing, and more likely to be found in the county hospital's emergency room with knife or gun wounds. Then there was the delightful younger children of the town. Instead of running away at the sight of the patrol car, they ran toward her, chattering and excited.

"You won't get those filled out by thinking about it." Hank's voice startled her.

"I'm almost done." Marlene twisted in her seat and

looked up into her boss' smoky eyes. Amusement twinkled in their depths, and she felt a twinge of desire. Embarrassed at her reaction, she cleared her throat and tapped the clipboard. "You're sure I need to do this?"

"Standard procedure. Get all the preventive medicine you can. Our workforce is too small to have someone get sick."

She sighed and resumed filling in the boxes. "What are you doing here? You got your shot this morning, didn't you?"

"Yup. Piece of cake. I just wanted to tell you that I have to run over to Hagerstown for a court hearing."

"Who's on patrol? Someone from Myersville?"

"You're not in Dallas, remember? The criminal element won't overrun the town if we stop to take care of ourselves."

"No, of course not." Why did he always make her feel like she overreacted to everything?

He turned his hat around in his hand. "How is Katrina?"

"She's managing." The question caught Marlene off guard. Hank had never asked about his deceased friend's widow before. In fact, his seeming lack of interest in the family's welfare made Marlene angry on occasion. "Thanks to you."

"I do what I can. She's the daughter of a cop." Marlene shrugged. "She's tough."

"Officer Frye!" A starched nurse beckoned from the doctor's office door.

"I guess it's my turn." She stood.

"It's just a flu shot." He grinned up at her.

Annoyed, Marlene put one hand on her hip. "Doesn't anything scare you?"

"Plenty, but nothing that comes in a needle." He jammed his hat on his head. "I'll be back in a couple of hours."

Marlene nodded and watched him leave. The nurse, still waiting, grinned at her.

"Ready, Officer? I promise, it won't hurt."

Feeling a little foolish, she took one step forward when

the room exploded in a shower of glass. She hit the floor, her service revolver filling her hand at the same time. Images of gang violence flashed through her mind. She glanced over her shoulder and shouted for everyone to get down. Both of the boys, yelling, tottered on their crutches and waved their magazines at something out of Marlene's sight. The receptionist screamed.

One hoof appeared beside her, then two, then four. A wide-eyed young deer stared down at her, blood dripping from one shoulder where the window glass had sliced into its flesh. Another yearling trotted past, hesitated, then bolted for the hallway that led to the examination room.

Marlene jumped to her feet. She re-holstered her weapon and stared around the room, wondering what to do. Her gaze fell on the front door. She ran to it and propped it open with a magazine rack. The wounded animal bounded out into the street.

From the back of the building, came more yells and screams, followed by the sound of pounding feet. Hank brushed past her into the room. "I saw the deer leave. Anyone hurt?"

"I don't think so. There's another one in the back."

"All right, everyone outside." He turned and gestured to the boys.

The track star grabbed Hank's arm. "Chief, let me go get my bow."

"Out. Now." Hank kept his voice even, but his look sent the boy hobbling through the door followed closely by the receptionist.

Marlene watched the small procession then froze as the other yearling re-entered the room. Hank stepped in front of it, silent, his hands relaxed at his sides. The frightened creature watched Hank with a wary stare. He moved closer, soothing it with nonsensical words spoken in a low, soft voice.

As it calmed and its breathing slowed, Hank managed to

guide it through the doors and outside. Marlene followed, relieved to see the released yearling head off across a field to the mountain. She gaped at Hank. "How did you know what to do?"

"Same thing happened at my house last year. My golden retriever spooked a yearling. She came right through my living room window. She stood in a corner, too afraid to move." He chuckled. "After an hour of staring at each other, I picked her up and carried her outside. I didn't think that trick would work twice." He cocked an eyebrow at her. "What made you think to open that door?"

"I don't know. Seemed like the thing to do."

"Like moving here from Dallas? Taking Phil's job?"

"Something like that." The questions caught her off guard. Why did he bring that up now?

"I want to tell you something." He glanced around then jammed his fists in his pockets. "Phil was going to leave the force. He gave me his notice the night he died."

Marlene stared up at him, too surprised to say anything.

"Phil was a good cop, but his heart wasn't in it. Katrina wanted him to be a policeman, so he was. He would do anything to make her happy." He hesitated, swallowed, then looked toward the mountain. "Phil answered that call about the drunk driver, and he shouldn't have; he wasn't even on duty. He had already turned in his resignation. I was the one who should have gone. I asked him to stop on the way home. One last favor." He rubbed his forehead.

"I heard that glass shatter just now, and I thought there'd been a shooting. Another officer killed. Funny how your mind works when someone you care about is involved."

Marlene's heart skipped a beat. "You care about me?" The words rushed out, full of disbelief.

"Yes, I care about you." His voice was low, husky with emotion.

Just then, people from the medical office started to gather around them, rehashing the incident, marveling over the outcome. Hank glanced at them, then lightly touched Marlene's arm.

"Can we discuss this privately? Over coffee?"

Marlene lifted an eyebrow. "Why Chief Covell, that's not standard procedure."

"Maybe not, but you're always griping at me to change things."

She laughed. "Nothing wrong with instigating a few new standard procedures."

"No," he said, smiling down at her. "Nothing at all wrong with that."

SHORT CHANGE

Betsy Norman

Mr Boom Box and Boxer Shorts came back.

Terri had been alone tonight at the Laundromat again, tucked snugly into her favorite cracked, red-plastic seat, when he elbowed the door open, balancing his burdens.

She spied on him covertly from behind her novel and tried to make herself invisible. Too late. His smile caught her staring.

He tried sweet-talking a single into the slot of the vending machine, but the detergent dispenser didn't budge. His dollar bill went in. The machine spit it out. In. Out. In. Out. A flutter of nerves twisted inside her stomach when she realized his patience gave out, and he was ambling toward her.

He dragged a hand through breezy black hair, a resigned

sigh deflating his chest. "The machine seems to think my money's no good." He fluttered the limp, "left in the jeans pocket last washday" dollar in his hand. "You wouldn't happen to have a few extra quarters I could bum for this single? It's not counterfeit, honest." He held his palms up in guileless surrender. "Just—laundered."

The lopsided grin and deliberate pun inched a smile out of Terri. She quickly brought up her hand to form a protective fence over her mouth, a habit acquired during four humiliating years of braces.

"S... sure." Terri set aside the behemoth novel she kept perched in front of her like a shield. Pawing into the back pocket of her baggy jeans, she produced a handful of quarters. She surrendered them palm up and chin down to hide her flaming cheeks. "I always come prepared with plenty of change, but Pete's Grocery across the street has detergent, just so you know."

"They close at midnight." His warm hand scooped the quarters from hers in an unmistakable caress. A chocolate brown eye winked at her. "Thanks!"

He plunked the quarters into the machine and retrieved a small box of Biz. Flipping the music on, he went about the machinations of starting a load, tossing kaleidoscope-colored boxer shorts and t-shirts into the washer drums. Each movement was an exaggeration to the be-bop beat. He continued a rambling chit-chat, apparently oblivious to the fact Terri had hunched back behind the protective cover of her book, staring over it at him as if he were crazy.

"This place is too quiet, don't you think? A little piped in rock'n roll would shake it up and draw more customers. Like that place downtown." He began snapping his fingers to the rhythm and whirr of the washer.

Terri knew the place he referred to. The new combo bar-and-laundry lured most of the late-night crowd downtown and away from this calm little Mom and Pop neighborhood. She liked it that way. There was only the occasional sleepy customer for company.

Until last week, when the Dud's-N-Sud's woke up to the boogie of his boom box. She had assumed it was a fluke. Why would a handsome guy with a duct-taped basket full of boxers and Biz show up at an empty tomb like this on a Saturday night, when he could be mixing it up with the college crowd? Seeing him here again sent her pulse into spin-dry.

"Name's Brad, by the way. You lit out of here last week before I could introduce myself." He held his hand out expectantly.

Terri was tempted to reach for it in return but didn't. Her fingertips still tingled from the last time their hands touched.

"Terri." She muttered beneath the overlarge rim of her baseball cap, pushing wire-framed glasses up higher on the bridge of her nose to avoid the handshake.

"Well, hello, Terri! Mind if I get a better look at you? There's been something I've been wanting to know."

Brad reached for the bill of her cap. His tilted smile mesmerized Terri, rendering her mute and staring like a frozen titmouse.

He eased the cap backward to reveal her face. "Thought so! Pretty copper-penny haired girls like you always have adorable freckles. Peaches and cream. Shame you try and cover 'em up so." An affable shrug accompanied the mock admonition.

Terri was speechless over his opinion of her carrot hair and awful complexion. Her dryer buzzed. Saved by the proverbial bell, she jumped out of the cubbyhole seat tucked between the snack machine and folding table, grateful for an excuse to escape.

Her nervous hands missed the handle twice before dragging the squeaky door open to snatch out her clothes. Their radiant heat added to the brilliant blush already advancing over her cheeks. She loaded her basket and bolted for the door with a flustered wave goodbye.

"Goodbye, Terri!" Brad called in her wake. "Thanks again!"

Next week came, only to find Brad using a hanger rack on wheels for a dance partner when Terri walked in. *This guy is outrageous!* But gorgeous, and incredibly uninhibited. She was almost a tad envious. He ended his dance routine with a flourish, and Terri felt compelled to offer timorous applause.

She gave Brad a quick smile, then ducked behind the row of washers to the farthest one to start separating her clothes—most of them muted or pastel, and all of them shapeless and concealing.

Brad zig-zagged to the beat of his music up beside her. Her sorting halted when she came to a trim, light denim blouse plastered with brazen sunflowers. Brad's dubious look ping-ponged between her usual baggy attire and the glaring shirt.

"Yes, it's mine," she confessed. "It's ugly and loud, and my brother bought it for me with some ridiculous notion I might actually wear it." Terri cringed. She thought she had wadded up that ugly billboard of a blouse and tossed it onto the closet floor. It must've been gathered up with the rest of the laundry.

"I like it." Brad confiscated the shirt for a Samba step.

"You would. Just look at those—shorts you wear." She whispered as if speaking the observation aloud would condemn her for noticing.

Brad grinned. "So you have sneaked a peek, eh? There's nothing wrong with my shorts. They're my secret, you know."

"Secret?"

"Uh-huh." He didn't elaborate any further than to broaden his grin.

Terri watched in horror as Brad tossed the shirt aside and beckoned for her to dance with him. "Please, Brad! I can't." Terri quailed at his advances.

"C'mon, I'm not an axe murderer you know. Just a

regular guy, doing his laundry and practicing my moves to kill time." He did a ha-cha-cha and extended his hand once more.

Terri shook her head, rapidly stuffing her clothes back into her basket.

"Seriously, Terri, I'm from the neighborhood. I've seen you in Pete's store across the street a dozen times. I'm the second-shift manager. You'd recognize me too, if you weren't so busy camouflauging yourself and concentrating on the bottom shelves."

"I'm not like you, Brad. Just bouncing about like that. I don't even know how to dance!" Terri snatched up her laundry and marched toward the door. He was right about her behaviour, and it hurt.

"I'll teach you how!" Brad followed her and started flagging something from the doorway. "Wait!" he called.

She only braved a quick glance backward, shaking her head 'no' before hopping into her compact car and speeding away.

Two weeks later, her fingers pruned from rinsing delicates in the sink, Terri returned to the Dud's-N-Suds. A drive by the window front showed the place was deserted. A good sign. She'd waited a full hour later than when she usually went, so Brad most likely had finished and gone home by now.

"You forgot these."

She'd barely entered when Brad's familiar voice initiated a prickling shiver down the back of Terri's neck. His tall frame looked ridiculous scrunched up in her habitual corner nook, hidden from view of the street. He dangled a pair of granny white cotton panties from his index finger and flashed a Cheshire-cat grin. Terri groaned in humiliation.

Brad uncorked himself from the chair and returned the panties to her laundry basket. "I'm sorry, Terri, I didn't mean to scare you away. I've got something for you." He retrieved a small wrapped package from his basket of folded clothes and slid it over the top of a washing machine.

"What's this?" Terri recoiled from the gift expecting it to bite.

"We may be more alike than you think." He hooked his basket over one hip and loped in an easy gait out the door, dazzling her with a mysterious smile before disappearing down the block.

Terri reached for the package, then jerked her hand away. Her nails drummed over the hollow lid of the washer. She spidered curious fingers back to the gift to grab it up and begin ripping at the paper.

Inside was the craziest pair of boxer shorts she had ever seen, size extra-small, and a photograph of a geek with taped glasses, slicked-back hair and... Omigosh, a pocket protector? Upon closer inspection, she realized the geek was a teen-age Brad. On the back, he'd written a note: It's what's underneath that counts, Terri.

What on earth did that mean? Wearing Day-glo underwear gave you some sort of inner confidence? Like Superman? Underneath the glasses and shy nerdiness hid the man of steel.

When she got home, Terri cautiously tried on the outlandish boxers, tucking her cotton camisole inside, and stood in front of the mirror.

"Oh, this is silly!" She waved a dismissive hand at the ridiculous image of herself and trod sock-footed to the bathroom to fetch her nightshirt. Once she flipped on the light, the blaring design emblazoned across the reflection of her rear end commanded Terri's attention. She couldn't help but smirk and waggle her hips a little bit. It was too irresistible not to posture and pose and make a face before she broke into giggles behind her hand.

"I guess they do make you feel kind of kicky, don't they?" Terri confessed to her palm, then dropped her hand and sharply scolded herself for perpetuating the habit. "The braces are long gone, Terri, along with the baby fat, so why do you keep hiding?"

She looked at herself closely for the first time since high school. The stark contrast of the boxers only accentuated the fact that her timid smile was indeed white, and no longer tinsel. The huge glasses she wore used to hide round cheeks, now they looked owlish over her sleeked out features. A package of contact lenses lay unopened on the counter. She'd shed the shapeless cocoon of adolescence but kept her feminine wings of adulthood pristinely folded around her.

It's what's underneath that counts, Terri.

The next Saturday night, it was Terri who waited huddled up in the chair when Brad ambled in. She saw the disappointment on his face at finding her huddled in her usual sentinal post.

"I guess you didn't get the meaning of my note, huh?" Brad said with a sigh.

With deliberate slowness, Terri closed the behemoth novel and dropped it to the ground with a loud plop. Next came the baseball cap and glasses. She shucked the baggy sweatshirt to reveal the sunflower blouse and stood, biting her lip, unable to squelch the tiny bit of nervous anticipation she still harbored.

Brad's broad grin of approval bucked up her confidence. Terri moved toward him and flipped the switch on his boom box. She boogied her shoulders a little hesitantly to the beat.

"Oh, I don't know. I think I understood. I guess it meant I shouldn't be afraid to make a change, even if it is a 'short change.'" She copied his penchant for puns with a giggle. His own laughter joined in, warm and robust.

Brad took her hand in a disco move, guiding her into a spin then back to hug snugly against his chest. Brow to brow, he asked, "Does this mean you'll be my dance partner now?"

Terri's unfettered smile blossomed. "I thought you'd never ask."

MOONLIGHT MADNESS

Su Kopil

"That blouse is mine," argued a plump woman.

"I saw it first!" responded a frazzled blonde who held her handbag poised at the ready.

Keri Matthews skirted the aisle where the two shoppers tugged on a yellow blouse. Moonlight Madness sale was right. Shoppers went crazy!

In a matter of hours, Hall's Department Store became a shambles. Hangers stuck out at odd angles from racks. Clothes lay strewn across the floor.

Noting the long line at the cashier in the women's department, Keri made her way to the men's section where the destruction wasn't quite so bad.

"Paisley or stripes?"

Keri jumped at the sound of the husky male voice behind her.

"I'm sorry, I didn't mean to startle you."

"Are you speaking to me?" Clutching the dress in her hands, she turned to find a handsome, broad-shouldered man with unruly dark hair, holding a tie in each hand.

"I'm sorry, I don't usually accost strangers." He smiled. "I thought you worked here. I can't seem to find a salesperson in all this madness."

Kerri laughed. "I know what you mean. I nearly lost an arm fighting for this dress."

"Would you—never mind." He shook his head. "I don't want to impose."

"What?" Kerri asked, fascinated with the lone dimple playing hide and seek on his right cheek.

"I could really use some help deciding which tie to buy. Would you mind?"

"Of course not." Her ex-fiancé always needed help picking out clothes. It seemed he'd needed her help for everything. Unfortunately, he'd never been able to return the favor, and she'd grown tired of being the only one doing the giving.

She leaned closer, eyeing the two ties he held. The scent of his cologne teased her nose. Deciding to approach this in a businesslike manner, she asked, "Is it a casual or formal occasion?"

"Formal."

"What color suit will you be wearing?"

"My brother lent me his black pin stripe, tie and all, but…"

Keri glanced at him. "But?"

"But my garbage disposal ate the tie." He flashed her a sheepish grin.

She laughed.

"I only meant to try the suit on," he said, defensively. "Then the phone rang and I dropped my pizza crust in the sink. The disposal backed up and—well." He started laughing, too.

"It could happen to anyone," Keri said. She studied the racks arranged at eye level on top of the glass cases. "Here! How about this one?" She selected a red tie. "It'll hide any stains in case they serve Italian food."

He reached for the tie. Their hands touched.

A tingle of excitement shot through the pit of her belly. She saw his eyes widen slightly and knew he must have felt it too.

Oh, no! She stepped back. This man already showed signs of needing a caretaker. Attractive or not, she refused to risk getting into another one way relationship. She dropped the tie as if the red fabric scorched her fingertips.

"I've got to run. Good luck with your shopping." She hurried back to the ladies department. Better to wait in line than to allow her foolish heart to fall for a man who ate pizza in a borrowed suit.

Forty-five minutes later she stood next to her open car door in the middle of the parking lot. A full moon shone brightly on people rushing in and out of the store. Shopping carts rattled on the pavement and horns blared.

Just her luck, her car had to break down in the middle of a Moonlight Madness Sale. Cursing her low cell phone battery, she searched beneath the floor mat for the change she'd dropped.

"Excuse me, do you need help?"

Startled, Keri jumped, bumping her head on the doorjamb. Rubbing the sore spot, she turned to face her Good Samaritan.

The tie man. Her pulse quickened with pleasure. Was this coincidence or had he followed her?

He reached out to touch the bump on her head. "Does it hurt?"

She winced from the pressure of his fingers. "Only when you touch it."

"Sorry." He dropped his hand. "Let me see if I can get her started."

"Do you know anything about cars?" She eyed him skeptically. "I was just about to call a tow truck."

"Cars I can handle but ties, no." He laughed. "By the way, I'm Tim."

"Keri." She stepped away from the door, looking everywhere but at him.

"If you rather I didn't help you, Keri, I understand." His voice trailed off. "You seem nervous."

"Nervous? Me? No." At least, not in the way he meant. The parking lot was well lit and filled with people besides, something about him made her feel safe—protected.

Tim handed her his package, then climbed in the driver's seat.

She noticed his collar stood partially up in the back, probably from trying on too many ties. She resisted the urge to smooth it down and stifled her growing attraction to him.

He turned the key. The engine clicked. Jumping out of the car, he popped open the hood and peered at the motor.

Keri tossed his package onto the seat, next to hers, and followed him. Trying to ignore the whisperings of her heart, she turned her gaze to the man in the moon. The soft glow lent comfort and strength confirming his status as guardian of the night. She smiled at her foolishness. Here she'd been so wrapped up in not becoming someone else's caretaker that she didn't even realize when it was she who was being taken care of.

A loud thunk brought her out of her reverie.

"Try it now," he said.

Skirting around the open door, she slid behind the wheel and turned the key. The engine roared.

"You did it!" She glanced up as Tim appeared.

"Your starter's bad. You'll need to have it checked. Be careful not to turn the car off unless you plan on staying put." He turned to leave.

"Wait! How can I thank you?"

"Well—" he hesitated.

"Yes?" She leaned toward him, wanting to prolong the moment for some reason she couldn't fathom and didn't want to ignore.

"You already did. The tie, remember?"

"Right." Her shoulders sagged.

He gently closed her door, then gave her a quick wave.

Shifting into drive, she slowly pulled away. She'd found a man who'd already taken care of her better than her ex-fiancé ever had and here she was driving out of his life. Was she mad? Her foot hit the brake the same moment she spotted Tim running toward her in the rearview mirror. Her breath caught in her throat.

"Package," he panted when he'd caught up to her. "Can't forget my tie."

"Oh." She opened one of the bags on the seat next to her and spotted the red tie she'd picked out for him. And here she'd thought he was running after her. "Sorry."

"I'm not." He grinned. "It gives me a second chance to work up the nerve to ask you to dinner tomorrow night." He hesitated. "I know a great Italian place. I'll drive."

The dimple appeared in Tim's cheek. Funny, how he reminded her of the man in the moon. Her very own guardian of the night.

"I can't wait," she answered and smiled. Everyone said she'd find something wonderful at the Moonlight Madness sale. How right they were.

SWEET HEARTS

Tami D. Cowden

"Valentine's Day is just a rip off invented by florists and greeting card manufacturers." The large man sneered.

"Aren't you forgetting the candy makers?" Clarissa Hart frowned into her fruit punch. Why had she let Sandy talk her into coming to Cupid's Ball this year?

"Yeah, that's right. Guys are expected to shell out big bucks for boxes of chocolates every February 14. Sheesh, the hype is worse than Christmas." The man with whom she'd felt obligated to dance took a big bite of cake and another swallow of beer.

Clarissa sighed as she looked around the brightly decorated ballroom. "Not that I'm really interested, but if you don't like Valentine's Day, why did you come to this party?"

"It's a good place to meet pretty ski bunnies, of course. But no dates until after the 14th. I'm not buying any woman any flowers or candy." He leered down at her. "So, what does a lovely lady like yourself do when she's not dancing?"

"I make chocolates." She smiled blandly back at him. "I make them, and then I put them in big red velvet boxes, and put huge price tags on them just so guys like you have to shell out big bucks." She took a sip of her punch as she watched his face fall. "I don't ski, though. Lots of locals don't, you know."

"I, I didn't mean any—," he sputtered.

"Don't worry. There are lots of lovely ski bunnies here." She waggled her fingers at the press of people in the crowded ballroom. "You can opt not to buy flowers or candy for any of them, either." Red-faced, he melted into a nearby group.

"So, Rissa, meeting any cool guys?" Clarissa's friend, Sandy, suddenly appeared. Judging by her flushed face, she'd been dancing up a storm.

"Not exactly." But then, Clarissa hadn't really expected to meet the guy of her dreams at Snowden's annual Cupid Ball. Not again. Been there, done that, had the scars on her heart to prove it. Carefully hidden, but there all the same.

"C'mon, take a look around." Sandy danced in place, her body moving to the beat of the swing band. Despite her addiction to Clarissa's raspberry truffles, the ski instructor's figure was lithe and graceful. "There are gorgeous men from all over the world here."

True enough. The ski resort attracted winter sports enthusiasts from all over. But when the fun was over, they went back home.

"I'm sorry, Sandy, but I'm just not in the mood. And I really should be at Sweet Hearts. Maria's sick, and I have to get ready for Monday. I'll be working all day tomorrow."

"All the more reason for you to enjoy yourself tonight."

Clarissa didn't have to turn around to know who spoke.

She knew Rick's deep voice. She also recognized the thrill that ran down her spine at the sound of the rich tones.

"Wow!" Sandy actually stopped chewing her gum, her eyes wide. "Hey, I'll give you two some privacy." Clarissa reached out a hand to stop her friend, but too late. Sandy darted off to be quickly welcomed by a trio of well-dressed athletic types.

No point in delaying the inevitable. Taking a breath in preparation for the whoosh of a stomach flip flop, she turned to face the man who broke her heart.

He hadn't changed in two years. Maybe a line or two had appeared around those dark eyes, and his sable hair was cut a tad shorter, but otherwise, he was the same old Rick. He looked entirely at home in his tuxedo, even though she knew he wore jeans and cowboys boots with the same ease.

"Hi, Rick." With one hand, she pushed back the strands of hair that had escaped her attempt at a chignon. Her other hand tried to smooth the creases in her silk skirt.

"Hi, Clarissa." His lips parted into that smile of his, the one that would melt all the fudge kisses in her store. "You look fantastic."

Despite herself, she could not resist the rush of pleasure that surged through her at his compliment. Damn. How could she still care what he thought? She searched her mind for some innocuous topic for conversation. Fortunately, one subject was always available in this town

"Skiing's great, I hear." She bit her lip. Her voice had a tad too much crispness for the air of unconcern she wanted to convey.

"I don't know. I haven't been on the slopes yet." His eyes, so like her best molasses candy drops, seemed to search hers.

"Just get into town today?" There. She gave herself a mental pat on the back. The question had just the right amount of indifference.

"No, I've been here a few days. I stopped by at the shop,

but the clerk told me you were out." He cocked his head. "Were you? Or were you too busy making candy to talk to an old friend?"

Again, that traitorous pleasure surged through her, this time at the knowledge that he had come to see her. Still, she squirmed. The past few days, she had told her employees to tell anyone asking for her that she was out. She confessed the truth, adding, "I was trying to keep salesman away, not," she hesitated over the word, "friends."

Rick looked away for a moment before returning his gaze to her eyes. "I guess I didn't expect you to be any less devoted to Sweet Hearts now than you were two years ago."

"Well, as I recall, I wasn't the only one devoted to my work." The words came out in a dry monotone, quite unlike the bitter tones she used the first—and last—time they'd had this discussion.

"True enough. It's something we have in common." Rick reached for her hand. "One of many things, as I recall."

Clarissa pulled her hand back. How dare he think he could waltz back into her life this way! "I wish I could say it was good to see you, Rick, but honesty is one of those traits we share." All thoughts of keeping her cool forgotten, she slammed her cup of punch onto a table and strode out of the hotel ballroom.

Rick stared after her, pleased with her reaction. Her coolness at first had made him fear she felt nothing for him anymore. But the furious sway of her retreating form told another story. Indifference would have been an uphill battle. But anger? Oh, yeah, he could work with anger.

"So much for happy reconciliations, huh?" The sympathy in Sandy's voice from behind surprised him. He turned to assess her.

"Do I sense a possible ally?"

"Oh, sure. I thought the two of you were a great couple. I even told her she should go with you when you asked." She flicked her eyes over him and grinned. "I would have."

"I guess we both should have known she wouldn't leave Sweet Hearts." He frowned. Would she even forgive him for asking? He'd simply assumed she would drop everything to join him in Dallas. He'd been astonished when she'd balked at leaving her shop. She'd been indignant at his presumption that she would walk away from her dream.

"No, that shop means more to her than anything." Sandy patted him on the shoulder. "So, how long are you here for this time?"

"This time? For good."

"For good?" Pale blue eyes widened, and she gave a low whistle. "For Rissa?"

He set his jaw. "No. For Rissa and me." He shot her a glance to see if she was going to argue.

But she merely raised her glass to the huge red silhouette of a dimpled baby holding a bow and arrow dangling above the dance floor. "Nice shot, Cupid."

This was only the fifth year since Clarissa'd bought Sweet Hearts, but the pattern was well set. The holiday for lovers was definitely the season for lovers of chocolate. She'd worked well past midnight the night before and had come in early that morning to get a jump on the Valentine's Day crowd. Now only two large trays of chocolates still waited for the finishing touches.

She carefully placed tiny swirls of white and dark icing onto the tips of the small brown domes. Long practice made the task run smoothly, and soon she was sliding the trays into the refrigerated cases.

But now that her tasks were finally completed came the moment she'd been dreading—the moment she had time to think about the return of Rick Denton.

Why had he come back? Sure, Snowden Ski Resort was one of the best, but Vail and Aspen weren't exactly penny candy.

She looked around her shop, designed to resemble an old-fashioned soda fountain. Shiny black and white tiles covered the floor, laid out in panels of joined hearts. The same pattern, mixed with bright pink tiles, decorated the back walls. Windows filled the other walls, flooding the store with the bright Colorado sunshine. Display cases were crammed with the chocolates and other candies, all brightly beribboned for this sweetest of holidays. In honor of Valentine's Day, she had many special molded confections, including various hearts, cupids, and even small boxes made from chocolate.

She breathed in the sweet smell that permeated the cozy storefront. Even though she had some clerks quit after a few days because they just couldn't stand it anymore, she never tired of the scent of chocolate. Inhaling the heady aroma always helped her center herself. Clarify things.

But not today. Today, every intake of breath reminded her of what she had passed up.

For two years, she'd told herself over and over she'd done the right thing refusing Rick Denton's proposal, doing her best to ignore the doubts that kept creeping back. And the question had been moot, after all. Rick had gone back to Dallas alone.

But now he'd come back, and what's more, he'd sought her out. Was he going to try to rekindle their romance? What would she do if he did?

These questions made her long for more chocolates to decorate. Anything to keep busy and stop thinking. The shop wouldn't open for another two hours. She started to putter in the work kitchen.

She'd barely noticed the time had passed when her clerk, Brian, came in the employee entrance.

"Hey, Rissa! What you got going?"

She looked up from the chocolate lollipops she'd been molding freehand. Working without conscious thought, she'd created heart lollipops. When the chocolate was almost, but not quite, cooled, she'd laid one heart onto the other, slightly off center, so they appeared to interlock. Both were outlined with white piping. She'd liked the effect so much, she'd quickly made a few dozen more.

"What do you think, Brian?"

"Pretty cool! Sweet Hearts! These could be like a trademark kind of thing." He lifted one of the dual lollipops. "They'll be a big hit! I'll start wrapping them."

She nodded absently, but kept the first she'd made separate from the hardened lollipops Brian collected. She held it up. Two hearts, joined, but each with a separate identity.

She had not been able to make Rick see that both were possible.

Within minutes of opening the doors, the crowds rushed in. Recently smitten swains mixed with forgetful husbands to procure sweets for their sweets. More and more, bold young women, and even a few older ones, made purchases for the gentleman in their lives. But by four-thirty, the crowd had thinned considerably, and knowing Brian had a date planned, she allowed him to take off early.

But she'd certainly raised her brows to see who his date was. Sandy? And why the glances she could only call conspiratorial? What were they up to, anyway?

But she'd forgotten the mystery by the time closing time rolled around. Nearly all of the special Valentine's confections were gone, and most of the regular chocolates, as well. Clarissa went into the kitchen to pull one last tray of raspberry truffles from the refrigerated cases.

Hearing the tinkle of the shop door's bell, she hurried out. "We've some raspberry truffles left, but—" She stopped short, barely managing to hold on to the tray. Standing in the doorway, Rick held a single red rose.

"Raspberry truffles? Love 'em." He smiled, and held out the perfect bud.

The flower blurred before her eyes. She could not believe

the urge she felt to drop the tray and run into his arms. How could her own heart betray her this way? After a moment's inner battle, she pushed back through the swinging door and slammed the tray down on a work table.

Her hands squeezed the edge of the table as she leaned heavily on it, trying to slow the rapid pace of her heart. Two years, she thought. Two years, yet still he had the same power over her. Tears streamed down her face, despite her angry attempts to stop them.

"Rissa."

She felt his hands slide up her arms to her shoulders. She wanted to pull away, but instead, leaned back against him.

"Rissa, don't cry."

She sniffed and brushed the moisture from her eyes. Turning toward him, she pushed him away. "Why did you come back? I was fine."

"Because I was miserable without you."

This stark reply left her bereft of words. But only for a moment. "There's no point. I am not going to go to Dallas to be your helpmeet. I have a life here."

"So do I."

Heedless of his interruption, she waved her arms. "I love this shop, I'm not—what did you say?"

He grinned. "I said I have a life here, too."

"Here? Here in Snowden, Colorado? What life do you have here?"

"I just accepted a position with the ski resort. You're looking at the new Vice President in charge of marketing." He straightened his tie, looking very corporate.

She clasped her hands together. "You quit your job with Boyton Industries? You loved that job."

"I love you more."

"Oh, Rick!" She found herself in his arms again. But she pulled away once more. "Rick, I can't let you—"

"Too late. It's done." He pulled her close. "Look, my job with Boyton was a great job, but," he shrugged and gave a crooked smile, "this new one comes with a ski pass." He slid one finger along the line of her jaw. "Besides, Sweet Hearts is unique. Like you. I can work anywhere, but I only want to live with you."

Their kiss was long, slow, and tasted even better than raspberry truffles. As her eyes slowly returned to focus, she caught sight of her newest creation, the dual lollipop.

Sweet Hearts. Not bad on their own, but terrific together.

PLAYING THE CARDS RIGHT

Carolee Joy

"I can't believe you're going at the last minute again."

Wendy sighed. Here it came. Every time Ed called, she had to listen to her roommate's lecture.

Sara popped another chocolate in her mouth. "Where's your pride?"

"Wherever it is, it's not worried about playing cards with a few friends." Wendy paused on her way to the shower and glanced back at her roommate.

Sara scowled. "Why do you let him treat you this way?"

"What way? They need a fourth, I'm not doing anything special, what's the big deal?" Sometimes Sara's logic escaped her. Ed was just a friend, after all. Besides, she was sick to death of dating games. Which was why she was home with her roommate on a Saturday night instead of doing something more interesting than watching snowflakes drift past the window.

She preferred that to bores or braggarts, which seemed to sum up the last few dates she'd had. Ed was a nice, quiet guy she'd been friends with for ages. With Ed, she could be herself, which was why she never minded his last minute invitations for cards, volleyball, or a softball game.

Sara shrugged as if Wendy were making a huge mistake. "You're only kidding yourself, but okay. If you say so."

"I do. Have you seen my Vikings sweatshirt?"

"No, but you're welcome to borrow my angora sweater. Or are you afraid that would send the wrong message to your buddy?" Sara teased.

Twenty minutes later, dressed in Sara's fuzzy pink sweater, Wendy stood by the front door and applied lip gloss. Why had she let Sara goad her into wearing her sweater? Because the wind was howling and the temperature had plummeted in the past half hour, that was the only reason. Certainly Sara's little digs hadn't made her reflect any deeper on her feelings for Ed. His four-wheel drive vehicle swung into the driveway.

"He's here! Catch you later, Sara." Gathering up a new pack of cards, Wendy prepared to bolt.

"You should make him come to the door, Wendy!" Sara called out before the wind caught the door and slammed it shut.

Letting her parka flap open, Wendy hurried to meet Ed. He stepped down from the truck and grinned just as her boots hit a slippery patch, and her feet shot out from under her.

"Whoa!" He caught her hard against his chest.

Wendy looked up into his bemused gaze. Funny. She'd never noticed before how good he smelled, like pine trees and winter.

His gaze flicked to her mouth, then he cleared his throat and set her down on unsteady legs. "New sweater? I like it."

He opened the driver's door and motioned her inside. "Sorry. The other side is frozen shut."

Wendy slid across the seat, hesitating for an instant in the center. What would he do if she stayed there in the middle?

He'd think she was crazy, that's what he'd do. Banishing the surprising impulse, she scooted over to the window and buckled her seatbelt. Ed got in and smiled at her as he started the engine. Was there just a little more depth, more warmth to his smile tonight?

Of course not. Ed was—her buddy. Nothing more, and she didn't want him to be. That's what she got for letting Sara's talk get to her, it had her making ice castles out of snow flurries. If she wasn't careful, imagined feelings would get in the way of real ones and spoil a perfectly good friendship. She wouldn't do it. No matter what Sara thought, she and Ed were just friends. Wendy relaxed and smiled back. He launched into their favorite topic, the local college hockey team and their chances to take the state championship.

A short time later they were at Brian and Dawn's cozy apartment. Seating herself at the card table, Wendy let the warmth of the fire and friendship wrap around her.

"Ed is so lucky to always be able to count on you for a last minute date, Wendy." Dawn dealt the cards.

"That's because we're just friends," Wendy felt compelled to explain again. "Besides, I always like seeing you and Brian." She picked up the hand and began arranging her cards.

"Still, it's shameless the way he takes advantage of you."

Before Wendy could retort, a sense of awareness prickled across her skin. Looking up, she caught Ed's gaze on her, mysterious and intent, as he hefted a tray of soft drinks and chips in from the kitchen. If she didn't know better, she'd think there was more going on behind his quiet look.

What was wrong with everyone? Cabin fever, that must be it. Seemed to always strike this time of year.

Around midnight, Dawn stood and peeked out the window. "Uh, Ed. You did drive your truck here tonight, didn't you?"

"No, we came by sled dog," he joked as he joined her.

"Good, because that's the only way you're getting out of here before morning. Look at that wind! And your truck must be under that huge drift. Guess you'll have to spend the night."

Stay here? All night? In this one bedroom apartment? Wendy hurried to the window as Dawn let the curtain drop. She bumped into Ed, startled when the contact sent a current of electricity racing through her. Must be static from Sara's sweater. Certainly not from the way he was looking at her as Dawn and Brian pulled out the sofa bed and made up the mattress.

"I'll use the cushions on the floor," Ed said softly.

After showing her where to find clean towels and a new toothbrush, Dawn said goodnight, leaving Wendy and Ed alone in a room lit only by firelight while a double bed crowded out rational, sensible thoughts. *Stop it,* she scolded herself. Ed stretched out on the couch cushions on the floor, his feet sticking out beyond the blanket.

Trying to ignore the guilty pang she felt, Wendy climbed fully dressed into the bed and pulled the covers up to her chin. Once the fire died down, he would really be cold there on the floor. She flopped to her side. "Ed, it's okay if you want to share the bed with me. I mean, you can use your blankets on top of mine, I'll just stay under the covers."

He leaned back on his elbows. "I'd sure appreciate it. This is a quick trip to backache city down here."

Wendy scooted over to make room. A moment later, Ed dropped his pillow next to hers, then cautiously lay down on the far edge of the bed. She dissolved into giggles.

"What are you laughing about?" Ed's voice started out gruff, then he joined in her laughter.

"How silly we are, acting like it's some big deal just

because we're snowbound overnight."

The awkwardness gone, they laughed and talked long after the mantel clock chimed three. As always, his sense of humor delighted her while his comfortable companionship made her wish the snowstorm would last for days. Wendy drifted off to sleep thinking how lucky she was to have a friend like Ed.

She awoke hours later in his arms. Pale light filtered past the window shades. Face relaxed in sleep, Ed held her close, his breathing even and steady.

Wendy's heart slammed against her side. Maybe she was kidding herself that all she wanted from Ed was a casual friendship. Were there sparks between them that other people saw, and she was too stubborn to acknowledge?

Tentatively, she reached up and traced her finger over the red-gold sprinkles of beard covering his chin. Her finger skimmed over the fullness of his lips, and her breath caught. She could kiss him, and he would never be the wiser. That would settle this once for all, put this nonsense out of her mind.

Raising up slightly, she brushed her mouth over his and started to move away. There. She'd done it, and now she could quit worrying about it.

His hand caught hers and held it against his chest where his heart hammered beneath her palm. His other hand cupped the back of her head and drew her mouth back to his. This kiss rocked her to her soul, shattering the innocent notion that her feelings for him were merely those of friendship.

Oh, no. What had she done? How could she face him now and pretend to be just his friend?

Tears stinging her eyes, Wendy pulled away and jumped off the bed. Jamming her feet into boots, shoving her arms into the sleeves of her parka, she rushed out into the cold, still morning. A city bus, chain-clad tires singing in the still, clear air, lumbered up the street. She caught it at the corner and headed home.

Mercifully, Sara was still asleep when she arrived. Wendy stood at the window, contemplating the new snow and her own stupidity. What had she done? Their friendship was ruined.

The snowplow lumbered by. Ed's truck followed behind it. Heart thudding, Wendy went to the door.

Ed stood on the porch, the pack of cards in his hand. "Thought I should return these."

"Oh, sure. Thanks." When he made no move to give them to her, she swallowed nervously. "Do you want to come in?"

"Yeah. I do." Once inside, he fell silent, juggling the pack of cards from one hand to the other. "About that kiss."

Wendy pressed her palm against her chest. "I take full responsibility for that."

A grin played at the corner of his mouth. "Good. Because if I had started it, it would have been more like this." Gathering her to him in a fierce embrace, his mouth descended to hers in a powerful kiss that blazed hotter than a roaring fire. The deck of cards fluttered around their feet.

She rested her forehead against his. "Sara says you take advantage of me by calling at the last minute."

"I was afraid anything else would seem like I was asking for a date. And I figured you'd never go for that."

"Oh, Ed." She sighed and let herself be pulled further into his warmth, relishing how right it seemed. "What a couple of dopes we've been."

"I never meant to be disrespectful." He brushed his fingers over her cheek. "I think the world of you, Wendy. Can we be more than friends?"

Being with Ed was one of the best parts of her life. She couldn't wait to see where this led next. Nestling her face against his palm, she smiled. "Keep playing your cards right, and I'd say that's more than a definite possibility. I'd say it's a reality."

ABOUT THE AUTHORS

SUSAN D BROOKS began her career as an accounting clerk, rising to the position of assistant controller before giving it up to stay home with her son. What does that have to do with writing? Nothing. Except that she learned that accounting is not what she wants to do. Today she writes book reviews for an online publication and has sold several short stories. She is a member of the Romance Writers of America and the Ohio Valley Chapter of RWA.

TAMI D COWDEN always wanted to be a writer but became a lawyer instead. Now, she is finally pursuing her dream. She has taught writing at the University of Colorado, the University of Denver, and Arapahoe Community College and presented two programs at RWAs 1998 National Conference. She has been writing for several years, has completed one novel, and has sold articles and fiction to international print and on-line publications. She has won two awards for her short stories. She co-authored THE COMPLETE WRITER'S GUIDE TO HEROES AND HEROINES, to be released April 2000 by Lone Eagle Publishing Co. Visit her website at
www.members.aol.com/tamicowden

CAROLEE JOY has been writing short stories since she was ten years old, but spent many years as a CPA spinning tales for the IRS until she became serious enough about her writing to abandon her calculator and seek publication. The author of two published novels, the award winning WILD ANGEL and SECRET LEGACY, several of her short stories have been included in anthologies, as well as appearing in on-line magazines. Now she pursues her writing dreams full-time, when she is not refereeing her three boys and two dogs. The millenium will see two more of her romantic suspense novels published, as well as another anthology from Dream Street Prose, LOVE MYSTIFIES, in the fall of 2000. Visit her website at www.caroleejoy.com

With a curiosity rivaling that of her pet ferret, SU KOPIL loves to enter the minds of her characters and the authors she interviews. Her articles and short stories have appeared in a variety of online and print publications. You can find her column, "Ask The Authors," in Calico Trails magazine. "A Home For The Holidays", her first historical short story, appears in the anthology, 'TIS THE SEASON, available from Neighborhood Press. A firm believer in dreams coming true, Su loves to hear from readers. You can write her at SuKopil@aol.com

BETSY NORMAN is a multi-published short story romance writer both in print and electronic form. Her monthly column, "Wit and Wisdom," appears in Romancing the Skyze. She teaches a course on the anatomy of the short romance at the Wisconsin Writer's Workshop. Betsy invites you to visit her web site at http://members.aol.com/bgreaney/page1.htm

Watch for LOVE MYSTIFIES

Prepare to be thrilled and chilled with spine-tingling, toe-curling stories of the inexplicable mystery called love.

Available Fall 2000 from DREAM STREET PROSE.

Visit our website: www.dreamstreetprose.com